Soul Survivor

by

Phil Groves

 **New Generation Publishing**

Dedication

I would like to dedicate *Soul Survivor* to my father and nephew.

My late father has been an inspiration in my life and has always had time to listen and when I need someone to talk to, I still turn to him.

This novel would not have been started if not for Keith, my nephew. You are a thoughtful, courageous and a good friend.

Acknowledgements

It's not every day I get a chance to be proud of something I have accomplished but the truth of the matter is I did not write this story by myself. I had help from many colleagues, family and friends and it would only be fair that they get a mention for their support. Before I do this, I would like to thank a lady who I have followed for many years enjoying her work in music. I would like to make a special thank you for her album, *A Little Soul in Your Heart*. The music gave me inspiration and brought out my creative side - thank you Lulu.

I would like to thank Kate Gettings, Jill Groves and Lesedi Vine for their input and editing skills that have greatly improved the flow of the story.

For their support, Alex, Trevor and Kevin, my three brothers and to my mother for giving me the right environment in her home to be able to put pen to paper without interruptions.

I thank Scott, for his beautiful artwork and especially his illustration for the cover of *Soul Survivor* and for Faye, for her kind and inspiring words.

To all my friends who have given their support and a big thank you to Tinkerbell, who has always inspired me to be the best I can be.

To Captain J. Peter Hoerr, Commander Patrol Operations and The Belmont Police department for their help and advice.

One person I could not leave out who made this happen, Darin Jewell, my agent for believing in my work, for his encouragement and knowledge that have helped improve my writing.

You need chaos in your Soul to give birth to a dancing star.

Friedrich Nietzsche (German Philosopher)

~~~~~~~~~~~~~~~~

There's no such thing as a Soul. It's just something they made up to scare kids, like the boogeyman or Michael Jackson

Bart Simpson (The Simpsons)

Chapter 1

"Please, please, pretty please. Five minutes, then I promise I will let you rest. I want you. I don't ask much. Please! Last time I swear."

"Yeah, you said that the last time and the time before and you got your way but this time, I won't break and I won't bend to your carnal needs."

"You don't love me anymore. You think I'm fat."

"Well you have gained a few pounds over the last few months!"

Karen hits her husband Steve across the shoulder.

"Hey! I was only joking; say you're sorry young lady," Steve responds rubbing his shoulder while trying not to smile.

"I'm sorry baby," Karen replies with her slow, but rich Southern Belle accent, "Did I hurt my poor baby?" She snuggles up to her husband, her hands playing with the buckle of his belt.

"Karen! I love you more than life itself," says Steve, keeping a stern tone to his voice "but, right now, in case you have forgotten you're eight and a half months pregnant with our baby and you know there is nothing more I would like to do than entertain your needs, but there is no way we're going to have sex. There is a baby inside you who kicks me every time I press myself to your body and I think he will not take too kindly to being kicked by his supposedly protective father."

"You mean when she kicks you. We are having a girl or have you forgotten?" Karen pouts.

"As neither one of us actually knows the sex of our baby, I'm afraid it is left in the hands of fate and stop trying to undo my pants! I am not going to have sex with you. We both know this is your hormones playing up, making you crazy and I understand all the weird stuff you keep doing, but baby you are to me the most beautiful and loving person I know and ice cream and carrots aside, you are going to be a great mother."

"You really know how to kill a girl's lust. You're off the hook for now buster, but we've still got time. The doctor said it was safe to do it and I hate to be like this with you, but you still have such a great bod and I am fat and I need you to want me."

"OK! I'm sorry baby." Steve gives Karen a long hug, "But admit defeat and stop tugging on my belt!"

"Oh come on. You can't punish a girl for trying." Karen pulls a face and sticks her tongue out at Steve, then follows it with the most gorgeous smile followed by a playful pout as she gently runs her fingers across his strong torso, following the contours of his body around to gently squeeze his behind, a hint of mischief awakening in her again.

"Come on Karen, you know nine times out of ten, you will always get your way and you know you always make me pay when I win so let's not pretend you're not already planning how to win this as you always put it. It's your journalistic instincts to dig deep and uncover the truth, so I already know you're going to make me feel guilty about something and get your way."

Karen, a natural blonde, had the beauty and the clear unblemished skin that many women would pay a fortune to have. She never let her beauty go to her head and many people who met her remarked on how intelligent and easy it was to talk with her. She was slow to anger and quick to laugh and as long as you didn't talk politics, you would always be welcome.

"Honey, you are my handsome thirty-four-year-old and half responsible for getting me in this condition. Know this; when baby comes, you, my big baby, will not get another crack at this for a long, long time, so get it whilst the girl is hot," Karen replies as she walks away.

Steve watches her walk away, trying to swivel her hips almost comically as she tries to push out her ever growing breasts and thinks back to when they started dating. Barely out of his teens when he met Karen, he had been a single male and single-minded, his only love affair at the time was with engineering. Karen changed his way of thinking and he had never looked back.

"I almost forgot," Steve calls from across the room, still trying to keep a straight face. "I have to go to the pharmacy to pick up your prescription."

"Steve, you have an eidetic memory, so don't give me that forgotten stuff. You're let off the hook for now but, this isn't over. You're only delaying the inevitable and the more you hold out, the more I want you and I never lose!"

Steve laughs as he opens the front door. He was so close to giving in, only he's very aware of Karen's condition and even with all the medical knowledge telling couples that it is OK to still have sex at this late stage in the pregnancy, he is not willing to risk it. Karen has more than an appetite for food and he is so surprised with how much energy she has. She looks beautiful with her bump and she can't wait to be a mother. As soon as she knew she was expecting, she just dealt with it, never worrying. There was only one issue she was having trouble dealing with and he had recently solved that.

Steve wishes he could make decisions as easily as Karen and he hopes the one he has made recently was the right choice. Protecting his wife and their baby is his top priority as he thinks about his recent decision to come away from work and the project that was close to finishing. He knows he has upset a few people but, he feels it was the right decision and if they want him back, changes will have to be made. Those are his terms.

He regrets that his work had taken up more and more of his time and Karen has been very patient with him. They have had their patchy moments in the past, only for Steve, waking up in the morning before Karen opens her eyes is one of those special moments in his life; watching her sleep, always enjoying the cute way she wrinkles her nose, the little things that make you want to protect the person you are with. When people talk about the All American Dream, he found his the day he met Karen.

Twenty minutes later, Steve strolls into the pharmacy. He's enjoyed this walk over the last eight or so months. All the work he has put in at the lab, trying to cram in some free time at the local gym and on top of that a baby on the way has led to less hours of sleep than he would like. For now, the important thing is to support Karen.

Looking around, he notices that access to some areas of the pharmacy have been closed off and some of the lighting had been taken down. It looked like electrical work was being carried out.

Steve makes a detour through the pharmacy to the rear, looking for the health section and almost collides with one of the shop assistants. Steve recognises the girl he had almost fallen over, bent down in front of him placing new stock on the lower shelf, "Hello Tina, looks like a building site in here."

Tina recognises the voice without looking up, "Hello Mr O'Neil. Yes, it does; our manager had hired an electrician to put up new lights and unfortunately he hit a water pipe when he was drilling and he had to stop work until the pipe's been fixed, so be careful where you walk."

Steve, surprised to hear her use his surname, says, "Tina, you know you can call me Steve. How long have we known each other?"

Tina whispers, "I know, but Keel, our manager, does not like us being familiar with the customers. He caught me this afternoon with Mr Harris. You know, the nice old man who comes in every other day for his prescription. He likes being called Carl and I guess he probably doesn't have many people to talk to, so he usually hangs out here for a while before he leaves. He just likes it when we give him some time, unfortunately the boss only sees the dollar sign."

"Well, do you want me to have a word with him? Make him see the point of having a good relationship with the staff?"

Tina giggles.

"What did I say that was so funny?"

"If you go and tell him about a relationship with us, he's going to think there's more to it. You should see him when he doesn't know we're watching, checking us girls out, he just makes us feel uncomfortable."

"I hope you don't think the same about me?"

"Are you kidding Steve? Most of the girls here wouldn't mind if you checked them out. God! Did I just say that? Please don't say anything. God! Me and my big mouth," Tina shrieks and blushes.

"That was very sweet Tina, and your secret is safe with me." Steve gives her a reassuring smile.

Tina was just playing with him as they had a good banter together and she loves talking about baby things with Karen when they both come in together. She and Karen are thick as thieves and they both usually end up talking about girl stuff which just gets him flustered.

"Well?" Says Steve.

"Well what?" says Tina, though she knows what Steve is asking her and giggles as she can't keep a straight face. "Yeah I passed the first aid. It wasn't really that hard and as you said, the more I learn about things, the easier it is to study."

It was Steve who had recommended that she take any opportunities to learn. Presently she is studying IT at evening college as she wants to take a business course at university. The pharmacy she works for is part of a chain and Tina has been sponsored by them as they had seen potential in her. She had just completed her first aid course and she had been asked to carry on working with the company when she eventually starts university, as they will offer her a position in management after completing her course, depending on her results.

She was talkative with him from day one and he assumed she had a crush on him. He later realised that it was just her friendly nature. When she told him about her plans to go to university, he had immediately offered to help in any way possible. He felt like a surrogate father at times as he had heard that she had lost her father when she was a baby. Times were difficult for many people. Tina's mother had brought up the family on her own and a year ago, she had fallen ill and was off work for a month. Tina decided to delay university and help with the bills. She applied for the position as shop assistant for the pharmacy and was hired on the spot.

Steve would normally chat longer but he didn't want to leave Karen alone for long in her condition and made his excuses to catch up later. He made his way to the back, at the same time glancing at the time on his watch, a present several years ago from Karen, remembering the time when she presented him with it. It was a chronological watch with a black leather strap in a classical design, made by Dalvey, in Scotland.

Steve had visited many parts of the UK when he worked there, and one weekend, he took a trip with Karen to Bath, a town famous for it's Roman origins. They had wandered through the many Victorian style shops, the city had to offer and had come across a shop selling stylish mariner gifts.

Karen had noticed the watch in a display case and instantly knew what to get Steve for his birthday. Steve was surprised they had left Bath without buying another pair of shoes to share the closet with Karen's other prized possessions. When Steve opened the box, he remembered seeing it in the shop and realised why Karen had not purchased more shoes. He was so pleased with the watch that it rarely came off his wrist.

As he locates the health section, he finds it difficult to pick out the various products as there is inadequate lighting at the rear and he ends up walking through a puddle on the floor, not noticing the wet floor sign until he almost trips over it, stopping fast, and almost slipping on the wet surface.

Steve decides it would be a good idea to have words with the manager before someone else has an accident; at the same time he hears a noise and looks up, catching movement as a ceiling light had come away on one side and was dropping down. Steve flinches, immediately ducking. Broken plaster was hitting his head then suddenly the whole light gave way with a thunderous crack as it breaks away from the ceiling, swinging down towards his head. Steve swings into action launching backwards and rotating his body as the light narrowly misses his head. At the point his feet leave the ground, the light makes contact with the water, the electrical cable trailing above, followed by a blinding discharge of electricity as it is still connected to the mains and sparks are discharged as the lights in the shop go out. Steve lands on his shoulder narrowly missing the water. Tumbling over, his feet collide with the shelving, bringing items of stock crashing down around him as he carries on his journey, hitting the end isle and bringing more stock down on top of him as he instantly reacts to save his head from falling items. His breath is knocked out of him as something heavy crashes down on his left side. Steve, winded, listens, his eyes tightly closed as objects roll off him as he drops his head back down on the floor, aware of the pain in his side but also aware of how close he was from getting fried.

The silence is cut short by a scream as Tina, calling out Steve's name, comes rushing to the back and nearly runs straight through the puddle. Steve immediately grabs for her, causing her to scream again, at the same time jolting his side and bringing a spasm of pain causing him to almost let go as he grits his teeth, holding on tight to Tina.

"Hold it my hero girl, I'm OK but you won't be if you put your foot in that puddle, although probably the lights are dead, but let's not take a chance."

Tina hugs him, at the same time, helping him up, off the floor as some of the objects that had landed on him, fall, clattering across the floor. He notices a large box with foot spa on the side, realising it was this that had winded him. Towering over Tina, her arm around his side, he suggests they make their way to the front where there is light and he can check his injuries.

Walking back towards the front, Tina's nonstop chatter reminding him, he could have almost died. She is trying to hold back more tears, her face already a mixture of running make-up and tears. He stops her and wipes her face, at the same time she embraces him causing him to stiffen as pain again shoots down his side as he returns the hug for a second and then unfolds himself from her grasp, giving her a reassuring look and telling her that she should be more cautious before she goes running in to give aid. Tina shakes her head as she looks at Steve, who had almost died and all he could think about was her. She jokes about how he is always lecturing to her and he should have been a teacher. Steve looks at her wondering if she was clairvoyant as that was something he was thinking about doing and taking after his father, who teaches.

The people in the store come rushing over, except for Keel. Steve looks around to find him still behind his counter. The man had not made a move to help and he was looking over with a blank look across his face.

"Excuse me," Steve calls to catch his attention. Keel comes out of his dream state to acknowledge Steve, mumbling about something Steve couldn't quite hear before asking him if he was OK?

"I'm fine," Steve calls over "and so is your assistant if you're interested," admonishing the man and making a point that it wasn't safe in the shop for people and to get everyone out before there was another accident.

It takes a second for this to sink in and then Keel starts calling for everyone to leave. Steve is about to usher Tina out when she leaves his side and runs around behind the sales counter.

"Tina," he calls "let's go now please."

"One second Steve," she says smiling and rushes back around with a small paper bag in her hands.

"What have you got there?" Steve asks as Tina passes the bag across.

"Your wife's prescription," she replies, as Steve looks inside the bag. Tina hugs him again.

Keel is the last to exit, closing the door behind him and locking it. He looks around, noticing that the crowd has formed a circle around the man Tina knew and stares hard at her. Steve catches Keel's eye and the man quickly looks away before coming over, making small talk with some of the customers who were gathering around him, Steve looks at him for a second more before being drawn back into the conversation with Tina and putting out of his mind, the cold stare he thought Keel was giving Tina, putting the feeling he had, down to his imagination.

Steve looks down at Tina, asking her if she is OK and she nods, laughing at the same time as she thought it was him that almost was electrocuted and whispering conspiringly in his ear that Keel will now be worried that he might try and sue. He laughs, shaking his head at the blame culture they all live in, thinking back to a story recently where a teacher had tied a pupils shoes and the lace had come undone tripping the boy and giving him a black eye. The parents had sued and won.

Chapter 2

That night Karen is constantly in and out of bed, running to the rest room to pee and although Steve can normally sleep through a force ten hurricane, the constant nudging from Karen to wake up, means he is having trouble drifting off and especially as Karen kept forgetting about his injury. The one good thing about his graze is that Karen has forgotten about her needs and is playing mother to him, concerned at seeing his bruise.

Around 3 a.m., Karen finally manages to go to sleep. Only by this time, Steve is fully awake. His mind is as usual running through all types of problems that might possibly arise in the future and finding that nothing really makes sense. These are the joys he is now starting to understand of being an expectant father.

He thinks back to recent months with work. He has been losing confidence with the people he worked for over safety measures he had wanted put in place, which would have cost the company more money and time to implement. He had been project managing a team of Scientists and engineers for several years and was worried that things were moving too quickly and important issues were being overlooked, so eventually made a decision to come away from the project after discussing it with his father and Karen. His father, Christopher, has been a great influence in his life and the only other person other than Karen whom he could discuss his problems with.

Steve's mother had died when he was a teenager after suffering for years with an incurable illness that left her muscles weak and eventually her heart had given out. Steve and his family had been heart broken by this but had grown closer together and since then Steve has never made any serious decisions without consulting his father.

Karen has talked with many experts in similar fields to Steve's and is a great advocate for pushing the boundaries of science but, for some unknown reason, she is petrified of the work Steve is involved in. Women's intuition, sixth sense – call it what you will, but Karen has worried so much over the last several months about Steve's work that he decided finally to make the decision to leave.

In the end, it all came down to Karen and the pregnancy. She has always suffered with a mild case of the shakes, but when she got pregnant, the shaking became worse and eventually her GP prescribed her a course of beta blockers which helped to keep everything under control.

Steve had put blood, sweat and tears into his role as team leader, a role he had not wanted, but unfortunately was forced on him after the accident four years ago that had killed a great man, Kenneth Mitchell, his mentor on the project.

He had been head-hunted by a small company specialising in nuclear waste containment after some of his work ended up in a science journal from his university. He had worked for the company for nearly two years when a position came up to work in England. Companies in England were looking for a cleaner source of energy. They were finding money thrown at them by the then Labour Government and companies were jumping on the band wagon because of this. There had been a great many different fields of research into alternative fuels: bio, wind, water turbines. The problem was not the lack of money, but the lack of where to put it. A lot of money had been spent by all, but it was like putting a pot load of money in a peanut bag and giving everyone involved a peanut each in return and much of the investment was wasted. Some very important research got started but much of it fell by the wayside as the money eventually started to dry up.

Steve was given a position with a company researching nuclear waste. They were contracted to find a better solution to deal with spent fuel rods and how to transport them safely. It was here that he had met with Kenneth Mitchell, who had been with the company for the last ten years and was now looking to return to the States as he had been working on alternative power sources and one in particular. Both men had worked closly alongside each other and before he left for the States, Kenneth had told Steve that he was impressed with his ideas and let him know that if he ever needed a job, to contact him.

Kenneth had let him know that the future for this industry was, in his eyes, coming to an end and that they should be looking to the future for new forms of safe energy. He believed, the way forward, lay with fusion and he had an idea that they could use colliders to help achieve this aim.

Fermilab in Illinois was built in the 70's and was somewhere he could try out his theory, but it wasn't until a larger collider was being built that he could see his dream evolve and the collider at CERN, in Geneva, on the borders of Switzerland and France, is where he needed to take it.

In 2002, six years before his accident and the year the Hadron Collider was finished, Kenneth had gone back to the States to work with plasma, the science of fusion. This was a great time for theorists working in this field and Kenneth was one of the thinkers of his time and someone had to be first as the world of tomorrow needed fusion.

He was fifty-nine at the time of the accident. It was kept quiet about what had happened back in 2008 at CERN, just another experiment, an unfortunate accident was the verdict. Unfortunately, Kenneth was the casualty. Things had got out of hand and the system had to be shut down quickly. Only it was not shut down properly. Kenneth had gone to investigate inside the collider. A system for cooling the miles of magnets from overheating had not been safely turned off and he died instantly as he was hit by a wall of liquid nitrogen.

Steve had been contacted by Kenneth, asking him if he would like to come and join his team. He had remembered some of Steve's ideas and one in particular. Steve didn't need to be asked twice. He had four years behind him learning more about containment and Kenneth remembered about a particular idea of Steve's, one he thought, would be the break they needed in fusion.

Karen didn't need to be persuaded to go back to the States. She was homesick and within a couple of months, they were back on home ground and more importantly, back at the university where he has studied for his degree in science and technology: MIT, the Massachusetts Institute of Technology.

Steve looks across at his wife in bed, quietly snoring, which she always denied she ever did when Steve brought it up, when he was in one of his teasing moods.

He remembered that when he first left the States to work in England, though he had made friends easily, there was something missing in his life and he knew that he couldn't be without Karen. It had been driving them both mad being separated and he had proposed over the internet. Only a few months after arriving in

England, he was back on a plane for a quick wedding arranged by his sister Carrie. Two weeks later, as man and wife they were both living in accommodation close to where he worked. It took Karen some time to get used to downsizing. Financially, they both had to adjust as they only had Steve's wages to live on. Karen felt a little homesick at the start and missed her family. Steve suggested that her degree in journalism might come in handy with the local science paper. A few months later, she was writing up reports and earning a wage.

Steve had been working hard and unfortunately not paying Karen the attention she deserved as a new wife, which had cost him financially as Karen had one expensive weakness she could not give up, shoes and not just any shoes. If Steve had not left her alone on all those weekends working in labs, they would be a little less poor.

Window-shopping in London by herself, Karen was maxing out the credit cards and in four years in England, had managed to accumulate over sixty pairs of expensive shoes and the debt that goes with them. Unfortunately to Steve's untrained eye, they all looked alike as he watched her walk around in her pairs of Jimmy Choo's or Burberry or Gucci or some other names he could not pronounce. All he knew was, they were costing him a small fortune. He thought gold was probably cheaper in weight than her shoes. This was payback for leaving her alone and it took him a further two years to clear his credit card.

Karen found another job within the science world, working for another science magazine. After two years, she had worked up to editor and although she loved her job, felt that there was another job she wanted, to be a mother. She was starting to get broody. She herself was an only child as her mother and father were only able to have one child. Karen knew all her life that when she got married, she wanted to have more than one baby as she remembered not having a sister or brother to play with. She had enrolled for a place at university to study journalism and unlike many of her friends at university, was able to concentrate on her studies, not having to work as her father had set up a trust fund for her. Money was never an issue for her. All she ever had to do was ask her dad and she was a little spoilt for it.

Steve was reminiscing again about how they met. He remembered how both of them had jumped at the chance to visit the Big Apple the same weekend, Karen with a group of friends and Steve by himself for a science fair.

She found Steve in a comic shop, head down in the latest edition of Spiderman. He knew it was geeky, but he had spent years in the real world reading nothing but science and engineering journals and on his walk in the Big Apple, passing the comic shop, he found himself going in. It had been years since he had picked up a comic and it was nice to get a little fantasy in his life.

Steve noticed the smell first. It was like spring meadows and intoxicating. He looked up to the most beautiful smile belonging to the most beautiful girl he had ever seen. Karen was standing before him, silently looking him up and down and making it obvious that she was enjoying the sight before her. Steve was struck dumb by her stare and others in the shop had noticed her. After all, this was a comic shop and geek heaven. Most customers in here were men in ill-fitting clothes and it was clear, a girl like Karen only existed in art in art form in comic books or in their imaginations at night when tucked up alone in bed with a roll of toilet paper.

Karen was first to speak, "Hi handsome," were her first words and then glancing at his comic, "I'm looking for a superhero to escort me around. Are you up for the job?"

It took Steve a second to put his mouth back in place before he replied. "If you're asking me to give up this comic, can you wait a few minutes until I've finished reading it?" He immediately thought "stupid thing to say," but Karen laughed and said, "You have two minutes, then I want the rest of your time."

It took him two seconds and they were out of there laughing and enjoying the attention they were getting as they left.

Over the years they had laughed about her finding him. Karen made fun of the fact that she found Steve in a comic shop when there was the whole of New York to look at. He then made the point that neither of them had made any attempt to look at New York as they spent most of their time looking at each other.

They spent the rest of the weekend together. Steve never ventured anywhere near the convention as he had discovered there was more to learn about chemistry.

It was difficult for them both when the weekend finished. They had spent many hours talking through the night and into the morning. Leaving the hotel was difficult and Steve felt a little guilty over the mess of the room. There was takeaway pizza scattered across the bed and towels thrown across the floor and he thought it right to leave a good sized tip for the cleaning maid.

He chuckled to himself remembering how Karen had misinterpreted the money.

Karen thought he was making a bad joke leaving money on the side. "This is for the cleaning women," Steve replied. "For you, I'd have to sign over the rest of my student grant."

After that weekend, they met up when they could, spending a great deal of time between the sheets.

Karen's mother was easily won over by his charm and good looks. Her father was a different matter and made Steve work for his approval.

When Karen had confronted him about wanting to have kids, she had made it quite clear that the right time was now. Fine, Steve had said, as long as Karen was not going to wake him up or call him back from work because some star sign was in the right constellation or there was a full moon. With a big smile Karen had instantly removed all her clothing, forgetting that it was the middle of the day and she was right in front of the window, naked as the day she was born and better still as he stared out of the window at the people who had stopped and were glued to the spot. The old guy with his wife was not happy to leave as his wife screamed at him, pulling him off down the street. Karen had turned and instantly dropped down pulling Steve down on top of her. She was too horny to care.

Unfortunately they found it hard to conceive and not getting anywhere with the pregnancy, they made a visit to the doctor's and were told that they were both healthy and just to keep on trying as sometimes, for no reason, getting pregnant was easier for some people more than others.

Karen, unfortunately, blamed herself and they went through a rocky patch. Steve, being pig-headed, believed nothing was wrong. His mind was not on the game as he was getting more and more involved with the project, as some of his ideas were paying off.

It was never a case of them splitting up. They were very much in love and that hadn't changed at all. Steve feels more strongly for Karen every day and he cherishes the moments when they're together and now, as he looks down at her, he wonders how he could ever live without her.

Karen went out a lot for a few months and was drinking more than usual. One night she came home with her sleeve ripped and said it was just an accident in the taxi. She looked like she had been crying and couldn't look Steve in the eyes when he asked her about it. After that evening, she had stopped going out. Her friends had tried to get her out, but she made excuses and eventually things improved between them and those past few months were forgotten.

Eight months ago, Karen had called him at work. He could not understand a word she was saying. There was just the sound of her crying. He thought she had hurt herself and he was five miles away. It took him fifteen minutes to get through the traffic and three red stop signs to drive back and run through the house, shouting for Karen and panicking when she didn't immediately answer, only to finally find her curled up on a bench at the back of their condo, just smiling up at him. She wasn't the same person he had spoken to not more than fifteen minutes earlier. She was just sat there calmly, looking very pretty, smiling in her usual beautiful way and then she said. "The first member of your soccer team has just signed up and will be with us in a little over eight months." Steve had been a little slow on the uptake as he stood there looking at this wife of his, wondering what the hell she was on about and then the penny dropped.

Here they are, eight months later, waiting for that member to arrive and he or she is a good kicker for sure, thinks Steve as he realises his chances of going back to sleep that night are pretty much nil and praising the fact they were into Sunday and he could relax, at least he hoped he could relax, depending on Karen's needs. He made a mental note to keep playing the injured party.

Chapter 3

Sunday afternoon is dragging along quite nicely as Steve, feeling very relaxed is slouched down on the sofa in front of his 52-inch flat screen TV with all the latest technology built in, watching re-runs of one of his favourite shows that he had been introduced to by a colleague six months earlier.

He has been very busy over the last few years and if he has any spare time, he makes sure that Karen gets his full attention. The programme gave him a little time to himself, though Karen didn't mind as she could always hear him laughing in fits and it was her moment to reflect on how much she loved him. The Big Bang Theory was the show he loved to watch and in her mind, anything that could get Steve to laugh that much was OK with her.

A call comes from Karen, behind him, letting him know that she's going down to the basement to do some washing. Steve springs up from his chair as he knows she will be carrying a load of washing. She anticipates this with a firm "No! Sit yourself back on your ass. I am not an invalid and there isn't much to carry, so sit!"

Steve obeys with a smile. He notices she has a book under her arm, a new one she had recently purchased. It stars her favourite character, Jack Reacher, built like a tank and tall. "A girl's dream for a while until they decide they want kids, they then look for brains and security," thinks Steve, as he smiles to himself.

When Karen first met Steve, she assumed he was the Reacher type. He's glad she wasn't disappointed. As she put it "with my man, I can indulge my fantasies without having to think of Brad Pitt." Steve wonders if she will still feel the same reading future stories about Reacher, after the film had come out. She has made a point about this but is open-minded regarding the actor. Her words, "Height's not everything but he's going to have to do some good acting to pull it off, or there will be a lot of disappointed girls out there," thinks Steve. It's funny thinking about that, remembering the time when he and Karen were talking through their vital statistics just after they first met, he'd told her he was only 5'11 and a half. She had laughed and said ."Don't worry honey, that other half got put elsewhere and trust me if a girl says size don't matter, then she's lying."

Steve can hear the washer humming in the background. He gives a small smile to himself thinking, "Karen with her book and a washer. I bet she's in heaven right now." Seconds later, Steve hears his name being shouted. He's up immediately and takes three stairs at a time going down to the basement, only to come to an immediate stop at the bottom. Karen is standing by the washer looking at the puddle on the floor. "Damn!" Steve mutters, "broken again." He turns and starts to walk over to where he keeps his tools when Karen calls him back,

"I don't think it's the washing machine this time."

Steve looks down and notices that the puddle is not coming from the washer but is directly under Karen. All the planning for this day immediately kicks in for Steve. They already have a bag packed for Karen in the back of the car. He carefully guides her up the flight of stairs and grabbing a coat to wrap around her, they make their way out of their home, a condo they had recently purchased several months ago. They had been living in Cambridge, near Boston, renting an apartment close to the university, but with a baby on the way, decided that they would not like to bring up a child in a big city with such a high population. They wanted a smaller town as they had liked the quaint towns in England.

Within two months, they had visited many of the local towns and were about to give up with Karen getting sick every time they travelled, when they found a place in a small town in Belmont.

A two bed Colonial style condo built in the 1920's, positioned on Flett Road and close to Pequossette Park. They had both fallen for it's period features and were equaly pleased when entering, as they walked across the polished hardwood flooring and looked out through the bay windows. The price was good and they just about had the budget to put down for the deposit and get a mortgage. Five weeks later they were living in their new home.

When we next return to our home there will be three of us, Steve thinks to himself in amazement. Little does he know how wrong that image is.

On route to their hospital in Newton, Karen rings ahead, letting them know that they are on their way. Unfortunately, unless you're having your head examined, Belmont does not have the facilities to bring new born babies into the world. Karen and Steve were not happy to be just a number in one of the big hospitals in the State and opted for the facilities that one of their neighbouring towns could offer. They went for the maternity hospital in Newton as it was not too far to travel and they could not have picked a better day to give birth, than a quiet Sunday. Karen also makes a call to Steve's father who lives several miles away in Milford. Carrie, Steve's sister, has been living with her father since she'd split up with her partner. Steve loves his younger sister and they love to talk to each other on the phone, but Carrie tends to let her heart rule in her relationships and unfortunately some of her boyfriends have not been so forthcoming and have been less than honest.

Her last boyfriend she found out was still married, living with his family and having fun on the side.

Steve feels very protective of his family and intends to confront the man. He is waiting for the right moment to do this. The boyfriend was a little hostile with his sister when she challenged him about his cheating but Steve plans not to let the guy forget his discrepancy.

On nearing the hospital in Newton, Steve's mobile rings, the name showing on the caller ID is his friend and colleague from work, Nigel Shanks. Steve hasn't spoken with Nigel since he had made his decision to leave the team. Nigel was next in line to replace Steve, but he took the news badly about Steve pulling out of the project and had tried to persuade him to reconsider his decision. Steve was adamant that he was leaving and things between them got a little fraught.

Steve had decided it was best if they didn't talk for a while as he needed to focus all his attention on Karen. He figured that after the baby was born, he would give Nigel a call and try to clear the air.

"Hi Nigel, look I can't talk," he says quickly before Nigel can say anything. "I'm driving Karen to the hospital. I'll call you later, OK?" Steve cuts the phone off before Nigel can respond.

Karen looks at Steve who shrugs. Karen isn't happy about the call and Steve can see it. For some reason, Karen isn't happy with Nigel full-stop, but she refuses to talk to Steve about it. He had been to their home on a couple of occasions and it seemed Karen would always have an excuse to either go out to see friends or make some excuse about having a headache and heading up to bed.

A few minutes later, Steve pulls up in front of the main reception. "I'll be quick," he says as he gets out of the car and runs into reception, where he is immediately greeted by an orderly pushing a wheelchair. Together they exit the building, pushing the wheelchair around to Karen's side of the car. She takes one look at the wheelchair and is about to complain when Steve immediately instructs her to, "Button it!"

They had decided earlier on that when this moment arrived, Steve would take charge until the baby was born as Karen was so up and down with her emotions, it would basically save a lot of arguments and tears in the long run.

They had picked this hospital because it provided a personal touch that they wouldn't get from the larger hospitals. The doctor that they had changed to, six months ago was completely different from the one they had originally been seeing. Dr Witherspoon was not as young as their previous doctor, but he came across as someone who enjoyed his work and had been with the hospital for over twenty years and everyone seemed to know and respect him.

Steve helps Karen into the wheelchair and they're immediately directed to one of the rooms on the first floor. Steve is told that he can come back to reception to fill in the paperwork when he has the time.

Karen is carefully lifted out of the chair and helped onto the side of the bed. A hospital gown is lying on the bed and she is asked to undress and put the gown on. Again she gives Steve a look that says "no way," but Steve gives her an equal look that says "don't argue."

Once dressed in her gown and lying back on the bed she is immediately greeted by a nurse who tells them she will be on hand for the duration of the pregnancy. They have met the nurse a few times before with their doctor and feel they are in good hands. Of Irish descent, Nurse Williams is petite, but has a firm manner and also a wicked sense of humour. They like her as their nurse and Karen has been made to feel less fearful as this is her first baby.

"Mr O'Neil," says the nurse. "I am going to be checking your wife now to see how far she is into the labour." Karen is aware of the procedure, as Is Steve and the nurse carries out her inspection, asking Karen how close together her contractions are. Karen tells her they're about five minutes apart and the nurse judges that the labour may be a long one, "You'll just have to be patient and allow nature to proceed at its own pace."

Dr Witherspoon arrives at this point and asks how the patient is. Karen politely replies and they have a short conversation. Dr Witherspoon, leaves them five minutes later after reassuring them that they will be cared for by Nurse Williams and that he will be back later to check on the progress of her contractions.

Karen and Steve are left alone. Steve sits on a chair beside Karen holding her hand and reassuring her. They have been at the hospital for forty-five minutes and Steve checks the time. Steve's father and sister will be at least another hour. Then there is a knock on the door and Steve gets up to answer. Standing outside is his friend Nigel who he has spoken to not more than fifty minutes ago.

Nigel puts his hand up as a gesture and immediately tells a shocked Steve that he guessed Karen was having the baby and that he thought Steve might need a little moral support as a friend. "This has nothing to do with work and we should let our argument rest." Steve immediately smiles and shakes his friend's hand.

Nurse Williams comes back into the room and asks if the man is family. "No!" says Steve.

"Now we can't be having anyone in with Mrs O'Neil. You should go into the waiting room or the canteen. If you would like to go with him Mr O'Neil, I will stay with your wife until you get back as long as you're not too long."

Steve pops his head back in to ask Karen's permission to grab a coffee. Karen mouths the words "Why is he here?"

Steve mouths back, "He's being a friend."

Karen mouths again, "Go!" but at the same time she points at her wrist warning him not to be too long.

Steve and Nigel make their way to the canteen and Nigel orders a couple of coffees while Steve finds a table. He glances at his watch and sits down waiting for Nigel to join him. Nigel arrives with the coffees and Steve tells him he can only stay a few minutes as he wants to get back to Karen.

Steve was introduced to Nigel by Kenneth when he had first joined the team. Nigel was a MIT man and for Kenneth to get his full funding, he was asked to have Nigel in his team. There was nothing wrong with Nigel's credentials and with a high IQ, he would have been considered anyway. At first Kenneth was not happy with the decision but Nigel had proved himself in his field and in the end had made a very good team player. His one downside was his lack of patience and he could be a little short with people, but on the whole he was a likable man whom Steve got on with very well and they had the occasional beer together. Nigel was six years older than Steve and taller, outweighing him by as much as 25 Lbs., most of which was muscle.

"That's understandable," says Nigel. He goes on to congratulate Steve and says that he will stay around for a few hours in case the baby comes early, as Steve has informed him that it may take some time as it's their first baby.

Steve looks again at his watch and begs to be excused. He thanks Nigel for coming and tells him that they will have a long chat regarding their work another time and discuss the business regarding Steve's work. Steve had made a decision not to completely hand over all his material for his design as he still needed to evaluate some of his ideas. The design was considered to be years ahead of the competition and there had been attempts to steal his work. He had made a tough decision after some lengthy discussions with friends and colleges and was sticking by it. They shake hands and part company.

Steve, walking swiftly on his way back to Karen, almost collides with two large men wearing orderly clothing. Looking back over his shoulder at the two men, one of whom is taking a call on his mobile, Steve apologising as he walks on.

When he gets back to Karen he is immediately given the cold shoulder and it is five minutes before she relents and holds his hand. Shortly afterwards, Steve starts yawning and he puts his tiredness down to a lack of sleep with Karen up most the night.

"Am I boring you?" says Karen. Steve apologises and tries to make a joke of it but it falls flat. The nurse feels that she can leave Karen alone for a while and excuses herself telling them that she will be ten to fifteen minutes, but if they need her to just use the call button. Steve keeps on yawning and is having trouble keeping his eyes open. Karen looks at him and wonders what is going on. Her husband can't be this tired as she has known him to go forty eight hours without sleep. A few minutes later, Steve is fast asleep and no prodding from Karen can wake him. She is too preoccupied with Steve to notice her door opening.

The two men that Steve had almost collided with have entered the room and make their way to Karen's bed, one on each side. The one closest to Steve gives him a shove.

Karen looks up at the two men.

"Is there a swinging door on my room? Can't you see I'm having a baby here? I don't think you two should be in here." Karen doesn't like the look of the two men and is about to press the button to summon assistance when in one quick movement, one of the men grabs both Karen's arms together and the other man places his hand over her mouth to stop her screaming out. Karen immediately starts to panic, looking back and forth between the men. "This can't be happening?" were her thoughts as panic sets in.

The man with his hand over Karen's mouth takes something out of his pocket as Karen watches alarmed as he displays the item he has removed. He uses his thumb to flip the end-cap off the syringe as he bends over Karen, a smile, leering malevolent across his face. He holds the syringe in front of Karen, who is pleading with her eyes for him to stop, no words to describe silence in the room as neither man has uttered a single word the whole time.

Karen has tears clouding up her eyes and in a severe state of panic as she looks over at her husband, asleep in the chair, willing him to wake up and stop this nightmare.

Unable to look away, she follows the point of the needle down to where the man is about to inject her. Without slowing, the needle enters Karen's abdomen, through her navel. Karen immediately winces as the needle tears through her skin and the contents of the syringe are injected into her body. She can't fathom why this is happening to her and is frightened for the life she carries inside her as she is unable to defend herself. What had they just injected her with?

A few seconds later she starts to feel faint and her body starts to spasm. She is having problems breathing and pain is shooting through her body. She is starting to have problems controlling her movements and spittle in her mouth starts to accumulate.

At this point the two men let her go. Karen tries to cry out but she can't form a single word as her tongue is swelling up.

The two men release Karen and stand towering over her, their expressions showing no emotions. One of them reaches for her handbag and checks the contents, then nods to the other. They both stare back down at Karen and then turn as they walk to the door, opening it and walking through, neither one looking back as the door closes slowly and quietly behind them.

Chapter 4

Steve was blissfully unaware of all the commotion going on around him.

The next thing he was aware of was an ammonia smell irritating his lungs. With a sudden reflex, Steve regained consciousness as he deeply inhales. Disorientated but starting to come around he could hear a female's voice.

"Karen. I am so sorry. I must have drifted off."

"This is not Karen Mr O'Neil. This is nurse Williams."

"Nurse Williams," Steve focuses and finds the nurse standing over him. He caught movement from his right as Dr Witherspoon entered the room.

Looking around him and finding no sign of Karen, Steve immediately asks where his wife is.

The nurse ignores his request and asks him what had happened?

"I have no idea what you mean. Where is Karen?" He asks again.

Steve stands quickly and almost falls over as his legs nearly give way. Both the doctor and the nurse take his arms and sit him back down.

Doctor Witherspoon immediately takes over the questioning. "Can you please keep seated Mr O'Neil? It is important that you answer my questions. Your wife has been taken to emergency. We had received a call button request from your room. A nurse found yourself asleep and your wife on the floor. She had fallen off the bed and was in an unconscious state. We found your wife's tongue was swollen and she was not properly breathing. We immediately had her taken to emergency where she is, I'm afraid, undergoing a tracheotomy to open up her airways. Her tongue is too swollen and we had to make a decision as we could not revive you. We need to know, did your wife ingest anything recently?"

Steve, not wanting to believe what he was hearing, but the scientist in him taking all the information in, immediately answered the Doctor. "My wife has only been drinking the water from the jug in this room that I am aware of. She had earlier today taken her Beta Blocker for her condition." Karen, since birth, had been suffering from a mild case of tremors and her doctor back in Cambridge, prior to her moving to the new practise, had prescribed her a course of Beta Blockers. As Karen had a history of tremors, the doctor thought that the most likely scenario was that her small problem had increased brought on by the pregnancy and was just down to a nervous reaction with Karen having her first child. The medicine was prescribed to help with her tremors and should not affect her pregnancy.

Steve immediately leapt up and crossed to where Karen's bag was on the side by the bed. Spilling the contents across the bed, rummaging through, he finds her pills and looks for anything else Karen may have taken. There was nothing else as he passes the bottle to the doctor. Steve tells him that these were a new prescription he had picked up from their pharmacist the previous day.

The doctor immediately passes them to Nurse Williams and asks her to get them down to the lab and have them immediately analyse the contents.

Doctor Witherspoon turns back to Steve as the nurse leaves. He has a questioning look on his face.

"Mr O'Neil. We had trouble trying to wake you. You seemed fine when you came in. Have you taken any sleeping pills recently? It is just strange that you did not wake up with all the commotion. Is there something I should know?"

Steve has had enough of the questioning and is anxious to get to his wife. "Doctor, I am not the one in trouble. What is happening with my wife? Where has she been taken and what the hell has been going on? I have no idea why I was asleep. Normally it's because of tiredness and right now I don't care, I just want to see my wife. Is that so hard to understand?"

Doctor Witherspoon ignored Steve's sarcasm and anger. He has learnt to deal with people in stress with years of conditioning and has learnt to stay detached from his feelings and focus on the problem at hand.

"Mr O'Neil. Your wife, as I have said, is in surgery. We are trying to find out what is wrong with her. Anything you can tell us will help your wife. Do you understand?"

At that moment there is a call over the intercom. Doctor Witherspoon is requested to go to emergency. He immediately asks Steve to wait but Steve is having none of that and insists on following. Arriving at surgery the doctor is met by the surgeon who looks past him at Steve.

The surgeon taken a deep breath and asks Steve who he is, though he already knows the answer.

Directing his attention to Steve, he breathes deeply, not happy about what he is now about to tell this man. He is wearing the face that all doctors put on when they are about to give bad news "Mr O'Neil, I am sorry to inform you that your wife did not make it through surgery. Your wife suffered a myocardial infraction although we had managed to get her breathing again through a tracheotomy tube. She seemed to be responding to her treatment and had opened her eyes. She tried to speak, unfortunately she relapsed into a comatose state. Her breathing had stopped again and we were unable to revive her." The surgeon gathers his thoughts as he has more news. "We needed to act fast under the circumstances and performed a caesarean on your wife. Your child is alive and has been placed in an incubator. This is just a precaution under the circumstances with your wife."

Steve is unresponsive, the shock of what he has just been told has left him speechless, now clearly having problems digesting what he had just been informed. He looks past the surgeon, his eyes fixing on the operating theatre. Steve pushes past leaving the surgeon trying to grasp Steve's sleeve, trying to stop him from entering. Steve shrugs him off as he enters the theatre. The surgery team are still present as they all stop their work and stand quietly, watching him. None of them want to make eye contact and keep their heads down. They need not have worried as they are invisible to Steve. His eyes are on the surgery table in the middle of the room.

Steve looks down at the body on the table. His wife covered to her neck with a white sheet. Blood had seeped through the sheet lower down. Her eyes are closed, her face a little swollen. Tears are forming in his eyes as he moves towards the body. Her hand is visible by her side. He places his hand in hers and brings it to his lips. His mind is overwhelmed with his loss and he whispers to no one. "Please wake up."

No one is brave enough to go to him and offer their condolences. They have seen this before and no words can help. Only time is the healer but it is also the curse.

The surgeon follows Steve into the room and he signals the staff to leave. The surgeon looks one last time at the body and shakes his head remembering the last words she had uttered to him. Her tongue badly swollen, she whispered something about "why Steve?"

and then something else. He was not sure but he thinks she said, "Get back to me."

Steve was left alone for a while to deal with his loss. There was no rush to remove the body from the theatre.

Doctor Witherspoon gives it several minutes before entering. He calmly speaks to Steve and gently places a hand on his shoulder and leads him away from his wife. Shoulders slumped, Steve allows the doctor to walk him out. He looks back as the team of nurses and orderlies as they return to the theatre to perform their task, to clean and take the body down to the morgue. Ten minutes from now, the room will be spotless, as if this tragedy had never occurred, waiting for its next success or failure. Steve's last view of his wife is her body on the table alone, Karen had already departed.

Steve is escorted and left alone in one of the private waiting rooms. He had earlier been taken to visit his baby. He had stood in the viewing room, looking through the glass at all the incubators lined up in rows, each one holding new life. A nurse had pointed out his baby and he had tried to feel something for this new life of his but was still too shocked from Karen's death to properly deal with the thoughts of raising a child on his own.

Now he is just sitting, facing the yellow painted wall, trying to understand and come to terms with his loss. Nigel appears at the door, knocking twice and pulling Steve away from his thoughts. Nigel enters, his eyes everywhere but on Steve. He eventually clears his throat, uttering a few words, making an effort to console him. "I don't know what to say buddy. I am so sorry."

Steve just looks at him, not blinking or saying a word, his haunted stare speaking volumes.

Nigel decides it is best to keep quiet and allow Steve time to reflect. This he thinks will take time to heal for

Steve and he knew his job here was to support this man and get him back to some normal life. Things needed to be done and time was important. Things have been set in motion now and he would have to steer them in the right direction. He pulls a chair up close to Steve and sits and waits.

It is much later in the day before Nigel again tries to get Steve's attention. "Buddy, it's not good for you to just sit here. Let's go and get a coffee away from the hospital."

Steve again looks up. Without uttering a word he nods and stands up. Nigel stands placing a hand on his shoulder.

They leave the room and walk through the corridor to the exit. Steve stops prior to them going through the main entrance and exit doors. Looking at Nigel, he pats his pockets looking for something, eventually pulling his cell phone from his breast pocket, he presses the re-dial, leaving Nigel wondering who he was calling.

Entering the hospital through the same doors are two paramedics. Both are looking tired from a long day and one of them is carrying a clear plastic bag with several items. The one carrying the bag accidentally collides with Steve, his eyes fixed on the bag he was carrying as he was trying to adjust the weight. They both recover, the paramedic first to speak, letting Steve know that making a call in the doorway inside the hospital is not allowed and he should wait until he is properly outside.

Steve had almost dropped the phone but had dialled the last number before the two of them had walked into each other. He had hit call. The cell phone dials out. A second later a ringing tone goes off in the bag held by the paramedic. Everyone stares at the bag. Steve stands straight and cuts his call off. The ringing in the bag also cuts off. Everyone is now staring at Steve. He again presses dial out on the last number. The ringing starts again in the bag.

Steve grabs for the bag and rips it open. No one tries to stop him as he grabs the cell phone from inside, hitting the answer button to listen. No one speaks. He knows whose phone this is but he has no clue why these men have it. He looks at the other contents in the bag. Personal items, he recognises.

He slowly turns to the paramedic who had the bag.

"Why have you got items belonging to my father and sister?" Steve, still in shock from his wife's death, is angry. He realises that his family should have been at the hospital hours ago and now some person is carrying their personal possessions.

The two paramedics look at each other. They do not want to be there. Their job is to deal with call outs. Not to speak to the public and they definitely do not want to speak to this man about what they know.

The paramedic who collided with Steve eventually chooses to speak.

"I am sorry sir. We are not at liberty to discuss whose possessions are in the bag, but if you would please wait here, I will get a doctor to speak with you."

"I do not need to see another bloody doctor," shouts Steve." Why are you carrying my father and sister's belongings?"

Other people in the area have heard the raised voices and people are drawn to the commotion by the exit doors, seeing four people gathered around, two in civilian clothing and one of them was clearly in a state, shouting at the two others, dressed as paramedics, both of whom were clearly seen trying to calm the situation.

Moments later, one of the doctors walks past heading to the front doors. Doctor Witherspoon was looking at Steve wondering how in hell he was going to tell this man that there is some more bad news.

Steve out of the corner of his eyes catches the doctor coming towards him. "What the hell is going on doctor? Why have these men got my family's belongings?"

"Mr O'Neil, can we go somewhere quiet to talk please."

"I do not want to go anywhere to talk. For Christ's sake, just answer my question."

Doctor Witherspoon takes a second, not happy with what he is about to tell this man. "Mr O'Neil I am afraid to inform you that there was an accident. Your father and sister were both involved in an accident. It would appear that the vehicle they were both travelling in had left their side of the carriageway and ended up on the wrong side. An articulated vehicle travelling on the opposite side had collided with your father's vehicle. How can I tell you this? Both your father and sister did not survive the accident and died at the scene." A few seconds pass and the doctor adds, "If it is any consolation, I am informed that they died immediately and they would not have suffered."

Steve cannot believe his ears, first his wife and now his father and sister. He stumbles to the side, those closest try to reach for him. He pushes their hands away, looking at each one in turn. Looking into their eyes and trying to understand if there is a God, then why has he not also been struck down. This cannot be happening, this nightmare that he cannot wake up from. His legs go first hitting the floor with his knees. The most horrifying sound eventually escapes his lips as he cries out, his face pressed to the wall.

Others around just look on helpless. Some wonder why the man is in so much pain. Those who knew, silently thanked God it was not their family.

Chapter 5

Two days had elapsed since the death of Steve's wife and family. He is sitting on his couch. It is the middle of the afternoon on Tuesday and there is silence all around him. He had hardly slept and when he did, waking up and reaching out, his hand patted the sheets but did not find the person who has shared his bed for the past twelve years and he remembered. Immediately tears flood his eyes as the memory of Sunday enters his life once more. He had closed in on himself and the only person he would allow to visit was Nigel.

Nigel had taken it on himself to help Steve. He had driven the two of them back to Steve's. He had made the suggestion that maybe Steve should not go back to his house and instead spend some time at his place in Cambridge. Steve refused and made it clear that he only wanted to return to his own home.

The journey back was covered mostly in silence and Nigel decided that it was best not to say much but made it clear that he would be there for Steve.

Nigel had stayed in the spare room that night and the following day had gone out and returned with a new cell phone. Steve's phone had been going off all morning with messages of condolence from friends and colleagues who had been notified by Nigel or had heard it through the media. The news about the tragedy had been picked up by the local radio and reports were repeated hourly. It would not be long before the local media actually started knocking on Steve's door once it was reported that the two separate incidences were from the same family. There is nothing like a tragedy to increase the sales of newspapers. People love bad news.

Steve had eventually pulled the phone from Nigel's hand after the last call the previous day and thrown it at the wall, smashing it into pieces.

Nigel had decided that it would be best to get a new cell phone if Steve needed to make a call and that he himself could call. Steve had thanked Nigel for watching out for him but had asked him to leave, thanking him for being supportive, but saying he needed to think clearly and couldn't do that with him constantly asking if he was OK. He'd told Nigel that he would ring him when he was ready. Nigel had objected but Steve had insisted.

On the table in front of Steve were his and Karen's photos and many letters. He had been watching their wedding DVD over and over, his thoughts on Karen, his father and sister, trying to understand how the lives of the people he loved had all so tragically ended. He had played the tragic day over and over in his mind, trying to change the ending, trying to figure out the meaningless of this loss. Nothing had worked and it was clear that he was having a problem coping with the tragedy, his grief, much too strong.

He had not eaten since his family's deaths and thoughts of eating made him nauseous. He had tried to make coffee but ended up making a hash of it. Once again with a cup of water from the tap, Steve makes his way back to his lounge when there's a knock at the door. He stands still, his hand tight on the glass, not wanting to answer it. The knocking continues until eventually someone calls out

"Mr O'Neil. Could you please answer your door? I am Detective Moralis. I would like to speak with you."

Seconds go by. "Mr O'Neil, answer your door please," the detective calls again.

Steve slips back into reality and eventually strolls to the door and opens it. Standing on the porch are two people. The man who had knocked was of Hispanic origins and Detective Moralis is taken a little aback by the ghostly form of the man in front of him. The other person at the door is an attractive female with a caramel complexion.

"Mr O'Neil". The man says, at the same time showing Steve his ID. "I am Detective Moralis and this is my partner Detective Washington." Carla Washington was blessed with perfect skin, her beauty attributed to her mother, who used to model in her youth and who now ran a resort in Florida with her American husband and Washington's stepfather whom she had married after her boyfriend had run out on her when she told him she was pregnant with Carla.

Hernando Moralis on the other hand would have been considered handsome in his youth, but age had not been kind, leaving him with worn features and a face that rarely cracked a smile unless he was in the company of his family.

"Sir, is it possible for us to come inside? I understand that you are probably not in the mood to want to talk to us, but we would like to ask you a few questions. We promise not to take up too much of your time."

Looking at Steve to reply, both officers can clearly see that he is having trouble digesting Detective Moralis' questions and it is Washington who takes over the conversation, clearly feeling that maybe a women's touch might be needed.

"Mr O'Neil. Can we come inside and speak with you? We have a few questions we would like to ask. We had tried calling first but we could get no answer."

There is a blinding flash behind the two officers and they both turn to see a man with a camera in his hands. He had clearly taken a picture and was about to take another. He snaps away at the same time approaching the house. Moralis is first to speak.

"Scholfield, I will shove that camera up your ass if you do not stop taking pictures. Take your camera and get lost."

Tony Scholfield was an independent local photographer and part time journalist who normally made a living chasing accidents and passing on information to solicitors looking to make a quick no win case for accident victims. He always wanted to be a journalist but after taking a bribe several years back, although it was never proven, he was never trusted again. It was clear that he had been passed information about the family tragedy and was looking to get a story. He figured that maybe if he could get the guy to talk to him he might get back in with the right people and he was clearly interested now, with the police on the doorstep.

"Moralis, I am just doing my duty like you. There is no law to stop me asking Mr O'Neil over there some questions".

"It is Detective Moralis to you." Moralis and Scholfield have a history and there was no love lost between them. Turning to Steve, Moralis asks, "Mr O'Neil, do you wish to talk to this man?"

Steve is now looking between the officers and the man holding the camera, not caring for any company. He just wants them all to go away. Without uttering a word he shakes his head sideways.

"That answers your question, now get lost or I'll book you for obstruction."

Scholfield is not a fool and knows it's not the right time. He'll wait for the officers to leave and try again. He turns and without saying a word waves with his hand up, two fingers distinctly higher in the V-formation.

47

Both Officers turn back to Steve, who is clearly not happy to invite them in but decides if he wants them gone to deal with them so that he can get back to his grieving in peace. He nods for them to follow him inside, Washington, the last one in, before closing the door checks no one else is lurking around.

They go through to the lounge, taking in the scattered photos and letters sprawled around the table. They clearly make out the photos of his wife and what looks like personal hand written letters.

Washington is first to speak, looking at the same time at her partner, not wanting to override the interview. Moralis nods with a look that says you can start but it's my interview. Moralis is the senior partner with many more years under his belt. His long term partner had recently retired and Washington had been assigned to join Moralis as his new partner. She has been in the police for six years as an officer and had applied to become a detective. She had passed her exams with distinction and had applied for the area and when a position came up she was posted in from her precinct in Florida. She was looking for a change of scenery and was fed up with the drug scene and constant busts to the same rich kids, who were back out on the street the next day, trying to get their next fix, some finding it and others over cooking it. She was sick of the life and wanted a change. Moralis had been hard on her when they had been assigned together but he was a police officer with many years in the force and he played it straight, which she respected. He was a hard man to like but he had the respect of his colleagues.

"Mr O'Neil, do you mind if we sit?" Steve nods as he waves his hand at the couch, at the same time walking to the table and gathering his personal belongings together, moving them from view. Washington continues, "Sir, we have been asked by the local police in Newton to ask you a few questions in relation to your late," Washington pauses as she knows this will be a difficult moment for O'Neil, "Your Wife's death." Washington stops to makes eye contact with Steve.

Steve stops what he is doing and turns to look at Washington, wondering where this is going. Washington carries on with her questioning occasionally glancing at her partner. "The circumstances of your wife's death has not been confirmed Mr O'Neil and we would be grateful if you would fill us in with all that you can remember prior to your," again a pause, "wife's death. I can understand that this will be hard for you but while it is clear in your head it would be helpful if we can get all the facts."

Steve, still looking at both officers, wonders why they are here and why they are questioning him. His wife is dead, his father and sister killed in a car accident and now he has to bring up his child by himself. He shouts out at them, releasing the anguish he feels at the world for taking away all that mattered to him and telling the two officers in front of him that he doesn't have a clue what the facts are.

The officers look at each other, slightly lost for words but they knew this was going to be tough, questioning a man after his wife's death, no matter what the circumstances were, but they were there to do their duty no matter how distasteful it seemed. They had been briefed by their superior prior to the task and had been told that if they did suspect any wrong doing that it was at this point that people tend to feel guilty and open up.

Washington carries on, trying to ignore the look in Steve's eyes. Questions need to be asked and she knows that the questions she asks are upsetting. "We understand your wife was taking medicine, Beta

49

Blockers for her condition. You had told the doctor that you had recently picked them up the previous day from your local pharmacist?" Steve complies with nods. "You checked the medicine when you received them prior to handing them to your wife." Again Steve nods." You said that she was not on any more medication that you know off?"

This time Steve answers. "Yes, my wife was only taking the medicine I picked up for her."

Washington continues." Why was it that when your wife was having difficulties, you were found asleep? The nurse had problems trying to bring you around. Can you explain why you did not wake up with all the commotion going on around you?"

Again Steve is hit by the guilt of why he did not wake up. It had been going through his mind why he had fallen asleep and why he did not wake up. It plays through his mind, over and over, why he had not woken up when clearly Karen would have tried to get his attention when she was suffering. He could not make any sense of it and he punished himself mentally because of it.

"Do you think that I haven't asked myself that a thousand times over? If I had woken up my wife might still be with me. Those precious moments of her life could have been saved if I had not fallen asleep. I have never fallen asleep like that before and it does not make any sense that I did not wake up. I had very little sleep the previous night because my wife," Steve pauses before carrying on, "My wife was up most the night," Steve reminisces over the memory, "and I was feeling restless, the thought that I was going to be responsible for a baby, new to the world. The point is, I work long hours in my profession and I have never just fallen asleep like that. It makes no sense to me and I feel it is my fault she is dead!"

Detective Moralis enters the questioning at this point as he wants to get a picture of this man when he asks this question. It has been his experience that certain questions will decide if a man is guilty or not and he thinks this one will decide for him if this person had possibly had something to do with his wife's death.

"Mr O'Neil, can you tell us why your wife had a life policy taken out on her only a few weeks ago."

Steve stiffens, confused by the question. "What policy? I don't understand, my wife does not have a policy. We never had a life policy. You must have your facts wrong"

"According to our records, your wife has a life policy for the amount of $200,000, taken out last month on a card in your name." Moralis pulls some paperwork out from a folder he had been carrying and hands it to Steve. On the paperwork are details of a transaction for a life policy made out for his wife and the card number he recognises as his own.

Steve has had enough. "What the hell is going on here? I have never seen this before in my life."

"Mr O'Neil, it would be prudent if you answer our," before Moralis can finish Steve has jumped up, not wanting to hear any more from these two as it is clear where they were heading with their questions.

"Please go. Get out!" Steve shouts as he points towards the front door. "Out!"

Both officers look at each other. This is not the first time they have been asked to leave an informal questioning and won't be their last.

Moralis and Washington stand, Moralis taking the document back from Steve. Both officers want to ask more questions but they know they cannot push it and walk to the front door. Moralis turns as he opens the door, one last try to talk and finds no one there. They exit, closing the door behind them and head for their patrol car, neither one utters a word until they are both seated in the car.

Moralis, first to speak, asks his partner what she thinks.

Washington thinks about her answer. They have been on several of these questionings with previous investigations and she has always relied on her instincts. As a rookie detective, she was quick and she always had a feeling if a person was guilty or not. Mr O'Neil is the first person who has left her undecided. The evidence looks suspicious but something about this man does not connect with the evidence and she tells Moralis that it's too early to say and they need to investigate further.

Moralis agrees, telling Washington he has the impression it was the first time O'Neil had seen the document. He has an idea that they may get some answers from the pharmacist and get a list of prescriptions the O'Neil's may have had. He hopes the person there will cooperate.

Washington asks about something in their report regarding the last words to the surgeon from Mrs O'Neil.

"They could mean anything. She was dying. I would not read too much into them," was his reply.

Moralis starts the car. He looks around and moves away, taking a last look in his rear mirrors.

Several cars down from the police car sits a blue Honda. Inside, someone watches the patrol car drive away. Scholfield watches them leave, thinking to himself, what's the best approach to take with O'Neil, before some other reporter beats him to it. Sometimes you can't always play fair. He has a hunch that there is a story here as he reaches for the door handle.

Sat further along the road is another car and the two occupants are also watching the patrol car leave. They

52

turn to look at the blue Honda, watching the man get out and walk towards the condo.

Steve has sat back down, feeling mentally exhausted, again thinking about Karen and for the moment, he has stopped thinking about the police. He sits back, remembering times with Karen on this sofa, thinking about the times he used to rub Karen's bump, talking about a name for their baby and he bends forward hands over face trying to hold back the grief.

Chapter 6

Tina was placing new stock on the shelves. Her boss was in his office. She was not too happy about being in the pharmacy alone with him. Every time she looks around, he's their watching her and she has caught him a few times staring and then he looks away suddenly caught in the moment for Tina to notice the intensity of his stare. Creepy guy she thinks.

Tina reminds herself that it's the end result that counts and she is only there to earn enough money to go to university. She hopes by next year, she would have saved enough to go. She always thinks it's ironic that she is on the door step of two of the most prestigious universities in America, MIT and Harvard and occasionally students from both these universities come into the pharmacist. A few of them come across as spoilt and arrogant, born with a silver spoon in their mouth and many of them half as smart as her. But she feels that circumstances make the person and character building comes from life's adventures. She makes a point not to dwell on her own upbringing. Her father was a big drinker and after Tina was born, youngest by five years to two sisters, her father decided that he was not cut out to look after an all-girl family and the drinking increased. One day in Tina's first year, her father had decided not to come home and two months later he was dead. It would appear that alcohol got him in the end but for a different reason. There was a delivery to a local bar down town in the early hours. The delivery man, down in the cellar, recognised the sound of heavy objects crashing. He knew instantly what had happened but could not figure out why his delivery of barrels of beer had fallen off his truck. Running up the steps of the cellar to the rear of the building, he finds Tina's Dad, crushed but still alive under the barrels. The delivery guy could not believe what he was seeing; the man was trying to push the plunger in on the end of the barrel to get a drink. He was so far gone, he did not realise he was crushed and bleeding internally. He died before the medics arrived but when they did arrive they were surprised he had not died straight away. Her mother never shed a tear and the state buried him.

Keel, had asked her if she would work the two days while the shop was closed to the public after last Saturday's incident in the shop with Steve O'Neil almost getting electrocuted. Keel had been a little jumpy ever since then. She had overheard him on the phone talking, she thinks, to the electrician. Something about possibly going to see a lawyer just in case Steve comes back with a claim against the pharmacy. Only she thinks it's the electrician who wants to do this as her boss is not too happy about seeing a lawyer and seemed really skittish about the idea.

Tina does not like what she hears and thinks about telling Steve what she has overheard. Tina was pulled away from her thoughts by a knock on the window. Looking up were two people, a Spanish looking man and a very attractive lady were stood outside looking at her. The lady was smiling but the man looked stern. He was showing her something through the window. Not a wallet, Tina thinks, looking closer at the badge pressed to the window, a police badge.

There was a sign on display outside telling people that the pharmacy was closed for two days while undergoing a refit. The officers had actually read the sign. Most people had been banging on the door trying to get in, not noticing the very obvious sign right in front of them.

Going to the door and unlocking it, Tina pops her head outside politely telling the officers that the shop was closed.

"My name is Detective Moralis, and this is Detective Washington. We are here to speak to the manager, a Mr Keel. Is he here?"

Tina invites both officers in and shows them to the office and knocks at the same time, opening the door and poking her head around the door, telling Keel that two police officers were here to speak with him.

Keel, standing behind his desk, looks a little agitated when he's told this and tells Tina to show them in.

Moralis and Washington enter, closing the door behind them. Tina stands for a while trying to hear what was being said but she could only make out muffled voices. She was tempted to put her ear to the door but dismisses that idea straight away. Giving up, she strolls back to where she was stocking the shelves. Her cell phone starts vibrating in her pocket. Tina reaches inside her pocket and retrieves her phone, opening up the message. It was from her mother.

Tina's mother was still a striking woman, born Elena Marino in 1967, in Chicago. She was half Italian on her mother's side and on her father's side, half Irish. It was because both her parents were Catholic that they were allowed to marry. Tina's father, Sean McElroy, was a lively person, tall for an Irish man and her mother had fallen for his good looks and wild ways. He was a drinker when she had met him, believing she would be able to tame him. She was loyal to him throughout their marriage even when she found out about his affairs. Elena had vowed never to marry again after his death.

Her mother had been in a long relationship with a local man and had decided to end it as she thought it was unfair to carry on the relationship. She knew that she would never marry him after he had asked her for the umpteenth time and like Tina, was again enjoying her freedom.

Tina was blessed with her mother's looks and her father's deep blue eyes. Her two older sisters had married young and were now both mothers themselves. Tina vowed not to follow in their footsteps. She was born with a head on her shoulder and her mother did not want her to make the same mistakes she had made and prays that her other two daughters would not regret their choice to marry young.

The message, was for her to meet her mother at their hairdresser's after work. Smiling as she answers the message, she shakes her head thinking for the thousandth time about her mother, who would rather give up eating, than getting her hair styled. Tina is staring out the window, just as she sends the message making eye contact with a young guy who she had seen hanging around. She assumed he was the boyfriend of one of the other girls. The young man is staring shyly at her and smiles. Tina could not help but smile back, blushing at the same time. The guy laughs and waves at her. She gives a partial wave back and turns again, smiling to herself. That's all she needs right now, she thought. Go out with some hot guy and kiss good bye to two years of planning and savings blown on lust. She cannot help herself and looks again. The guy is gone. She hears movement from behind her and turns to find the female officer standing quietly looking past her.

"Hi. Nice looking man, your boyfriend?" asks Washington, still staring out the window.

"My boyfriend, no, he's just someone that hangs out here," Tina answers a little too quickly.

"Well it looks to me like he was interested in you."

Tina smiled and asked Washington if she could help her with something, trying to change the subject.

"Maybe you can," said Washington, closely watching Tina for any signs of nervousness, "the other day, I think it was Saturday, a Mr O'Neil came in to the pharmacy and I believe you served him." Washington had just received this information from Keel and decided to follow up on it while her partner was still talking in the office.

"Why would you want to know about Steve? I mean Mr O'Neil."

"We are just following up an enquiry. It is nothing to worry about. I believe you served him when he came into the pharmacy last Saturday?"

Tina feels a little agitated, wondering if Steve was OK. Maybe he did get hurt when the light fell down. She remembered he was holding his side. "Is this about the accident? I thought Mr O'Neil was OK as he had moved out of the way before the light fell on him."

What light fell on him, thought Washington. It seems Mr Keel has left out something of his story. "Sorry Tina, do you mind if I call you Tina?"

"OK," Tina replies.

"I am not following you. Did you serve Mr O'Neil or did someone else serve him?"

"I got his prescription if that's what you're asking. I didn't do anything wrong did I? It's just that we all had to exit the shop just in case someone else had an accident as the electrician's work was left unfinished. All I did was retrieve Steve's, I mean Mr O'Neil's, prescription from behind the counter. He had come in for it for his wife. Anyway she's pregnant and I thought that it was important that she got her meds."

"Did you check the contents before you handed them over?"

58

"No. They are checked beforehand when placed behind the counter in the morning. We check the name of the customer, before we hand the prescriptions over."

"Thank you Tina. Tina, what did you mean when you said Mr O'Neil almost had a light fall on him?"

"A stupid accident," she explains to Washington about the incident describing how Keel had paid an electrician to put up some new lights, only one of them he had not been secured properly to the ceiling and it almost fried Mr O'Neil when it came down. The electrician, Neil, she thinks his name is, had hit a pipe earlier and water had gushed out. The water was turned off but it had spread across the floor. They had tried to clean most of it up but were pulled of the cleaning to serve customers. O'Neil was fast and jumped out the way or he might have been fried. That's why when they were leaving the shop, she had remembered his prescription. She didn't think and just grabbed it. It was on order so he was entitled to it as he's on account.

"OK Tina, thanks for the chat." Washington turns and heads back to the office, noting that Tina knew O'Neil by his first name and obviously used it when in contact with him.

Tina watches Washington return to the office, wondering what was going on. Why are they interested in Steve and that prescription and why do they want to talk to Keel? Behind his back the girls called him Keel the Heel on account that they thought he was the type of guy that likes young girls.

What none of them knew then was that he has a past, one that he would like to keep secret and he is not happy with the attention that he is getting from the police.

In the office, Keel was short on answers with the detective interviewing him and very careful with what he tells them as the last thing he needs is to draw any attention to himself.

"Detective Moralis, I can assure you there was nothing wrong with the prescription when I made it up that morning. The girls normally place the prescriptions on the back counter where they can be passed to the customers when they come in. If there was something wrong with Mr O'Neil's prescription then you had better speak to the girls."

Moralis had taken an instant dislike to this man in front of him as his answers were short and he could tell that he was unhappy to talk to him. He had already decided that when he gets back to the precinct, he would do a background check on Mr Keel. He remembers the name but can't recall why.

"Mr Keel, as I have already said. I am just enquiring into a few things and I have not said there is anything wrong with the prescription. It is just a line of enquiry that I am following."

Washington at this point re-enters the office and whispers something to Moralis.

Moralis gets back to questioning Keel on the new information. "Mr Keel, can you tell me what happened last Saturday in the shop with Mr O'Neil? I have just been informed that there was an accident."

Keel was afraid of this and makes out that it was nothing serious, explaining that there was a slight problem with a lighting unit. Moralis listens to his explanation, knowing full well it could have been serious, but decides not to push it and instead he asks something else.

"Mr Keel, I am sure you would like to help the police and I noticed that there are CCTV cameras around the shop. Would you mind cutting us a copy of the footage from last Saturday? We would be extremely grateful to you for your cooperation in this matter.

Keel makes a spluttering noise, knowing full well if he does not cooperate, that they would be back. He reluctantly picks up a spare tape and makes a copy of Saturday's footage. He hands this to Moralis who thanks him and decides that he's had enough speaking with the man. Both of them leave the office and head for the front door. Tina rushes over to let them out, at the same time asking Washington if Mr O'Neil was OK. Washington smiles telling her not worry and they leave.

Moralis is first to talk. "I don't like that man. He's hiding something. Do some digging when we get back. See if you can find any history on our Mr Keel. How were you with the girl?"

"She was polite. I got the impression that she seemed upset, that maybe there was a problem with O'Neil. I don't believe she is aware of what had happened last Sunday with his wife and on top of that his whole family." Washington added, "Either he is one of the unluckiest people I have ever met or he's hiding something."

Both of them return back to the car. Moralis is shaking his head trying to gauge everything they had learned and trying to see if there were any connections. He had previously asked Mr Keel for a list of all persons working in the shop. The list identified all the girls who were full or part time. The name Tina McElroy jumps out at him. He remembers a man by that name from years ago who was killed by falling beer barrels and he wondered if she was related.

Both officers are watched getting in their vehicle. The man watching them calls a number listed on his cell phone, the call is picked up on the second ring and he relays information to the person listening on the other end.

"The two officers who were at O'Neil's have just left the pharmacy. They were in there for about fifteen minutes. Keel and some girl are still inside. From what I could see, the girl was talking with one of the officers and I assume the other was talking to Keel. You were right about them suspecting O'Neil's prescription for his wife. It would be the only reason for the police to visit here. What are my next orders?"

After a brief conversation, he hangs up with his man watching the pharmacist. Thinking about how things were progressing he decided that maybe Keel should have a visit. See if they could use him as they had looked into his past at Belmont and found he had already had trouble with the police. Maybe they can use that if he wants to keep his job.

Chapter 7

Steve wakes up on the couch the following day. He checks the time, seeing that it is just after 12pm. He rubs his face to throw off a tiredness that did not come from fatigue but was more to do with a lack of will power. He realises he has neither showered nor shaved. Steve was starting to realise that he needed to get some order back in his life.

He had only been concerned with visiting his child in hospital and nothing else. The paediatrician he had been speaking too in the hospital had told him that for safety reasons, they were keeping the child under observation. A few blood tests for toxins and if everything checks out, they will consider allowing him closer access. Steve had not responded well to this, asking why he cannot take his own child home? He had been asked how he intended to look after his baby by himself and that there were professional people that he could call on to help him. Steve knew things were going to be tough and told them that he would manage.

Stretching, he wonders what time he had drifted off; somewhere around 7 am he thinks and the first proper sleep since Sunday. He was drifting again, allowing his mind to escape to the past and the life he had with Karen. God he misses her so much. His stomach rumbles and he realizes that he has not eaten since Monday, when Nigel was over. He had tried to get Steve to eat, but at the time he had no appetite. Right; he thinks, get your butt upstairs for a shower and shave, then try and get food in your stomach.

Moving slowly off the couch, Steve catches a glimpse of Karen in one of the photos and almost stumbles. He thinks, don't stop, move, you have to move. Heading for the stairs, one step at a time, he makes it to the shower room, grabbing a razor off the side; he undresses, kicking his clothes to one side, again thoughts of Karen as he remembers that she always complained that he needed a mother not a wife as he was such an untidy person. Bending down, he balls up his clothes and throws them in the basket. He is going to have to re-think his whole life as a single person. Passing the mirror, he stops and looks at himself, noticing the bruise for the first time, down his left side where he had collided with the shelves in the pharmacy. "You look like shit," he tells himself.

Half an hour later he's out of the shower and shaved, feeling a little better and thinking he needs to start acting responsible or he might as well just hand his child over to the state. Little did he know how true that thought would be.

Clean clothes on, he heads down to the kitchen, checking the fridge and finding a few edibles. As he sits back on a stool, not really tasting the food in front of him, but more out of necessity and with coffee to wash it down with, Steve looks from the kitchen to the lounge, taking in the many photos' piled on the floor. Shaking his head he concentrates on eating and drinking the coffee.

He is miles away, lost in his thoughts and does not hear the doorbell go and is only dragged back into reality when he hears the sound of a dog barking and someone banging on the door.

Wondering if it was another journalist, as the one yesterday had returned and Steve had almost lost it when the guy started to ask about Karen. What the hell was he on about asking about how he felt about his wife dying? What sort of question was that, he had thought. Steve had taken a swing at the guy, but he was quick or he'd had plenty of practice ducking people's punches. He was suckered into throwing a punch as the guy had his camera ready and got one off before running back to his car. Steve had picked up a flower pot off the front porch, thinking this is why people put these out front. He had sent it flying at the man's car catching the back windscreen. The pot shattered and lucky for the guy his car windscreen didn't. Unfortunately the pain in Steve's side came back to remind him not to be so stupid.

Before he opens the door, he wonders, stupid or not, if there is another pot to throw if it's the same man returning again.

Opening the front door, a blur hits him in the stomach and pushes him back. Trying to control his balance and almost ending on his butt, he is again reminded of his bruise as his side erupts in pain. Steadying his legs, at the same time trying to hold in the pain, Steve looks down at the canine face staring up at him, panting away, happy to see him and the tail wagging like mad. Steve for the first time smiles down at the dog trying to slobber all over him

"George!" cries Steve, happy to see the dog.

George was Steve's father's dog, a six year old, male, German shepherd. Sixty five pounds with a grey and tan coat. George has been in the family since his father had decided that he could do with some company and he needed an excuse to keep healthy. Taking a dog for a long walk seemed like a good way and since getting George, he and Steve's father were inseparable. George always seemed to know what Christopher was thinking as he always seemed to react before a command was given.

Standing on the porch, holding the lead and only just hanging on was his father's neighbour, Frederick Klein. Klein was a portly man in his late sixties who had been living next to Steve's father since he could remember.

"Frederick, you might want to let go of the leash or George will have your arm off." Just getting George to the front door from his parked car only 50 yards away, Klein was out of breath, a man happily overweight from his wife's cooking. Not a man to turn down second helpings.

"Hello Steve, I hope it is alright that I bring you George," Frederick stammers, trying to get his breath.

Steve looks over to Frederick's car, not seeing his wife Elsa.

Frederick reading Steve's mind, "Elsa did not come with me." Taking his time looking at Steve, Frederick tried to judge how he was doing. "Elsa sends her love. I do not know what to say Steve and I cannot imagine what you must feel."

Frederick explains how they found out about the accident and they were both still trying to come to terms with all that has happened. It has shaken them to the core, as they could not believe what they were hearing from listening to the local radio with reports of the accident. George had been barking all night, a dog's sixth sense that something was wrong. They could not leave George alone and so they went around with the spare key his father had given them. George was under the table and they knew he could not be left by himself.

Frederick stares at George, a sad smile on his face. "We have tried to look after George but we got worried for him. After Sunday he has not eaten and he just lies around watching the front door. Elsa thought it best if I brought George over. She is a smart woman and I think she is right. This is the first time George has been excited and looking at you, I think maybe that is your first smile. I tried to ring you to let you know but I could not get through, so my apologies for turning up unannounced."

Steve forgetting himself, takes in everything Frederick is saying and rubs George's head. Both are delighted with seeing each other. "I am sorry Frederick, I am forgetting my manners, please come in."

"If it is alright with you Steve, I will decline. I am sorry but Elsa is not very well and with what has happened, she has slipped a little more. I am very worried for her and I do not wish to leave her alone too long. The journey has taken me almost two hours. I am very sorry Steve as I am sure you could do with someone to talk too. I hope you understand?"

Steve understood, telling Frederick that he will be in touch about the funeral details. His friend Nigel had offered to organise the funeral and will be sending the cards out soon.

Looking down at George, Steve for the first time feels happy that he had some company.

Steve watches Frederick drive off, and waves as he passes.

"Come on George, let's get you fed. I feel both of us can do with each other's company." Steve's father used to come over, sometimes on unannounced visits to discuss ideas with Steve when his mind was set on something he was working on, so Steve made sure that there was always a few days' supply of dog food.

Tina was back in the pharmacy, watching the time. Things had been a little tense with Keel, after yesterday's visit from the police. Keel had come out of the office after the police had gone and had given Tina a long stare which had left her unnerved. Things had not improved when she had arrived earlier today. She was thinking of phoning in sick but decided against it as money was tight and every cent counts if she wants to go to university but thinks that once she finishes the stock take, she's out of there.

Her cell phone vibrates in her pocket, her bleak thoughts forgotten as she reads the message from her mom. Thank God for small interruptions she thinks. The message read, "Meet me at the movie house after you finish. My treat, Kisses, Mom," Tina replies. "Finishing at six. See you 6.15 Kiss. Kiss." Tina thinks about where she will finish up her stock check, looks like the small store room at the back is last on list. Some of that stuff has got to be out of date. That's got to be a couple of hours work. If she can get in there for four, that will give her a couple of hours.

There is a bang on the front door. Tina heads over thinking another customer is calling for their prescriptions. Tina had to make some calls to customers whose medicines were urgent. These were the only customers who were allowed in while the pharmacist was closed. Then she realised that the last prescriptions were picked up more than an hour ago. Another person who can't read the notice she thinks. Spotting the man at the door, Tina points to the notice. The man ignores this and beckons Tina over. Tina rolls her eyes as she walks over, again about to point out to another person the notice on the window to say they were closed.

The man looks to be in his fifties and getting a little on the large side, dressed in a suit and tie and smiling at Tina as she points to the sign. He shouts through the window, "Hello miss, I would like to speak with your manager, Mr Keel," at the same time, holding a card to the window. The card reads Shaver and Mills, Attorney at Law, with Paul Mills, printed under this.

Tina reads the card and looks back at the man, wondering if she should tell him to come back tomorrow when the pharmacy opens as she is not happy disturbing Keel after yesterday.

"Please young lady. This is important."

Tina closes her eyes and nods, telling the man to wait. Walking to the office, Tina thinks, here we go, another cold stare from Keel the Heel. If he has a go at me, I'm off, she tells herself, knowing full well she will bite her tongue.

Knocking on the door, Tina hears her boss shouting out, "Wait!" Followed by, "What do you want Tina?"

Tina enters, waiting for the boss to have a go at her, willing it.

"What is it Tina?"

"There's a man, a lawyer I think at the door. Says it's important and he wants to speak with you. He's still out front."

"What's it about," Keel asks?

"I don't know. He just says he needs to talk to you."

Keel gets up and walks out the office to view the man in the distance. Making a decision, he goes to the front door and opening it, he asks the gentleman what he wants with him.

Mills hands Keel his card telling him which firm he represents and asks that they have a talk in private relating to a matter of importance and telling Keel that it would benefit both parties if he accepts. He makes a point that with the pharmacy closed, this would be a good opportunity to have that talk and offers to take him for lunch as his firm would pay.

Keel thinks about this, wondering what this man wants with him. Free food also goes through his mind, and beneficial, what does that mean? "Can you tell me what this about? I am busy?"

"I will gladly explain sir; I assure you this will be in your best interests."

Keel tells Mills that he will lose money if he takes time away from work, knowing that he does not intend to honour that with his employees.

"Mr Keel, we will be happy to pay you for your time and as I have said, this will be beneficial to you."

Keel thinks again, looking at the time, and makes a decision, telling Mills that he needs to be back before closing.

Keel tells Mills to wait and fetches his jacket from the office. On the way out he speaks with Tina, telling her not to answer the phone or let anyone in and that he will be back before she leaves at six.

Tina watches as they both walk across the road and climb into the back of a limo, wondering why a lawyer wants to speak with Keel. Looking out the window she hopes that the young guy from yesterday was around .She could do with cheering up and if he's around what's wrong with a little flirting she asks herself. It's not as if anything else will happen.

Washington is sitting at her desk, writing up reports and still waiting for the toxicology report from the hospital regarding the chemical contents of the late Mrs O'Neil's prescription. They had a call from the hospital earlier to say it would be with them later that afternoon. She was also waiting on information on Keel. She had put a request out over the Internal Police network. She put it through normal channels to keep the cost down as last month their station had a visit from the local Mayor's office about their expenditure. They were only a small precinct with a police force of fifty four personnel. They were told to tighten their belts but not to take it personally as times were hard and they had to find ways to save on cost or more jobs could go. They had already lost officers in the last cutbacks and with elections coming up, budgets were always top of the list.

They had learned that Keel had moved to Belmont two years earlier and had rented a place on the outskirts of the town in a quiet neighbourhood. They had also found out, that he had been picked up for trespassing on a family home when the owners had spotted him prowling around, outside their teenage daughter's window. They had not proceeded against Keel as he was picked up walking away from their house by the patrol car that was sent. However, he was put on record, but no charges were filed against him. There appears to be little more information on him. They had his driving licence and social number on record and put these through the system and were patiently, still waiting on this information.

Detective Moralis may be the team leader, he also makes a mean coffee and was back at his desk handing across her coffee, asking her at the same time if she had finished the report she was working on. She throws him the report and he quickly scans it then passes it back and before he can ask, she tells him for the umpteenth time that nothing has come in from the net, thinking that no matter how quick the system gets, it will never be quick enough.

They both turn when the door opens from the main office as the secretary comes out holding a few files. She walks to a few tables dropping some of the files off, talking with some of the officers and one in particular, Officer Richards, a good looking man with a close resemblance to Brad Pitt and known for being a bit of a Casanova with the ladies. He had tried to flirt with Washington, when she had joined but she had seen right through him. Not a rank thing, she had told him, just that she likes grown up men. Washington smiles to herself when she remembers the look of hurt on his face, not used to being rejected, so once in a while he tries again. She decides to watch herself at the Christmas party; reminding herself not to have too much to drink otherwise Richards might have another notch to his belt.

The secretary finally stops chatting to Richards and heads over to their desk. She has a smile on her face as she's thinking about the weekend she is planning to have with Richards, thinking maybe she would be the one to land him, after all, she had held back before and didn't give it all away. Keep them coming back until their hooked was what she had been taught by her mother.

Without so much as a glance at either Moralis or Washington, she drops a file on their desk and turns heading back to her office giving a big smile to Richards on the way.

Moralis snatches it up before Washington moves and glances through, turning a few pages before handing it to Washington.

She does the same, then glances up at Moralis. The toxicology report had been sent and the screening showed the pills had not contributed to Mrs O'Neil's death as the contents showed they were as prescribed. Moralis and Washington were not just waiting for information on the Beta Blockers, but as there was a death in surgery, before a body can be released, the coroner has to perform a post mortem to find out the cause of death and they were waiting on the results.

Reading the findings of the toxicology report, the coroner states that trace amounts of a substance normally associated with bees, were found in her blood cells. The coroner also states, that in his opinion, the substance found, may or may not have contributed to death of Mrs O'Neil and that other trace substances found in her body were too small to identify. It would appear that Mrs O'Neil suffered a trauma as it is quite clear that she had suffered a systematic shut down of her internal organs, leading to a cardiac seizure and stopping her heart. There are signs of burnt tissue in her upper torso and this concurs with the surgeon's report of using a defibrillator to try and restart the heart.

The report goes on to say that it is not clear how some of the substances had entered the body and the Coroner had left the cause of Death as Systematic Organ Failure, but he could not fully account for the cause of this. Further tests were needed and samples from the body will be sent to forensics for testing.

No one liked reading coroner reports but they helped clear up police cases, unfortunately this one was left open and Moralis was impatient as it could take weeks for another Toxicology report to come back. There was another file under the coroner's report that he almost misses.

This one was a report back on Keel. The first couple of lines ask if they had put the social number through for Keel correctly as the number given, was for a Peter Stanley Keel, from Maine, diseased 2003. A photo showed a man they had never seen before. Looking further through the report, they come across a photo showing what looked like their Keel. The report states this man is wanted in connection for the possible rape of several teenagers in the State of Minnesota. The name was Peter Sean Keel. A different social number was shown.

Both Moralis and Washington turned to each other as Washington had leaned over to read the report with Moralis. "That's our Keel," they both said in unison.

The report goes on to include, that Peter Keel, had disappeared after being questioned by officers back on the 14th of March 2009. Forensics had taken DNA from a girl who had been assaulted and it matched DNA taken from Keel. Before they were able to arrest him, he had fled and his whereabouts were unknown. The report goes onto mention the statement given by Keel at the time of the interview. There was a signature with this. They read on and find that other teenage girls had come forward with stories of assault and Keel was identified as the perpetrator.

Moralis turns to Washington. "We need a new sample of his DNA and a signature to match so I want him brought in for questioning. Get a patrol across to the pharmacy. When we leave here I'll let the captain know who we may have. We will need a warrant for a search of his house and car. Check to see if we have had any reports in the last few years concerning unsolved rapes of teenagers. Say a radius of twenty miles. I can think of two off the top of my head."

"Why are we not picking up Keel? "Washington asks.

"Don't worry. It will be our bust if he is this rapist and our interview. I just want to clear things with the captain first as I want to get O'Neil in for questioning as well and I don't want uniforms picking him up, if he's innocent, I do not want the neighbours alerted to gossip with uniforms bringing him in. We are just requesting he comes for another interview and you can work your charm. While we interview O'Neil, I want Keel to sit and sweat until we're ready for him."

"What about the girl?" Washington asks. "Don't you think we should interview her?"

"I was just thinking about that. Again I do not want her brought to the station in a police vehicle. Get some plain clothes out there as well."

This could be a major bust, Washington thinks, at the same time getting back on the police net for unsolved rapes in the past couple of years.

Tina is finishing up the last of the inventory. She has managed to find that almost half the stock on the shelves was out of date, some of it several years and wonders when the last stock take was carried out. Some of this should have been recalled years ago for termination. Certain medical products were classified for termination if not used within the life of the product and Tina had found several that had leaked. Checking the time on her cell phone, she sees that it is almost 17.45. Keel should have been back by now, she thought.

She hears movement in the shop and calls out, letting Keel know where she is as she carries on checking the inventory.

She stops suddenly as the door swings inwards almost catching her arm. Keel stands in the doorway, one arm holding it open. He is staring at Tina, not saying a word.

"God Mr Keel. You almost hit me with the door bursting in like that."

Not a word comes from Keel and Tina feels bumps spread out on her skin. Keel has a look on his face she does not like. Only it feels more threatening in such an enclosed space.

"Mr Keel do you think you can let me out. I have finished the inventory and it's almost time to go." She also adds, looking at Keel, that her mother was coming to the pharmacy to pick her up at any moment. She doesn't know why she has said this, only that Keel is making her feel nervous and he does not look right. He seemed to be swaying on his feet and she realizes that he has been drinking.

Keel looks back at the front door ignoring Tina. He moves forward into the room, blocking any chance for Tina to get out, at the same time as catching the door and throwing it shut behind him. He stands swaying before reaching across to the light switch and turning it off.

From inside the store room comes the sound of breakage followed by shouts of panic and a high pitched scream.

Outside in the distance is the sound of a police car with its siren blaring.

Chapter 8

Tina's Mother, Elena, had been waiting outside the cinema for twenty five minutes and Tina was late. The movie that they had talked about seeing would start in five minutes. looking again at her watch, she pulls her cell phone from her pocket and for the third time in five minutes, she dials her daughter's phone. After listening and waiting for her daughter to answer, the phone goes straight to voice mail. It was unlike Tina not to answer, as you could hardly keep her daughter off her phone. Elena knows her daughter would not have forgotten to come and would have called if she had changed her mind.

Looking at her watch again, Elena decides to head down to where Tina works. She could walk it in fifteen minutes or five if she drove. Deciding to choose her car, she knows that as soon as she leaves, seconds later her space will be occupied and thinking they would miss the 18.30 show, but maybe they can catch a later show.

On arriving across the road from the pharmacy, many of the shops had already closed and there was plenty of parking.

Elena had met Tina's manager only once before. The man had barely looked at her when Tina introduced them. A rude man, she thought, remembering what Tina had said about him.

Going to the front door and checking the handle, she presses down on the lever and the door opens. Tina had told her that she was the only girl asked to work while the work was taking place. All the electrical work, she said, was being carried out after six and Tina was asked to carry out a stock check and take in the deliveries as well as phoning customers to let them know their prescriptions were ready for picking up.

Elena was about to enter, when someone calls out from behind telling her to stop. She looks around at the police officer walking quickly towards her. He was beckoning her to come away from the pharmacy.

"Sorry lady, the shop is closed. You shouldn't be going in there."

A little startled, Elena composers herself, "I am here for my daughter as she works here. The door is open, so she must be still working."

"Can you tell me your name please?"

"Why do you need to know my name?" Elena is inpatient and is less than happy to tell the officer who she is as she feels it's none of his business but she eventually complies, telling him who she was and adding who her daughter is.

"Sorry Mrs McElroy, do you mind waiting here for a few minutes? I need to speak with station. I won't be long."

Walking away from Elena, Patrolman Joseph Lieberman is on his radio calling dispatch, letting them know that there is was no sign of Peter Keel. Also they were questioning the electrician in the car and he had told them that he was late arriving for work. He had some work to finish off and should have arrived before six.

The police had arrived earlier and had stopped the electrician from entering the premises. They had brought him back to the patrol car where his partner was asking him questions about where Keel might be. They had turned up around six and had found the premises to be open after trying the door. They had stepped inside and quickly looked around and finding no one around, they decided it was best to just wait and see if Keel turns up. Another patrol had been dispatched to Keel's house where they would meet up with a recently issued warrant to check the house and Keel's car if he showed up there.

Officer Lieberman, also lets them know that Tina McElroy was meeting her mother at the cinema house but had not shown up and that maybe she had gone home. He knew a car had been dispatched for her and let them know to send it to her address. Dispatch tells him to hold for further instructions.

Elena had not waited and had entered the pharmacy, looking around the dark interior and calling out her daughter's name. Moving further to the back, she removes her phone and pushes redial to ring Tina. Listening, she hears the muffled ringing tone, one she recognises as she has heard the sound before on her daughter's phone. It stops and she redials again listing for the direction the sound was coming from. It sounded like it was coming from the back and she walks to where the sound seemed to be emanating from and stops in front of a door, listening. The ringing had gone off and she dials once more and the ringing starts up from the other side of the door. The door has a name plate with the words, Stock Room 2. Another door to the right was stockroom 1 and the room to the right of that is Keel's office, then kitchen, followed by restroom.

Elena opens the door just as the ringing stops. The room is dark as she searches the wall for a light switch, finding it, she presses it and a modern energy saving bulb slowly lights up. It would be minutes or so before the bulb is bright enough to properly be able to see into the room. Shelves were blocking her view and Elena steps through, walking hesitantly, trying to peer through the shelves. As she steps forward, her foot kicks something that sounds like broken glass. She stops and peers down to see what she had nearly stood on. There were glass vials broken and scattered on the floor. Elena catches a rustling sound from the back of the room. She peers through the gloom, spotting something in the shadows at the back. Unable to see anything, she calls out Tina's name. No answers. She tries again. This time she gets a response. A shuffling sound of someone moving followed by a response as Tina cries out to her mom.

Elena quickly finds her way to the back, calling for her daughter and finds her cowering down on the floor. Something about her does not look right in the gloom.

"Tina, are you hurt? Please talk to me."

Elena looks down at her daughter, concern etched across her face as she realises what is wrong with her daughter's appearance. Her clothes did not look right and, bending closer, she is shocked to find Tina's was not wearing her clothes and that she was holding them across her.

Tina looks up, ashamed that her mother has found her like this, pulling the items of clothing, tighter, around her body as if this would hide her embarrassment. She was sobbing uncontrollably and Elena pulls her daughter to her and holds her.

Elena, rocking her daughter, holds back her own tears and silently curses the person who had committed this act of gross indecency on her daughter, bringing back memories of her own past

Tina pulls away from her mother, trying to hold back a scream, wanting to forget what has happened to her and wanting her mother to see in her eyes that this was not her fault, as she recoils from her memories.

Keel had been fast, pinning Tina down. He had proceeded to remove her lower garments. Tina had frozen not believing what was happening to her. She was petrified of this man and he was very strong for a man his size. He was all skin and bone but toned and very strong. She could not believe how strong he was as she tried to fight him off. She remembers the smell of his breath, Whiskey, he had been drinking and the sickening smell had made her gag.

She had eventually passed out from shock and woke up soon afterwards. He was standing over her, just looking down, his eyes moving across her body. He bent down towards her, his eyes now fixed on her eyes. He wanted her attention, telling her to listen clearly for he wanted to be sure she understood what he was going to tell her. "You are not to tell anyone what just happened, is that clear. I have just received information regarding your boyfriend, the O'Neil guy. It appears that he may have killed his wife. Do you understand?"

Tina wants to pull her eyes away from Keel. She hears him speaking to her but is not listening as she is petrified until she hears O'Neil's name mentioned. Keel carries on.

"Your boyfriend may have been given something from this pharmacy. Do you understand? Only it turns out it may have killed his wife. You gave him the package and I remember you leaving the shop last Saturday with O'Neil. You two left together and you gave him the package. The CCTV shows you running around the counter and grabbing a package and handing it to O'Neil. Those officers here yesterday have footage of that film. I checked the film after they were gone. Now his wife is dead and the police think that she had taken something when she was in hospital having her baby. They suspect her husband, your boyfriend and guess who else. You!"

He lets this sink in for a second. "If you tell anyone what happened here tonight. Remember I can say whatever I want as a witness against you when this goes to court and trust me, they will try you as an accomplice to a murder. You will be an old woman when you get out of jail. Do you understand me?"

Tina nods, her face a look of terror. "Murderer, Steve a murderer. They think I helped him. Steve's wife is dead." She was confused. She could not think straight as she was in shock and it was painful between her legs. Tina starts crying, telling Keel that she will not tell anyone, not a soul. She had no intention of letting anyone know what had happened to her. People would judge her she thought. She has been brought up as a Christian, not a regular every Sunday Christian but she goes to church at least once a month with her mother who is a profound worshipper with strong opinions about certain men.

Now her mother is here looking at her, knowing what has happened to her and she feels like she wants to die. Her mother can never tell anyone, she thinks. Tina needs to make it clear to her mother, that she must never breathe a word about this to anyone.

They both turn, looking at the open doorway as someone calls out. Elena remembers the police officer and is about to call out, when suddenly Tina grabs her arm. She looks at her daughter and sees a frightened look on her face, her head shaking from side to side and whispering to her, "No mom he can't come in here." Thinking quickly, she lies to her that this is not what she thinks. Tina tells her mother that it was consensual and that she had just fallen over afterwards. Her mother can read between the lies and smiles down, telling her to stay calm and get dressed and she would try and keep the officer from coming in.

Elena tries to smile for her daughter, but turns away quickly before she starts crying as she stands up and walks out to the shop. She reaches the front door and lying, she tells the officer that she thought she had heard something inside and went to check it out, only to find someone had left a fan on.

"Mrs McElroy, you should not be in here, please come out."

Elena walks past the officer and out the front door. The officer looks back in the shop, and then closes the door, turning to Elena; he asks her when she had last made contact with her daughter? Elena thinks quickly, telling him that she had just been in touch and Tina was on her way home.

"Mrs McElroy, can I ask you to call your Daughter please as we have a car coming over for her. She's to go to the station. Just a police procedure, a follow up with the officers who spoke with her yesterday."

Elena thinks quickly, trying to decide what she should do. Her daughter is inside the pharmacy and she has now lied to the police. Taking out her cell phone, she presses buttons and speaks, telling the person on the other end to go straight home and wait as the police would like to talk with her again.

Lieberman thanks Elena and contacts dispatch, letting them know where they can pick up Tina.

He thanks Mrs McElroy for her cooperation, telling her not to worry and that her daughter would be dropped back at home afterwards. Elena nods and walks away. Officer Lieberman watches her for a second, and then crosses the road to his patrol car.

Elena is aware she is being watched as she walks to her car, her phone out again as she speaks to Tina letting her know the police are outside waiting. Tina tells her mother that she will have to sneak out and that she will need a distraction. Her mom tells her that she will drive past the officers and stall the car which will hopefully get their attention. Elena can't believe what she is doing and gets in her car. She passes the patrol car and slams on her breaks, screeching the car to a stop.

Looking out the door towards the police car, Tina sees both officers turn to face her mother's car. She quickly leaves and walks in the opposite direction, desperately wanting to look around but instead keeping her head down until she reaches the corner. She quickly turns to see if anyone is following, then darts around the corner. Tina walks on a short distance, then hides behind a bus stop and leans against the back. Shaking, she looks at her hands, trying to control her emotions, telling herself to hold it together, but she cannot get the thoughts out of her head. She has been raped and the police want to speak to her about last Saturday and they think she helped Steve Murder his wife. She can't believe it and she doesn't believe what Keel has told her, but why do the police want to speak to her? She is so confused. She is getting over her shock and is starting to feel angry. Anyone who was near Tina would have heard her cry out, "The bastard, that bastard raped me!"

Her phone goes again. It's her mother asking where she was. Tina, fighting back her anger, tells her to drive to the corner, to turn left and stop fifty yards up the road just past the bus stop.

The weather was turning colder and rain was on the way. Other people were walking past, their coats buttoned up. Tina ignores the cold as it bites into her. She stands still like a statue and waits.

Five minutes later, her mother pulls up. Tina walks over and get in. Looking at her mother, she speaks, telling her to drive them to police station. Elena nods to her daughter and puts the car in drive.

The man picks up the phone and listens. Three minutes later he puts the phone down and dials another number.

He asks his man if they are still following Keel. He had decided to put a tail on Keel. What he didn't know until a few minutes ago was what a bad boy Keel was. It appears Keel has a secret and this will be a problem for him if he's picked up. If Keel talks and the police go and speak to Paul Mills, then things may get out of hand. They had the statement they needed to get O'Neil in court. His man will make short work of the prosecution. But Keel is now a headache. He orders his man to pick up Keel and to be quick about it. The police want him for questioning and they are out looking for him. He makes it clear that on no account can Keel be found by the police and to use whatever force is necessary.

Chapter 9

Steve had earlier, returned from walking George around the neighbourhood and through Pequossette Park, a ten minutes' walk from the condo. Both of them had enjoyed the walk, both silent companions, Steve more so as he thinks about the last few days. He doesn't realise what the time is and checks his watch then looking at George, had asked him if he was hungry. George instantly barks as if he understood what Steve had just asked him. Steve had smiled and they headed back to the condo. George had run straight in the kitchen and had waited for Steve to catch up and feed him.

Steve was now filling his bowl and thinking about eating himself. For the first time he turns on the local radio. Music is playing and he turns his attention to getting some food started. Grabbing a pizza from the freezer compartment, he places it on a tray and then into the oven. In the background, the music has ended and the presenter is talking about the state lottery being the highest pay-out, with over $500 million in the pot for the lucky person or persons with the right numbers to win it this Saturday. More news is given and then the music resumes.

Taking his pizza with him to the lounge, George follows at his heels, his eyes never leaving the plate and his tongue hanging out. Steve looks down at the dog, knowing that he could never say no to George. His father was always telling him off for feeding the dog, telling Steve that if he keeps feeding the dog on top of his normal meals, then Steve can go and exercise George.

Sitting carefully down, watching not to catch his side and wincing slightly, Steve, for the first time, sits back, enjoying the smell and taste of his food. George is sat in front watching every move of the pizza, as it leaves the plate. Steve teasing, with every mouthful, unable to control himself from laughing as he looks down at George, the eyes, begging to be fed. "OK boy, you win again," he says as he breaks a slice off and drops it down where George snatches it in mid fall, tipping his head back, the pizza slice never touching the sides as it slides down in one swallow.

"George you're a pig." George looks up with a look that says, I don't care, feed me. George's head pops up suddenly, alert, his ears prickling, listening.

The doorbell goes, breaking the spell of the moment these two were having with each other. Steve looks at the clock, it is close to six, and thinks if it's the journalist again, he'd make sure he wouldn't miss this time with his swing. Standing, they both head for the front door and open it to find the two detectives from yesterday stood out on the porch.

Detective Washington and Moralis were about to ask him to accompany them to the station, when Steve speaks first.

"If this is about that policy again, I still do not know anything about it. I have checked my paperwork this morning looking for this so called policy. I have also checked my emails for the last couple of weeks and nothing has been sent or received from my laptop regarding this so called policy. As I informed you yesterday, I have no idea other than my wife." Steve stops himself from saying any more as he regains his composure.

Moralis looking from Steve to his dog is first to speak, "Sorry to trouble you again Mr O'Neil and yes this is about the policy and other things. We have a few more questions Sir, about things that have recently come to light and we would just like you to clarify a few things. Would you be willing to come down to the station and answer a few questions?"

Steve looks at Moralis, turning over what he has just been asked and for the first time thinking clearly about why the police were questioning him. At first, he had assumed that it was just policy after the death of Karen. Now he thinks it's more and asks Moralis, "What other questions? He tells them that he was going to visit the hospital and could it wait. He would drop in at the station on the way back. Moralis tells him that it would be in his interest to cooperate now and then he could go the hospital. Steve decides he has had enough, telling Moralis that if he has no authority asking him to come now, then he could twiddle his thumbs until he was ready to come.

Washington decides it's time to use a women's charm as she feels this might turn into a standoff between these two, looking now at the change in O'Neil's expression and knowing her partner can be a little abrupt, she tells O'Neil that they will not take much of his time up and that the sooner he helps them with their enquiry, the sooner they will be out of his hair. Explaining further to him, that it is just normal procedure, that it would help them with their enquiries and hopefully clear things up.

Steve slowly takes his eyes of Moralis and for the first time acknowledges Washington, thinking quickly and working out if he should refuse these two but deciding that he wants this to stop and whatever these two need clearing up. After all, he thinks, this is probably just normal procedure, though at the back of his mind he knows that life is not that simple. He just wants this week over.

Looking at his watch, he takes a deep breath and tells them, that if they want him now, he was taking George.

Moralis tells Steve that is not going to happen and before Steve and Moralis can start arguing, Washington tells him that it was fine, looking back at her partner, her eyes pleading with him to agree. Fine, he replies, telling him about the dog compound. Steve shakes his head telling them where he goes, George goes. Moralis laughs, shaking his head and telling him again that it was not possible. Steve smiles and tells them he will see them later when he is ready.

Both Moralis and Washington turn to each other. Moralis grits his teeth and tells his partner that it was not police procedure but they can make allowances and to call ahead to get something for the dogs leash to be attached too. Turning back to Steve, he sarcastically asks him if he has a leash.

Steve ignores the sarcasm as he looks up at the weather, asking them to wait as he nips back in for his coat and George's leash. He looks up again as he the closes the door, thinking the clouds look very unsettling and he shivers as if some dark malignant force had settled over him.

Keel had spotted the police cruiser outside his house. His first thought was that Tina had blabbed. Bitch, he thought. Should have done her again but now he has to disappear. Not the first time, but he knows he was stupid to do it at work. He knows he should never have got drunk. It was stupid to make that statement to that lawyer. At least he's got some money in his pocket. He can't now go back to his house and grab his things. The police will be looking for his car. He needs to go now.

The man following Keel wondered why Keel has stopped, away from his house. He looks across and just makes out the police vehicle. Before he can do anything, he sees Keel's car turning around. Obviously Keel does not want to talk with the police, he surmises as he once again follows behind Keel.

Chapter 10

Moralis is sat impatiently at his desk. He has made several calls and has been told several times that every available man and women is out looking for Keel and when they find him, he will be first to know and would he please let them get on with their job. There are other problems that also need to be addressed in Belmont and some of these also have top priority.

Washington has made her call to have Tina McElroy seen by their MD and as soon as she finishes taking a statement, Tina will be taken over for the medical. Tina with her mother had arrived at the station a short time after Moralis and Washington. They had taken O'Neil with his dog to one of the interview rooms and were just starting to ask questions when there was a knock on the door. One of the station officers had called Washington out to let her know that, Tina McElroy and her mother were taken to another Interview room. She had then been informed about the assault on Miss McElroy.

Washington re-entered the room to whisper the news to Moralis and the interview was put on hold.

The priority now was to take a statement from Miss McElroy and get her off to the MD for examination.

Coming back to his desk, Moralis spots a large envelope. Someone had recently dropped it off and it was marked urgent. The heading on the envelope was some attorney company he had never heard off, a Shaver & Mills Attorney at Law. Moralis sits back and opens the end of the envelope. Looking inside, he pulls out what appears to be a statement. It was only after he started reading it that he realised what it contained.

This was a signed declaration from Keel about what had happened last Saturday when Tina had given O'Neil the bag. He states in the statement that he spotted Tina dropping something else into the bag before handing it over to O'Neil and also states that he heard O'Neil say something about whether the contents would be picked up in an examination. Keel goes on to state that at the time, he would have brought this up with Miss McElroy but with all the commotion that day, it had completely slipped his mind and it wasn't until he found out from the radio that Mr O'Neil's wife had died in hospital that he thought it best to contact Shaver and Mills before speaking to the police.

Moralis reads some more and decides on a plan to arrest O'Neil and leave him sweating in jail for the night. Nine times out of ten people tend to reflect on what they have done and he hopes a night behind bars will make O'Neil admit his guilt.

Steve has been sitting in the interview room for a while. The officer in the corner is just staring blankly at the floor and occasionally looking up and directing his blank stare at him.

He looks again at his watch. Steve is worried about the time, thinking if he is not out of there in another half hour, he will not be able to visit the hospital. He looks again at George thinking, you're not happy to be here, are you boy?

He decides that he has had enough and stands. The officer immediately reacts to this and tells Steve to sit back down. George is also up looking from Steve to the door.

"No! I won't sit back down. I have been more than reasonable with the police and now I have been left to sit in here and no disrespect to you, but you're not the most talkative person. Go and find someone or I walk."

The officer looks at Steve for a second and then tells him to wait and he will check to see when they are coming back.

As the officer opens the door, Steve catches a glimpse of Washington walking past. Steve is taken back as the next person to walk past is Tina, with an older woman at her side and he calls out her name.

The officer turns as Steve tries to get past him as he tries to blocks his exit by positioning himself in the doorway, but Steve ducks under his arm and collides with Washington as she returns.

In the background, George is trying to pull from the leash as he thrashes about, trying to release himself from the table which is firmly attached to the floor.

Tina is stunned, seeing Steve coming out from the room, next door to hers, calling his name and immediately asks him why do the police think he's killed his wife.

Steve looks at Washington who instantly tells Steve to go back in the room. Steve ignores her and turns back to Tina to ask her who had told her he had supposedly killed his wife? Turning to Washington he asks if she had put that idea in Tina's head. Then he asks her if that was the reason they had him in the station, because they intended to charge him?

Washington immediately tries to calm the situation by telling everyone that no-one has been accused of killing anyone and turns to Steve, again asking him go back in and that Moralis will be in shortly to speak with him.

Steve again ignores her as he looks at Tina, asking her why she was at the station. Tina, with all that had happened to her, had bottled up her emotions and she burst into tears. Elena moves forward to console her daughter. Steve, surprised and confused by Tina's outburst, looks for Washington to explain.

Moralis was on his way back when he heard all the commotion and is annoyed at seeing Steve outside his room. He pulls Washington to one side and asks her what the hell was going on and then tells her in a whisper that he has just been passed a file from Shaver and Mills, Attorney at Law.

Moralis shows her the statement made out to a Paul Mills from Keel earlier today, stating that Tina had passed on something to a Mr O'Neil last Saturday and that they both were acting suspiciously and had stated that the item in the package was not the medicine that Mrs O'Neil normally has.

He turns around to find Steve staring at him. He had overheard what he had just told Washington and was shaking his head sideways, not believing what he was hearing. Then Steve says something before anyone else speaks, a sad smile on his face as he turns back to Tina, looking her in the eyes and telling her, that whatever she hears, it's not true. Turning back around to Moralis, he tells him to get on with it as he knows what is coming.

He looks at Tina, wondering why she is in tears, a sad look on his face, and stating that she looks like she had a rough day and this was not a place for someone as young as her to be in.

Moralis asks Washington to escort Tina and her Mother out or they will be late for the appointment. Turning to Steve, he asks him to step back in the room and walks in with him, shaking his head at the guard and closing the door. They both stand eye to eye and then Moralis informs him that he is being charged with the murder of his Wife and that anything he says will be taken down and used in a court of law. He asks him if he understands and Steve nods.

Unfortunately, outside in the corridor, Tina has started crying again and it has now attracted the attention of the station captain as well as other police officers. Captain Debra Childs is the first female to be given the role of captain in Belmont and has a reputation of being fair, as long as the rules are followed. She immediately empties the corridor of other officers with her stern look and was now focusing her attention on Washington and Tina.

Washington makes the mistake of asking Childs if she can help her and this infuriates her as she gives Washington a stern rebuke, asking her why a young girl was making such a racket and where was her partner? Moralis, hearing his commanding officer, shows his face and is immediately asked to make time later on as she would like a word with him and then she turns and walks away.

Moralis shakes his head and walks back into the room. Steve had sat down and was looking down at the table. Moralis looks at him wondering if he has done the right thing by charging him. They still need Keel to confirm the statement he has made, even though he is now a wanted man. However, the statement was made prior to their knowledge that he was wanted in another State for assault and now, the alleged assault on one of their own. He walks over, sits back down and turns the recorder on. He repeats the charge against Steve and then tells him that they have the statement from Keel accusing him of receiving a package from Tina, allegedly containing more than the Beta Blockers for his wife and which may have contained a substance that may have contributed to her death. He tells him that he has checked footage from last Saturday, showing the transfer from Tina to himself. That this was not normal practise and that it was witnessed by Keel.

Steve looks up and asks him if that was the case, then why did Keel not intervene last weekend? Moralis tells him that they will obviously ask that question but presently Keel is not available to be questioned.

Steve nods and then tells Moralis that what he has in front of him is bullshit and he should be spending his time looking for this Keel and not following false statements and that is about as much as he is going to say until he gets a lawyer.

Moralis figured this was going to happen. He tells Steve that he will be placed in lock-up until he makes his call, turning to the officer, he asks him to escort him to the duty officer. Steve is asked to stand and put his arms behind his back. The officer places cuffs on his wrists and escorts him out.

After sitting in the lock up with various other people, all in the same boat, waiting their chance to make a call, Steve gets his turn and is called out. The cell door is unlocked and he is taken to a booth where he is told that he can make one call. Steve has already decided who he's calling.

Nigel picks up the call on his cell phone, not recognizing the number but knows the local code and answers, hearing Steve's voice.

"Hi Nigel, it's Steve, I have a problem, I need your help and I need it now."

Steve tells him what has happened and that he needs a lawyer. Nigel tells him it's getting late but he thinks he knows someone who would come out to see him tonight.

Nigel is all business and tells him of a lawyer he has dealt with, who works for the company and although his work is more towards financial, he has some court experience and he could at least get things moving. Would Steve be fine with this? Steve tells him that at this point, he does not care which lawyer he sees as long as he gets him out. Nigel tells him that if he has been charged, that he would be fighting for bail first in what they call an arraignment and the earliest they would deal with that will not be until tomorrow some time and he would have no choice but spend the night in jail. Steve accepts this and tells Nigel to do his best.

Steve is escorted back to the cell. There are five other people there and he finds a corner to sit away from the others as he has no intention of passing the night away in conversation with these people, so he keeps his head down.

He sits there with nothing else to do but think. Only a few days have passed since his wife had died and his father and sister were killed. He is wondering why Tina was in the station and is unhappy that he could not make his appointment at the hospital. He is also feeling very sorry for himself.

George is also not having a good time, as he had also been placed behind bars in the local pound. He had been making a scene earlier but had calmed down.

Scholfield had been watching Steve's condo for ten minutes when the front door opens. A man peers out looking around and exits followed by another man. They make their way to a vehicle, placing bags in the rear. He watches them talking before they get in and leave.

Scholfield waits a few seconds then follows, keeping his distance. He thanks God for the rain as this will keep him from being spotted.

He had a call earlier from his friend on the vehicle he is following. The vehicle belongs to a company that specialises in personal security. The friend he spoke with tells him that these are people you do not piss off. They have friends in high places and people that have gone up against them are either permanently on medication or not available to comment. Nothing, it seems can touch these people and apparently they have very good defence attorneys. His friend tells him to watch his back and better still drive the other way and forget about it.

Forgetting about it was the last thing on his mind. He had the bit between his teeth and the more something smelled, the more he liked it.

Steve is wide awake. Some of the men in with him had gone to sleep. These were people who he thought spent a lot of time in this institute. He decides he was not going to be one of them.

It is after 21.30 and he thinks that he won't be seeing any attorney tonight. Nigel may know one or two, but it was highly unlikely that the sort of expensive attorneys that Nigel knows, dealing in multimillion dollar battles with other companies were going to give up their nice evening to come and talk to him. A slim to none chance, he thought.

Steve's name is called, taking him away from his thoughts. A duty guard is opening the cell door, looking across at Steve as he stands, unhappy from being taken away from watching sports. He ushers him out, telling him he was lucky as it wasn't procedure to have offenders receive visitors this late at night and that he must have a fairy god mother.

Steve leaves his cell and is escorted by the guard to a room similar to the one he was in with Moralis. He makes a mental note, if he gets out, that he will never be coming back.

A man wearing an expensive suit walks over to Steve and shakes his hand. He waits until the guard leaves before offering a seat. Steve's thoughts, as he looks at the attorney, are that he was strictly boardroom, a corporate lawyer. He had met many of these lawyers, always one eye on the dollar, the other trying to peer down their secretary's top.

He starts by apologising about his lateness and that he was in a meeting. He introduces himself as Richard Talbert and says that he works as one of the attorneys for Joseph and Mitchell. Being frank with Steve, he says that their law firm mainly practice corporate law and that he had been called out of a meeting because he had previous experience in the courts. He was just there until a more suitable attorney could be found and, he told Steve, someone high up at MIT considers him important enough to get him a hearing first thing in the morning.

They talk about Steve's side of the story and consider the evidence against him. Talbert feels that it is weak, flimsy at best and the testimonial by Keel seems a little suspect in his opinion. He has heard of the law company who had taken Keel's statement and rumours have circulated that they are under investigation themselves for fraud. He goes on to tell him that he is not surprised by events as there is $200,000 to be paid out. The insurance company will do everything in their power to hold onto it. The law company is in for ten per cent of that money and from what he hears, need every cent.

Steve is shaking his head as he tells Talbert that he never applied for a life policy in the first place.

Talbert, prior to arriving, had been informed that Keel had gone missing and that he was wanted in connection for assault on one of his staff and he asks Steve what he knew about keel. Steve asks him if he has the name of the person he assaulted but Talbert tells him he doesn't and he can only tell him that it happened sometime earlier today. Steve jumps up, angry, as he realises who the person was, that was assaulted. He tells Talbert and the attorney thinks, with

Keel missing and the assault charge, he can't see it going past arraignment. There is no way, without any more evidence against Steve, that this will go any further and that they should pray Keel isn't found. He thinks the police have made an error but not to get to overconfident and the best thing he can do is find out what type of judge they have tomorrow. Before Talbert goes, he asks Steve about his child as he was informed of Karen's death in the hospital and the birth.

A father himself, he wonders if O'Neil is aware of what might be happening with him being detained and tells him that it may be nothing, only in circumstances like this, babies are put under the ward of the local court. This may not be the case but, from what he knows, if social services have been informed of your arrest, innocent or not, you have a fight on your hands to get your child back.

Steve closes his eyes, wondering how bad can things get? Looking at the attorney, he asks him, if it happens, what does he need to do? Talbert tells him, right now to think about tomorrow first and not to worry about other things.

As he leaves, Talbert thinks that if it was a woman he was defending, then her child would normally be given back if she was found not guilty, but it doesn't work like that for men, he knows. Even as a lawyer, he has had to fight for every second to see his own child after a lengthy court battle with his ex-wife.

Keel finds a safe place to pull over. He needs to think things through. His best chance is to drive south. He can get lost down in the south but he needs to change his car. It's getting dark and now is a good time to do it before he leaves town.

He looks up in the mirror and spots a car. The car lights are on but he can't quite make out the model. If it's the police, he's had it. The car approaches and Keel watches in the mirror as it gets closer. He realises he has not taken a breath. His head down, he watches the car cruise pass, the passenger of the car looking across. Not the police, he thinks, and takes a breath and sits back up. The weather is getting bad outside and for once he's happy about this as it will hamper the efforts of the police to find him. Before he knows what is happening, his side door is flung open and a hand reaches in and grabs him by his collar and drags him from his car, throwing him down on the ground. Before he can retaliate, something hard is cracked across his skull. Keel's last thoughts were about Tina, a sick smile playing across his face as he falls unconscious.

Chapter 11

Moralis is nearing the end of his shift. He had pulled a late one as usual with all the running around he had to do. He knows that as things are with O'Neil, that he has a weak case against him.

A call came in from dispatch about finding a car outside of town belonging to Keel and there was no sign of the man. The keys were still in the ignition. Both Moralis and Washington had gone out to investigate and had forensics run their tests. Fibres were taken and the car was brought in for further investigation but nothing as yet revealed where Keel may have gone. It is Moralises opinion that the car was left as a decoy and that they should be looking closer to home. He has put a man on Keel's house and forensics will be out there first thing in the morning to do a thorough search.

Moralis knows if his man is not found by the morning of O'Neil's court date, the chances were that he was going to walk. Moralis had still not made up his mind on O'Neil. Things were pointing at him and yet in the back of his mind he felt something was not right with the case. His partner had already left and Washington was staying on the side-line on this one. She had taken Miss McElroy for examination and a DNA sample would be matched up with the ones already in the data base. If the samples match, it will tie Keel to the other assaults.

Moralis had checked the database on Shaver & Mills as he could not understand why they would want to get a statement from Keel. He thinks that the insurance group who gave the life policy to Mrs

O'Neil, is behind this. He thinks that if Keel has accepted money for his cooperation with the insurance agency, then the statement he gave will automatically be thrown out and the case against O'Neil will be dropped by the judge.

Moralis had tried to get the courts to postpone the hearing but he was unsuccessful and both himself and Washington will be at the court hearing. He is of the opinion that the hearing will be done and dusted within ten minutes and that the news will be back in the precinct before he is. He is sure of one thing, there will be another meeting with the captain in her office; about wasting the court's time, police time and police budget.

If the tests come back and prove positive for the death of Mrs O'Neil, then they can go through the whole process again and if O'Neil is the guilty party, he now has the best council money can buy and he will be thoroughly prepared next time.

Today was a total screw up and the blame will lie with him. It's not the first time and it won't be the last. Looking at his watch again, he thinks it is time to call it a night. His wife, after twenty four years of marriage, has stood by him with his late returns and phone calls in the middle of the night. She was born the daughter of a police officer and understands the responsibilities that go with the job. This job is not for the faint hearted. It takes the right type of person to live with someone who spends more than half the day and more weekends at work then he could care to remember. The job is a taker, not a giver but for Moralis it still means the same to him as it did the day he started.

Opening his wallet, he looks at the picture on the inside of his wife and three kids. Kids, he thinks, two boys and one girl, the oldest nineteen and in university. The other two a few years off, but all with their heads screwed on, Moralis thinks, pride showing in his eyes as he puts his wallet back in his pocket and turns off his desk light.

Tina was back at home with her mother. She had endured the tests with the doctor, who was very sympathetic, which helped with the examination. Her mother and Washington were left in the waiting area as Tina was too embarrassed for her to be in with her. The test lasted twenty minutes and Tina felt that she would never allow a man to violate her like that again, let alone ever have a man touch her again. She vowed she would fight back next time, even if her life was threatened.

Elena is very protective of her Daughter, and the last few hours in the police station, plus the possibility that her Daughter may be investigated because of something that had happened last Saturday at work with this man O'Neil, has left her shaken to her foundation. She had tried to get the detective who took them to see the doctor to open up about what is happening, but she had told her that she could not divulge any information about the case. "This is not a case," she had told the lady, "this is my daughter we are talking about." Elena has always protected her family and has always kept her own personal life away from her family. Whenever a man has shown too much interest in her and has wanted more from the relationship, Elena has always put a halt to it and cut all ties with the person.

She has asked Tina not to speak with this O'Neil man and although her daughter had agreed, Elena feels she will not listen to her on this matter. Who is this person her daughter knows from the pharmacy and what do the police think he has done? Tina will not speak on the matter.

What's important now is helping her daughter get over her ordeal. Elena has never told anyone of the many times her late husband had come home drunk and had made demands on his rights, as he put it, for a man to have his way with his wife. As a Catholic, Elena was brought up to obey her husband and the times she did not were the times she had to hide her injuries from her family and friends.

Elena had thought that she could protect her daughter from these types of men but she knows she cannot. Life, she feels, is failing young vulnerable women and modern life is making a mockery out of human standards. Technology has its benefits but it has brought with it many of today's problems with young people being denied their youth.

She thinks that God is losing his flock. Attitudes and people's expectations need to change. Not everything is on a plate. A person will only know him or herself when they have achieved success through the labours of life. She has instilled this in her family with a mother's love. Now though, she is thinking and worrying about tomorrow and what the day will throw at her daughter. All she knows is that she will be there for her.

Scholfield has been sat outside the building for more than an hour. Another vehicle like the first one has turned up all black and facing towards him, as if it is quietly challenging him to a duel. He had to slide down in his seat, as he did not feel like mixing it up with these guys. They were big and they certainly were not the type of people you would go up to and have a friendly conversation with. No one had come out since the first vehicle had arrived. It was getting late and he wondered why they had come here. They had driven out of town for some twenty or so minutes and had arrived at some buildings on a business park estate. He had again made some enquiries with his man in the know and was still waiting on his call. He knew that if he hung around much longer, someone would spot him. Other premises on the site were closed and most of the vehicles that were parked were mainly company vans. His car would not be too hard to spot among them.

Looking in his rear view mirror, he spots another car turning and driving towards him. Again he hunkers down and watches as the vehicle glides past. The side windows were dark and he could not see the driver. The weather was still bad. The wind had picked up and rain was lashing sideways on his windows. Pulling himself up for a clearer view, he watches as the person opens the car door, an umbrella appears and is nearly torn from the person's grasp. The heavy rain and umbrella make it hard to see who is getting out. He cannot make the details out of the number plate but makes a note of the car type, a very expensive one by the looks of it. European, he thinks, as he watches him run to the building, the others had entered. A door opens before he arrives and he steps through. Scholfield is not sure but he thinks before the man enters, that he quickly looks across in his direction. Just my imagination, he thinks, but he makes a point to be extra vigilant and locks his doors from the inside.

A short time later, the doors to the building open and two of the men exit, heading out to the second car. They open the rear door and between them pull a large bundle from inside and carry it back to the building. This was too much for him, as he was not going to see anything from inside his car and he was going to have to get wet. "Come on you hero," he tells himself as he steps out into the rain and makes his way to the building using the cover of parked vehicles and shadows. Arriving, he works his way around the side of the building, trying to look through the windows to see if he could spot movement. He heads around the back and notices that at the rear, there was smoke billowing out of a smoke stack. He cleans an area of glass from the last window and peers in. The room is dark but there is light filtering through from a half open door. As he peers in, there is a movement outside the doorway and something hits the door throwing it open. Scholfield's eyes widen as the bundle that was pulled from the car has fallen to the ground opening up and exposing what looks like an arm. The men quickly lift the bundle, not worried about the exposed arm and carry on down the corridor. Scholfield looks across to the smoke stack and shudders, realising what is going to happen to whoever is in the bundle. He hopes to God that the person is already dead and decides he should contact the police and let them deal with it. He wonders what their interest is with this O'Neil person. He decides that he has seen enough, but the journalist in him wants more as he looks back in the window. That was his mistake as his shadow was projected onto the floor, catching the attention of one of the people inside. Their eyes meet and as the man turns to issue orders, the shadow disappears from the floor.

Scholfield does not take a second to think about things. He is moving fast, his car is three hundred yards away and facing in the wrong direction. Seconds after clearing the building, he hears the sound of a door being flung open and hitting the wall rebounding back followed by a cry and the sound of running feet. There was no way he was going to look back, his thoughts on getting to his car in one piece. He collides with the side of the car, his arm outstretched, his hand finding the door handle and almost losing grip. He flings the door wide and jumps in ready with his keys in the ignition. The car starts and he pulls away, throwing his lights on and illuminating one of the men who he spotted going into O'Neil's house. Behind him is another person and in the distance he sees the lights of the second vehicle come on. The man in front of him has stopped and is bringing his arm up. He spots the gun in the man's hand and he does not think twice as he guns his car, aiming for the guy who makes the right decision and jumps out of the way landing in the scrub at the side of the road. With the wheel turned, he hits the hand break and immediately the car is thrown into a spin. The car comes around and again he jams his foot down on the peddle, while trying to control the spin. He heads towards the main road, almost losing the back end as he takes the corner, keeping his foot down, trying to find traction and eventually finding it. He glances in his rear mirror, seeing head lights in the distance and back to keeping his eyes on where he is going. His eyes darting in the mirror every second as he thrusts his hand in his pocket trying to locate his cell phone, eventually finding it and pulling it free only to lose grip as he narrowly makes it around a tight bend. The phone hits the floor face down on the passenger side. Without thinking, he quickly reaches out across to the floor, groping, his hand feeling for the phone and finding it. He is back in the rear view mirror and spots the lights now closer. Much brighter now and on full beam trying to blind him from behind, the vehicle, quickly catching up and he knows it won't be long before it's on his rear bumper.

Thinking quickly, deciding on whom to call first, the police he thinks, will leave him waiting on the line and he will need to speak to someone who can get through to them quickly. Scrolling through his numbers, he comes across one he's had for a while. A man he has recently bumped into, he quickly dials the number. It goes straight to answer phone. "Damn!" He quickly leaves a message and again tries fast dial for his friend. Carl picks up, seeing the caller ID on his phone, he absently tells him that he still has no clue to who owns or rents the building he wanted checking out.

Scholfield cuts him short, telling him to listen as he is in trouble and gives the route he is on to his friend asking him to get through to the police as he is being chased and they are not friendly. He cuts his friend off and immediately swears as he has forgotten to give the identification of the vehicle following.

Looking back in the mirror, he notices the vehicle has closed the distance. It is now only 200 yards behind him. He needs to get some distance. The other vehicle is twice the size with a much bigger engine. He looks across at the screen on his satnav; a view of the road he was travelling along showed all the side roads. He looks and notices a road a quarter of a mile away on his left. He would have to time it right with the vehicle chasing. It was now less than a hundred yards. He watches the satnav and gets ready to time his turn. The vehicle is now almost on his bumper. Fifty yards to the turn and he hits the breaks, instantly propelling his car at the corner and throwing it into opposite lock. The car loses traction for an instant before the wheels grip and he's around and gunning the engine once more, leaving gravel flying behind him in every direction.

The other car is not so lucky. Trying the same manoeuvre, but too late to make the turn, it runs out of road, ending up sideways, flying into a ditch and hitting trees ripping the right wing completely off. This throws the vehicle into a spin back across the other side, hitting trees again and this time stowing in the rear left passenger door, buckling the rear wheel and eventually bringing the vehicle to a stop. The engine bucks once then dies.

Scholfield, his eyes in the rear mirror, sees that the vehicle is not following and for the first time takes a deep breath. He tells himself not to get too complacent as there are still two vehicles out there and they are both faster than his. It won't be long before one of the other vehicles catches up and is right back on his tail. Concentration is what is needed and as much distance as he can get. His eyes again on the satnav, he wonders where the side road he is on is leading.

Twenty minutes later and with no vehicle behind him, he is back approaching Belmont. He starts to relax and wonders why the police have not been in touch. His friend would have contacted them over twenty minutes ago. Surely they are not that slow and he was sure he made it clear to his friend that this was a life or death situation. Keeping his eyes peering all around, he heads back to his apartment near the centre of town and parks up behind his building. He sits in his vehicle with the lights off trying to get his night vision back. Looking around and not seeing any sign of life, he gets out of his car, still keeping vigilant. Looking up to his apartment on the third floor, he heads to the dumpster and checks behind it, finding the step bar that he had placed there several months ago, when he had moved in. Picking it up and reaching up to the first floor, he snags the drop steps on the fire escape and pulls them down and starts climbing up to his floor. Outside, he waits, as he peers into his apartment. Clear, he opens the window and climbs in, looking around to see if anything is out of place. He almost turns the lights on then thinks twice about it, going to the front door and placing his eye to the viewer, checking the corridor. No movement and no lights on. The lights are set in the corridor to automatically come on when someone is on the floor. Going back through his apartment, he grabs his laptop and takes his portable camera out of his pocket. He looks through his pictures of the men who were chasing him tonight, though he was unable to take a picture of the last man to arrive. There was still the question about the body's identity and still no call from the police.

Scholfield again wonders why these people are interested in O'Neil and he feels the only way he's going to know this, is to confront O'Neil again. He knows he works in MIT as an engineer with a science and engineering back ground, but what type of work is he involved in? He has tried to find out more about his work, unfortunately whatever it is, it's classified and no one is talking. What about the death of his wife? She died from an allergic reaction and the police are looking at O'Neil. Maybe now they should be looking at the people who chased him.

Taking the films, he loads them to his laptop and as an afterthought he grabs a USB flash drive and downloads the film, adding a few words about the people on the film and their involvement with the body and Steve O'Neil. He could only describe the man he saw tonight but he would recognise his expensive car again if he ever saw it around. He pockets the flash drive and decides that he will leave the same way he came in, climbing through the window, he does not hear the tiny clatter as the flash drive falls from his pocket.

He climbs down the fire escape again, trying to keep the noise to a minimum, which was near impossible with the old fire escape, and eventually he finds his feet on the ground. Looking around, he makes his way to his car and opens the door. Climbing in, he inserts his key's in the ignition, when a sound from behind catches his attention and before he can turn around, a hand with a cloth is pressed to his mouth choking him. Another arm comes around his shoulders pinning him back. Scholfield panics and makes the mistake of trying to reach behind him for his attacker. The man holds on tight. The last thing he sees before he passes out is his

side door opening and a large man bending down, not a
word   from   him   as   he   reaches   in.

Chapter 12

Steve had been awake all night, the thought of going to sleep far from his mind. He wondered what the exact time was as his watch, along with his personal belongings, had been removed. He had an idea that it was possibly close to six in the morning as the sky was getting lighter through the small window in the cell.

Looking across from him, he could see two others that were awake, two young lads who were in for being drunk and abusing police officers when they were asked to go home. One of the lads had made the mistake of telling an obvious repeat offender to piss off after the guy had bumped into him. He bumped him again, leaving the young lad on the floor with a busted mouth and missing a tooth. His friend was wise and kept his mouth shut after the guy had turned on him daring him to have a go at him. All the others were still fast asleep, some on the floor and others sitting in the upright position.

Steve was thinking that it was only five days ago when he had lost Karen and his father at the same time. He was dried out from crying but still hurting from his loss. His thoughts were also on Tina. He hoped she was alright and then thought that of course she's not alright. She'd been assaulted by this Keel and now for some reason the police think she had passed him some dodgy pills or something. He knew she was innocent of any wrong doing but try telling the police that.

Now he was sitting in a cell, waiting to find out if he is to go to court for the murder of his wife and on top of that, he had just found out that he will have to fight to get his baby back. He is brought back from his thoughts by the guard waking everybody up, telling them to get ready as they will all be in court that morning. He looks at the two lads, obviously aware that one had an injured mouth but does not give a damn as he heard these two had been verbal about the police, and tells them that they had better lose their bladders here as they won't get chance at the courts.

It is 8.45 when they all arrive at the court house. They are taken around to the back and offloaded. Once inside, they are again placed in a waiting cell and each is told the order they would be called. When it's Steve's turn, he is escorted through where he is met by Richard Talbert wearing another expensive tailor made suit. They shake hands and Talbert quickly brings Steve up to speed with the process. This trial in front of a judge is an arraignment and depending on the strength of the case from both the defence and prosecution, the judge will make a decision for the case to go to trial or not. Before long it is their turn to face the court.

Looking about the courtroom, Steve spots Moralis and Washington. They are sat halfway to the back on the left side of the court. Talbert is asked to make his case and he asks for the court to drop all charges. The prosecution working for the District Attorney's Office, makes an objection but knows it is a feeble gesture as one by one Talbert wins the arguments as their prize witness is still missing and most of the evidence is pure conjecture. Eventually the proceedings are brought to a halt and the judge asks the prosecution if they have any other evidence. When the prosecution tries to get the case postponed to a later date, the judge puts a halt to the hearing and moves that all charges should be dropped. The prosecution tries to object against this but the judge overrules him and makes a point about coming into his court with so little evidence. Without another word, the prosecutor comes across, shakes hands with Talbert and leaves. Steve looks back to where Moralis and Washington were sitting. Their chairs are empty. They had already left. Looking around, Steve notices a few people with their heads down, their movement looking as though they are writing. Talbert notices him looking and tells him that it's just a few media reporters but as there is no case to answer, they probably will leave him alone.

Steve turns to Talbert and shakes his hand. Talbert, pulls his business card from his wallet and places it in Steve's hand. Before he leaves, he offers advice concerning Steve's child and that he should call if he needed advice.

Steve grabs a taxi when he gets out the door and heads back to the precinct, chastising himself for already breaking his promise on entering the station again. He has to pick up George from their compound, his personal belongings and his car.

Moralis, on his return with Washington, sits down at his desk waiting for his call from his captain. Hopefully he will only get a little ear bending and it will not go any higher. To take his mind of the morning, he attempts to organise some of his old files and gives up, asking Washington if she wants a refill as he needs another hit with a caffeine kick. Waiting for others to fill their cups, he gets out his cell phone to check his messages. He had one last night that he had not checked. The name that came up was Scholfield's and he was not in any mood last night to pick up his message as he assumed he was just after information. The two of them had fallen out a few years ago when Scholfield had reported a story in the local papers and though he had not named his informant on the story, the story backfired and fingers were pointed at Moralis, but nothing was ever proved. Moralis after that, had told Scholfield never to contact him again. He was close to deleting the message but curiosity got the better of him and he listened to the voicemail. A minute later he's back with Washington asking her to get in touch with dispatch over a call last evening.

Dispatch had confirmed a call had come in but not from a Scholfield, though the name was mentioned in the call. Moralis asks to review the call and it is put through to him. Listening, the caller withholds their identity and relays a message that almost matches the message Scholfield has left him. The shifts on dispatch were not due in until the evening and he asks for the private number of the person who took the call. After calling the evening operator at home, the woman picks up. She remembers the call and putting it through but she cannot remember who picked up. Washington in the meantime has been trying to ring Scholfield, but the line is dead. Other officers are asked if they had received a call but no one had. Moralis finds Captain Childs and gives her the news. Childs gets her staff to make calls to anyone who was working the late shift.

Moralis and Washington leave the station after finding out where Scholfield was living and headed over to his apartment. On arriving, they knock and wait. They try again with no luck and finally Moralis decides to check the back alley and tells Washington to wait. On entering the alley, he recognises Scholfield's car, one that he has had for many years and due to lack of cash, he has never been able to upgrade. Peering into the car he spots the keys in the ignition. He made a mental note of this as it was the second car in the last twenty four hours with keys left in the ignition. He was surprised that nobody had taken the car, considering where he was but it would appear that even thieves could be particular about what they take.

Looking across to the building, he wonders why Scholfield had parked around the back. He obviously did not want to be seen going through the front. Looking across at the fire escape he decides to check out the apartment. He knows it's on the third floor and goes to the dumpster, releasing the wheels and pushing it towards the fire escape. Climbing on top he manages to pull the steps down and climbs up to the third floor. Looking through the dirty window, he sees nothing out of the ordinary. Making a decision, he tries the latch and the window opens. He notices on the inside ledge several shoe marks and decides to step over these as he does not want to contaminate the prints. Moralis stands silently in the apartment for a second, looking around before going to the front door and opening it up for Washington. Together they go through the rooms. There are only three rooms in the apartment and it looked as though the place had never been dusted. The place was a mess. Washington made a joke about Scholfield not winning any awards as a domestic god.

Finding a pair of sneakers, Moralis checks them with the shoe prints on the ledge and judging by the size, they match except for one, which is several sizes larger. Moving away, he feels something small under his foot break. Looking down, he sees a small device. He picks it up and calls Washington in who immediately recognises it as a USB flash drive. Checking to see if it will still work, she tells him that it is only the outer casing that is damaged and hopefully the components are still working. He spots the telephone on the floor and picking it up, he checks the answer system, but finds it empty. Looking down at the coffee table full of books and paperwork, he notices a dust free area closest to the couch. Washington also looks at the table, then down at the telephone line, tracing it back to the wall. There is a router attached on the line. Washington tells Moralis that the space on the table probably held a laptop. Thinking things through, he tells Washington to go back to the car and check the flash drive out on their own laptop, thinking that there might be something worthwhile in the file.

Moralis carries on looking around the apartment but finds no other items of interest and decides that it would be a good idea to check in. After contacting the station, he decides that they should follow Scholfield's directions. He recalls the message mentioned, a road leading into a small industrial estate off Trapelo Road, the other side of the Hobbs Brook Basin just north west of Belmont. It would be a good half hour's ride from the centre. That would mean at least forty minutes from where they were, further south in Belmont.

Moralis this time, leaves via the front door and finds Washington with the laptop in her lap. Looking up, she informs Moralis that there were some interesting photos taken in the last few days. Pointing at the screen, she starts scrolling through the images starting with photos taken at their visit to O'Neil's, the other day. This is followed by other people. Two men shown entering O'Neil's place. Time and dates were on the photos and Moralis remembers picking up O'Neil just before for questioning. Washington nods agreement. Other photos show men entering a building and there are also photos of vehicles. Number plate shots were taken but were hard to read as the weather and lighting was poor. These shots, according to the times, were taken last night before the call message was left for him.

Moralis turns to Washington and tells her that he believes the building in the photos is possibly on the site that was mentioned in Scholfield's message and that there was only one way to find out.

Scholfield is woken up with a slap to his face. Coming out of his confusion, he finds that he is seated on a wooden chair. Looking around he finds that he is in a room no more than ten square feet, no windows and only one door. A single light bulb throws light down from the ceiling. There are two men in the room with him. Scholfield tries to stand but finds he is unable to rise from the chair. His arms behind his back appear to be tied together and his legs are also restrained. Looking down he sees a type of plastic cable tie, securing his legs to the chair. Scholfield knows he is in trouble and sweat breaks out on his forehead. At last he looks at his two jailers. He knows one from the photos. He is one of the men who broke into O'Neil's place and is a lot larger close up. The other man was the man who had spotted him in the window, the one driving the expensive car and obviously the boss. He is first to talk.

"Mr Scholfield. Glad to see you could join us. You gave us a little bit of a chase. Two of my men are not very happy with you. One has a broken arm and the other will not be walking for a few weeks. He will be lucky not to limp. Our friend here has been asked by them to return the favour." At this point the other man moves in front of Scholfield, a contemptible smile on his face and, with no warning, the man swings a right hook into his left shoulder, followed by a left downward punch to the top of his right leg. Both punches are extremely painful and Scholfield can do nothing to defend himself. The pain is unbearable and both men stand back to watch how he will cope, determining his pain threshold. They do not want to overdo things as they needed him to talk, but they want him to know that they mean business. Giving him a few minutes to recover, the man speaks again.

"That was just a little of what you will receive if you are unwilling to answer my questions. I personally do not like violence but unfortunately for you, my friend here does. He hopes you won't want to help me with my questions. Do you understand me?" Scholfield looks up grimacing and nods. His mind is working overtime and is thinking "How do I get out of this?" as he knows that he will be joining the man from last night in the furnace. He knows if he answers, his life will be over and if he doesn't, his life might as well be over. His only move is to delay and hope that someone is out there searching for him.

Chapter 13

Steve had driven straight to the hospital and had left George in the back of the car, making sure that that the window was slightly down and that the dog had water to drink. He knew that George would be unhappy about being left alone so soon after being picked up from a night spent in a cage, but he intended to make it up to him later.

Feeling like things may be improving, he tells himself not to get too excited. He still did not know if he was walking into more disappointment. He will know soon, he thinks.

On reaching the floor where his baby is being cared for, he signs in and makes his way to the viewing room. For the first time in what seemed like a millennium, as he looked in, once again, Steve felt a heavy burden lift from his shoulders, allowing the previous day and morning to disappear from his thoughts.

Time seemed to evaporate as he looked at the tiny bundle, asleep and peaceful, oblivious to those around, passing the days in a blissful ignorance.

For a time, Steve was left to bond as only a parent can, even with the separation of a glass window. He was pulled away from his silent thoughts hearing his name called. Looking down the corridor, a nurse was coming towards him. The nurse stops and asks that he follow her as he has been requested to speak with a liaison officer with the hospital. He asks the nurse what he's wanted for, but the nurse tells him that she has no idea. He starts to feel those butterflies you get when bad news is coming as he follows the nurse. He remembers what Talbert had said to him and had warned him that no matter how bad it seems, the only way he will keep his child is to comply with everything they throw at him.

Stopping outside a door, the nurse knocks. The name plate reads, 'Administrator' with the name Susan Megan. A commanding voice behind the door calls for them to enter. Susan Megan looks up from her work, a woman the wrong side of fifty with greying hair and an expression that tells of a life in paperwork and hospital politics and instantly dismisses the nurse without acknowledging her. The nurse turns and leaves. Turning to Steve, Susan Megan offers him a seat and he pulls the chair out in front of the desk, noticing that it much lower than the administrator's. She stands and walks to a side table where there is a glass decanter with water. She pours herself a glass and returns to her seat. He notices how short she is, almost as tall as she is wide. Too many late night microwave meals alone, he thinks, as he notices no ring on her finger.

She starts and Steve instantly adopts a relaxed appearance as he knows what is coming and he knows he has to keep it together.

"Mr O'Neil, we at the hospital, over the last few days have been in discussion with certain authorities over the best course of action for the safety and protection that your baby deserves."

Steve is about to say something but the women holds her hand out in a gesture that clearly tells him not to speak, but listen. "It is in our opinion that your child has not had the best introduction to life and there are outstanding questions regarding your wife's death, that need to be addressed. We feel and I am sure that you agree, that care and protection is needed here, so we have contacted the local DCF, who have looked into the care of your child. They have assessed the situation and feel it is their duty to put your child into their care.

The hospital agrees with this until certain matters can be resolved. I am sure that things will sort themselves out and I hope you agree with our decision."

Steve has no idea who the DCF are and asks. Susan Megan tells him that the DCF is the Department of Children and Families, run by Social Services.

Steve stays quiet for a while, deeply fuming, but he had prepared himself for this and he has his eye on this women's hand, which is poised over a button. He knows the heavy squad are just outside the door if he makes a scene and they will be straight in here if he gives this woman any indication that he's going to be trouble. He knows he will only get himself locked back up. He relaxes and takes a deep breath and stands, a tight smile on his face, telling the woman that he would like to go back to the ward as his time is short and that he will comply with the local authorities. The woman, expecting some verbal abuse is taken back by his actions and ends the conversation, asking him not to make any trouble about their decision. Steve bites his lip and leaves.

Outside, walking away, are two security men for the hospital. They had retreated quickly and show a lack of interest in him as he walks past them without glancing in their direction as he heads back to the ward. Deep down, he is fuming, but as soon as he spots his baby, life seems to improve for him as if there were forces outside his world giving him an invisible boost. Looking through the glass plate, he is more determined than ever.

Back in his car, Steve is straight on his cell phone to his attorney, remembering the number he was given. Talbert had expected the call and checks his calendar. Saturday is a no go but he fits Steve in for first thing Monday morning. Steve thanks him and sits for a while, thinking through things. Eventually he is pulled away from his thoughts by George in the back. He had forgotten about the dog. "Sorry George. Let's get you home."

Talbert was requested to phone his superiors when he was contacted by O'Neil. After putting the phone down, Talbert wonders why this O'Neil chap is so important to the company. Having heard gossip about past cases, he decides that it is best that he knows very little. He likes his life and will comply with the task he is given as long as it is lawful. He hopes this stays lawful, as he does not want to be the gossip of future employees.

When Steve arrives back at his condo, Tina is waiting at the front door. George is let out of the back of the car and seeing Tina, rushes towards her. Steve watches, thinking about the times when he has walked George in park and how he has always been very good with strangers.

Steve walks up to Tina, watching her closely as she is making a fuss over George. This was the girl who, a few days ago had been assaulted and had supposedly conspired with him to murder his wife. Steve thought, all it takes is a dog to take you away from all your troubles, and he smiles. Tina sees him smile. Leaving George for a second, she strolls up to him and gives him a long hug. They stand there for a while, then slowly they separate. Steve places his key in the door and they all go in.

They walk through to the kitchen and Steve puts the coffee on. George finds a place on the floor and watches them both. Steve is first to talk, asking her how she is and Tina shrugs before explaining everything that had gone on over the last few days. Steve tells Tina about his last few days with the court and problems at the hospital. Tina listens, never saying a word. When he is finished, she wipes a tear from her face and hugs him again.

Nigel had called earlier on his way back from the hospital and Steve had updated him on having to go back to the attorney, as social services were now involved. They need to talk about how he is going to be able to pay the costs. Nigel tells him that he has an idea and that he will need to speak to someone about it. If the people he talks to accept his proposal, then he will get back to Steve later that afternoon.

Before they hang up, Steve had asked about the funeral arrangements this coming Sunday. His father and sister are to be buried in the same cemetery as his mother. The only people he knows are going are friends of his father and sister. He has cousins around the world but no one close to the family. The casket will be a closed one as both his father and sister were badly injured in the crash. Steve was never asked to identify the bodies due to the injuries and they were identified using other means. Arrangements had already been made with a local funeral company, paid for by his father over the years. Steve had to find the additional cost for his sister. Nigel tells him that they would talk about it later.

Steve turns to Tina, his thoughts on the weekend coming and asks her if she would accompany him to the funeral. She tells him she would and they leave it at that. The radio is on in the background and the topic on the news appears to be about the President of the United States. It would appear that his daughter is involved with a disreputable person that has links to drug barons in Mexico. This has hit the President's re-elections prospects badly and has now put him behind another candidate.

Scholfield has been left for a while. He is shaking his head trying to clear the fog that clouds his thoughts. He has endured a half hour of beatings and knows that his body cannot endure any more punishment. He would rather die than go through the beating again. The two men had left him alone. He had told the man most of what he wanted to know. Mainly about what he knows about their organisation and who he has been in touch with since last night. He has tried to break out of his restraints but he is dealing with professionals. He tries again, trying to pull up on one arm and he thinks he hears the tie-wrap snap or at least partially break. As he tries again, the door opens and he immediately stops, watching, as the two men walk in. These were the two that he had seen together at O'Neil's and whom he had followed. One grabbed him by his arms, pulling him upright. The other bent in front and cut the ties around his legs. Scholfield groaned from the pain in his body and from the rough treatment of moving him. They dragged him from the room and into daylight that was streaming through broken windows of what appeared to be a large warehouse. The place was empty and from the looks of the interior, had not been used for many years and had been left to deteriorate. One of the men roughly pulls him up to his face, telling him that this was a place they used once in a while as the other one he had found out about was now tarnished as the police will be all over it. This gets Scholfield another belt to the back of his head and he blacks out.

Scholfield wakes up shortly after being bundled in the back of a vehicle. He has no idea where he is being taken, but he thought that wherever it is, he is sure that it was not going to be good for him. He is finding it difficult not to pass out again as he is getting thrown around in the back like a rag doll. He needed to focus and stay awake.

Trying to get his thoughts working, he realises that they obviously had finished with the interrogation. This is it. He is not coming back. Where were taking him? He remembers the tie-wrap retraining him and starts pulling again using all the will power he could muster. He is near to blacking out again when he feels the plastic tie-wrap give and then it snaps and his arms are free. His arms are bruised and his fingers feel tingly as his circulation responds to blood pumping properly through his veins to his fingers. He starts rubbing the wrists to get his circulation flowing. He checks his legs and finds they have not been re-tied. Now his thoughts are turned to the vehicle. How is he going to get out without alerting the two guards? He assumes that the two, were together in the front. It is quiet and he tries to listen to sounds. The road they are travelling on is smooth and he believes they are still on a main road and not some back road full of pot holes. He cannot see out of the vehicle as there was a canopy pulled across him. Daylight is trickling through gaps in the canopy and he looks around the interior for a weapon he can use. He comes across a wheel brace around twelve inches long thrown to one side. There is a little weight to it and it could certainly put a dent in someone's head. Scholfield knows he has only one swing in him. He might be able to stop one of the guys but not two. He needs some luck. All he can do now is rest up and hope that luck will find him.

It is another half hour when the sounds under the wheels change as the vehicle slows, turning onto a gravel road. They travel for short time, eventually crawling to a stop. Scholfield can hear two doors opening from the front and he can hear the crunch of feet walking on loose rubble. One set he realises is moving away, the other coming around the back. This is his chance. He places the brace quickly beneath his body to hide it. The back door swings open, pivoted on two hinges on the side allowing for easy access to the back. It also allows Scholfield wider movement to swing the brace with all his strength at the head that was bending towards him. The guy drops like a twig, a grunt escaping him as he hits the ground. The other man is alerted to this and looks back, seeing his partner fall. He is slow to respond until he sees Scholfield exit the vehicle, then he is up and running, chasing down his captive. Scholfield is not hanging around and heads off into trees that border the road. He runs flat out and he can hear the sound of snapping branches close behind him. He realises that he is in a mountain range with dense brush around him. He needs to get some distance from his assailant. He hears the sound of a cry from behind and everything goes silent. There is no one chasing him but he keeps moving, not daring to look around. He thinks the guy has fallen but he will be up again. Scholfield is much lighter on his feet and agile. He negotiates his run through the trees, ducking under limbs and jumping over fallen debris. He takes a chance to look behind him. No one in sight as he turns back around to face forward, finding there is nothing for his right foot to make contact with as the ground opens up to air. With nothing to stop his forward momentum, he flies through the air, his legs and arms flailing for what seemed like an eternity until eventually striking water, the breath knocked out of him as he rebounds off the river bed back to the surface, banging his head in the process. Scholfield is knocked unconscious as he is dragged through the torrent waters, rock formations narrowly missing him as he is carried along at a great pace, unable to help himself.

Chapter 14

Nigel finds a space to park his car a few hundred yards down from Steve's place. A minute later he's at the condo just as the front door opens and Tina walks out, almost colliding with him as she turns to say goodbye to Steve. Turning around to this new face at the door, she apologises and Nigel shrugs it off. Steve introduces the two of them and they all have a short, polite conversation before Tina leaves. Steve calls after her, reminding her about picking her up on Sunday. She waves back at Steve, who is holding onto George, stopping him running after her.

Nigel has news regarding his meeting earlier and asks Steve to keep an open mind. They both sit and Nigel proceeds with telling Steve that the company will pay the legal fees for him to fight for his right to bring up his child. The company will pay for a legal team to fight his case, but the company want something in return. They want Steve to finish his work on the project and that they are aware he has issues surrounding the safety of the design and the consequences if things go wrong. They will put a package in place, guaranteeing the funds for the improved safety measures to be adopted that Steve had previously asked for, so that they can move forward with the testing at Fermilab and over at CERT, in Switzerland. The devices for both the small and large projects are in place and they have a window of opportunity to proceed in the coming month, the first being in two weeks, at Fermilab. Steve is stunned by the speed at which MIT is moving. He, after all, had suggested that first tests should be at Fermilab as it was the second largest Hadron Collider after CERT. Tests at a smaller level could be carried out and would give the much needed results which they cannot achieve through simulation at MIT.

The big question troubling Steve is that, with the amount of money going into this project, if Fermilab doesn't work? Millions of dollars will be wasted trying to push ahead with the set up in Switzerland. If they have the green light to carry out the tests, how is it possible to implement the safety measures and finish the last remaining tests that he has kept under his belt? Nigel assures him that as long as he proceeds with his side, then he will personally concentrate on the safety aspect. Steve has doubts as the people they work for are looking for results. They are not interested in the time and research that goes into a project like this, ensuring that results can be achieved. They don't see the graft, just the results and if things fail, they're the ones you cannot find to back you up. They're hiding behind their fat cat lawyers, out of reach. Nigel assures him that they will have the safest security and extra funds are already in place to deal with it.

Nigel watches Steve, as he digests all that has been told him and he knows how his mind is working.

"Steve, I know what you are thinking and I can assure you that safer contingencies will be put in place. All those safety procedures you asked for will be implemented and with the extra safety nets, our safety margins will go from 80/20 to 88/12. That obviously leaves us with a 12 per cent risk factor, but you have to admit, that's a good safety margin."

Steve is impressed but it's the unknown factor that troubles him. This huge piece of engineering has been built not just by him, but by the engineers he has worked with. They all have a claim to be the first to obtain the unattainable. If it works, they will have created the most important piece of engineering the world has seen.

With the problems facing the world today, pollution increasing at a tremendous rate, especially in countries such as China with their increased industries pumping out more pollutants, the balance of nature will be lost. Things need to be done now or everyone loses. Steve knows the world is running out of time and this thought alone makes it easier for him to complete his work, but at the same time, elements of the project have not been tested and it is these that he objected to, as the company kept pushing for results, disregarding procedures. Other countries working in the same field were barrelling through with results and his company was adamant that coming in second was not an option. Steve knew that any one of them could cross the winning line. People on the inside knew it was just around the corner. The media had always been informed that it would be many years before a clean source of energy would be found and that we would still need to rely on nuclear power as our energy source. Countries with old nuclear power stations were still spending billions dismantling them and the clean-up bill was two to three times the cost of the original build. He should know, he had worked on projects dealing in this field.

The time is right and this new source of power is needed and hooray to the first country to enable it, but it needs to be properly tested, but only one month, he thinks, trying to get his head around how much time they have.

More important to Steve, is the promise he made to Karen and his father. They are no longer with him but in his heart, they will never leave. Bowing his head he has made his decision as he looks up to Nigel, he nods. Nigel claps him on his back and tells him he has made the right decision. He has to make a call and leaves Steve to his thoughts.

Sitting, head bowed, Steve is praying for forgiveness from his wife and father. He cannot lose his child and yet the people that will help him may never get through the gates of heaven. He thinks of the saying, better the devil you know. Well he would buy the devil a drink if that could get his child back. He's made his decision. At the back of his mind, he wonders if it the right one.

Moralis and Washington have been driving along Trapelo road for over fifteen minutes when they come to a sign damaged with age and half the print missing. A few hundred yards further up is a turning. Trees are blocking the view but they could see buildings through the branches. As they get closer, they can see industrial buildings. Turning into the road, they stop and view the board with the site buildings numbered. There are over fifty on the site with names of companies below. There were also signs showing empty premises. Looking at the buildings, they can see their problem. Most of them look like they have smoke stacks. Scholfield had not said which building, let alone if they were in the right place. Moralis thinks they are. He just knows that this will take time. He thinks about it for a moment, working out a plan to proceed. A lot of these units are being used. It would make sense that the building Scholfield mentioned would be one not used for normal industrial work. Look for a building that has not got a rent sign up and with it being working hours, one without vehicles in front.

They drive around the site looking for premises that look vacant. After twenty minutes they have counted five. Now they need to check them out and see if a smoke stack has been used recently in one of the five.

They will need a warrant to search each building and they will not get this from a message left by a missing man with Scholfield's reputation. They will just have to improvise and use their heads as well as their climbing skills. If a stack had been used as recently as last evening, then hopefully there will still be some heat transfer on the bricks around the stack. Someone was going to have to climb on the roof and check. He is Washington's senior partner but he knows he is going to have to do the climbing.

Stopping at the first one and walking around the back and looking up, at the walls, Moralis smiles. Fixed to the wall was a set of iron steps. Hopefully all of buildings have these. The buildings themselves must be over forty years old. Let's hope the steps hold, he thinks. Standing on the first step, he tests his weight. The steps groan but hold steady. One by one he climbs until he is on the roof. Walking across to the smoke stack, he passes sky lights and tries peering through the glass. Unfortunately none of the glass has been cleaned for quite some time and his view is obscured by a mix of moss and bird droppings. Coming up to the stacks, he places his hands on the bricks to feel for any sign of heat; the stack he finds, is cold. With the weather still cool from the night before and the sky threatening to open up again and give them a good drenching, any stack used will still have a residue of heat left in it.

Climbing down, they drive to the next one and repeat the operation. They have no luck with the second one or the third. That leaves two and, if no luck there, they will have to start knocking on other doors, asking permission to climb on their buildings. He wasn't looking forward to that as any refusal will delay and he was not in a good mood after their time in court that morning.

On the roof of the forth building, Moralis, his hands pressed to the stack, feeling the bricks, finds that they are slightly warm. Looking up he sees a small sign of smoke escaping. There is very little smoke and the clouds are reducing light visibility. It would be impossible to spot signs of smoke from the ground. This is the building, he is certain.

Back on the ground, after telling Washington, they both try looking through the windows, but try as they might to peer inside, visibility is too poor. They need to get inside but the place is sealed. No broken windows, the building is secured. They noticed when looking at the building that it has security. A lot of the buildings did but most of them used the same security company. This one was different and they made a note. There may be a record for entry into the building. Modern key pads have displays that show entry and exit times into buildings and this was a new system fitted.

They would have to head back to the station and speak with their captain. With this morning's court case still fresh on everyone's mind, Moralis would not be in her good books. Now they will try and press her to get them a warrant to search the building. No evidence to back them up and it's getting late, there won't be any chance of getting one today and if they get lucky, it will be Monday at the earliest. They also need to find who is paying the rent here.

Driving along Trapela road, heading back into Belmont, Washington notices a skid mark across the road and what looks like damaged foliage on both sides. She makes a comment to Moralis about people not taking care with their driving.

Once back, Moralis is in reception, the secretary is surprised that he's asking for a meeting. She looks at Moralis, asking him if that's wise considering he is not Mr Popular with the hierarchy. He acknowledges this and wishes he could leave it, but tells her that it's about this missing journalist from the previous night. She puts her finger up in a sign for him to wait a second as she buzzes through to Captain Childs. Childs answers and they have a short conversation followed by the secretary telling Moralis to go through. In the meantime, Washington is phoning around trying to find out who owns or rents the building they are interested in.

"Moralis, sit! You know why I'm in this chair and you're not. Because when I fart, no one notices. You on the other hand, like to leave a big stink!"

Moralis has always been amused by his captain's descriptive analogies, but today he is deadpan as he needs her on his side. He nods with agreement and is secretly happy that he actually isn't sitting in her chair. He can't stomach all the political crap that comes with the job. He's a front line man and will stay that way until they pension him off. He understands life on the streets. He's been at it more than half his life. That chair, he thinks, belongs to those who kiss ass and have given up wiping their mouths.

After giving a summary of last night's message and the missing journalist, followed by their trip, he sits back and allows Childs to determine if they can get the warrant to look in the building.

Childs is again reminded of the morning's missing calls made to one of her officers. She has listened to the message left and is in agreement that something is amiss; forgetting about the court case, she tells Moralis to write up his warrant and she will get it to a judge first thing on Monday. There is not enough evidence to push it today and if they want the warrant to get accepted, then she will present it first thing Monday. She tells him that a bulletin has gone out for Scholfield even though it has been less than twenty four hours and

135

to not get his hopes up. After all, they are still trying to find his other missing person, Keel. He has priority, but she thinks he slipped through the net and has gone to ground.

For the rest of the day, they sit at their desks, both phoning around, trying to find either the owner or who rents their elusive building. Frustrated, he wonders how hard it is to get information on such a simple quest. Washington across from him, is also shaking her head, giving the sign for another coffee just as her phone rings. Listening to the caller, she puts the phone down after quickly scribbling the message down. Drumming her fingers on the table, Moralis, sitting impatiently, waits for Washington to speak.

"That was a call from Lowell police department. They have a man in Lowell General with serious head and body injuries in a coma. He was fished out of the Concorde River this afternoon by some rafters coming down the river in an area of white water."

Moralis shrugs. "And?"

"This man was not wearing a life jacket and there was no boat or canoe with him. It looks like he came down the river in the clothes he was wearing. He had no ID on him, but he fits the description of our Scholfield." Moralis looks at his watch, replying to his partner, who anticipates his next move and grabs her jacket as Moralis grabs his. They are both aware that it's rush hour.

"Traffic's going to be a bit of a bitch at this time," says Washington.

After disconnecting the call, he thinks again about the mistakes his men were making. More bad news he could do without. These people working for him were screwing up and he had to sort the mess out again. Another man injured. Concussed, the fool should have known better. The other one suffered a twisted ankle. This one man has managed to take down four of his men in less than twenty four hours, leaving only one just about able to do his job. The other will be out of it for a few days.

It's funny how things work out. That story they found on his laptop about illegal fishing on the Concorde River. He thought it was ironic that they were going to throw him to the fishes anyway and then he decides to do it for them.

Other things have worked out well. There was no need, he thought, to bring in anyone else and he did not want to alert those he works for to the incompetence of his men. They might feel that he wasn't up to the job and have him replaced. If things are in place at the old workshop, then no evidence should be found. The main problem is his journalist friend. It's a good job they have a man in the right place. If his friend is in a coma, then they have a little time on their hands to organise his unfortunate accident. This time he thinks his man in the loop can deal with him. The police will put security on him. That might work in their favour.

Thankfully there isn't enough evidence to put together. But those photos will have to go. There's only enough there to show breaking and entry, nothing more; but it would be best that no-one gets picked up for questioning. If it looks that way, then they might have to send them on a long trip. The police are not going to try and pick two men up for entering a house if they're out of the state. They can help with things over in Switzerland. All loose ends can be cleaned up over there.

A smirk comes to his face, regarding his choice of words. Cleaned up! After all, that's what this is all about, a clean source of energy. He smiles as he thinks about the work ahead of him.

Chapter 15

It takes Moralis and Washington almost twice as long to reach the hospital in Lowell. The traffic was heavy on route with emergency vehicles busy dealing with multiple accidents due to unexpected heavy rain in the last twenty four hours. They had been hit by four inches of rain in a short period and this has played havoc with the drainage. A lot of surface water was flowing across major roads causing cars going too fast, to aquaplane.

Arriving at the hospital, they check with reception to locate their man and head to the emergency wing where they are met by the doctor treating the patient. They are given a brief summary of his condition and are allowed to check on his identification.

Moralis and Washington have seen accident victims many times in their line of work and from what the doctor has just told them, it is a wonder the man is still alive. When he was brought in, he was nicknamed by the nurses as the Pin Ball Wizard on account that he probably had careered off all the boulders in the river on his way down, then spat out. His face is a mask of bruises and cuts, barely visible with the bandages placed around the head and jaw area. He had suffered a fracture to his skull and broken bones from his toes up, including sustained internal injuries.

Moralis recognises Scholfield straight away, even with the damage. His left arm is in a sling but a tattoo of a bottle with the Jack Daniels slogan, being emptied upside down on his arm, is clearly visible.

Scholfield had told Moralis years ago, that he had this tattooed on him when he had given up the booze. It was his way of reminding himself that a good story will not come from a person who spends most their mornings puking into the toilet. Moralis was wondering what story he was chasing, remembering his past relations with the man. He was now wondering, who Scholfield had pissed off. He thought, "Why do I get the feeling that you now have a good story and this has got something to do with our friend O'Neil."

The doctor tells them that the next twenty four hours will be critical and even if the man does pull through, then there is the likelihood that he may not remember his accident. At least not straight away and he will need further treatment with the type of head injury he has sustained.

They ask the doctor about getting a statement from his patient, if he ever regains consciousness. The doctor tells them that his only concern, is treating the patient, but he will call them if he wakes up and will only allow them to interview their man, if he considers it safe to do so and that was final.

Moralis believes that it may be that Scholfield had not had an accident and that his injuries were due to other causes and that it would be wise to have him protected. Washington agrees.

Washington, sitting in the passenger seat on the way back, is thinking about the photos they had seen and in the back of her mind she has been trying to remember something she had read. It comes to her suddenly and turning to Moralis, she says "Here's a thought. Remember that accident we came across this morning on our drive back from the industrial units?" Moralis nods, remembering parts of a vehicle scattered across both sides of the road.

Washington carries on explaining about the fact there was quite a lot of wreckage left across the road and if that was reported, then would not the emergency vehicle have picked up most of the large pieces as well as taking what was left of the vehicle away? She goes on to remind him about the road accident involving the O'Neil's and what was in the report, an eye witness mentioning that she thought she saw a large black vehicle run into the side of the O'Neil's car, but she had retracted the statement saying she was not clear about what she had seen. Washington next reminds him of the photo taken by Scholfield, outside the unit they had just visited with the two large vehicles. She could remember that one of them looked like it had a dent in one wing. It was a poor picture because of the rain but what they saw on the side of the road earlier was wreckage from a black vehicle and according to Scholfield, he was being chased by one or both of those vehicles. If the vehicle chasing him had the accident and Washington knows it's a long shot, they could get forensics to check out the damage on the O'Neil's car and see if there is any trace paint in black. Then they could go back to their wreckage and get a scraping and if the paint matches, it will obviously still be coincidental, but they might be able to get the woman to verify if the car she thought she had seen matches. If she can and they can locate the damaged car, then the O'Neil's accident was not an accident.

Moralis quickly glances at his partner and for the first time, he is happy to be partnered with Washington.

"Let's also check with the local hospitals. Check to see if they have had any people admitted with injuries last night. It may be difficult as we have seen that the weather is adding to our problems with more than normal car accidents. Check with the local recovery people. See who came out to pick up the vehicle. Also, I want to check again with that life policy for Mrs O'Neil. What format it was sent in? If it went out via the web, there will be a trace on the email. Where was it sent from?"

Steve was returning from another visit to the hospital. He and Nigel had talked for most of the afternoon and into the evening, discussing the coming month. He had let Steve know that the company would put whatever finance package was needed in place and the necessary man power to fight his side in court. He had been reassured the process would be going full steam, even with him out of the country for a week working on the last part of the project and that someone would keep him up to date on the proceedings.

Arriving back at his place and turning the radio on to catch some late jazz, he remembers the times with Karen when he would return home, catching her in the kitchen, her head in the clouds with the music in the background giving a tranquil setting. These were the moments that hurt, He would just watch his wife in the quiet of the moment, eventually Karen turning to view him, both of them joined by warmth that only two people in love could ever understand.

After a while he turns the station to the news and takes a drink of his coffee, looking into his cup and thinking a lot of coffee was going to be needed by the team to keep the pace going. He knew, with the time frame needed to complete the work, long hours were going to be put in and tempers were going to fray. Nigel was a good organiser and he would make sure the project ran as smoothly as possible and on schedule. He was also good at judging people's weaknesses, ready to implement down time for those individuals he thought might be prone to outburst, as they all at one time or another, had suffered from that. In this field of work, there were more failures than successes. Steve was thinking that Nigel was going to be very busy with the team, keeping their spirits going with a project as immense as this and on its final leg, concluding one way or the other. Many of the original team were still in place, handpicked by Kenneth all those years ago. This last push was going to be both a momentous occasion as well as the end for the project, though most of those working on the team would still be working over the next few years to get the system properly in place. Something like this cannot just be put on the market to use. Further tests will be needed to finalise the design, but his job would be done.

Tonight was his last night to sit back and think. Tomorrow is the restart for him, working Saturday, with a short break on Sunday, to put his father and sister to rest and then back to work. In a way, he is looking at this as a blessing in disguise. At least that's what he keeps telling himself, as it will get his mind off thinking about his family. He will need all his attention focussed on the project and more importantly on getting justice in an unjust world where fathers have very few rights to their own children. He felt there had to be a balance to all of this and he had to believe deep down that right would prevail and his child would be given back to him.

In the background, the news is reporting flash flooding in many areas, with a bridge collapsing, plunging three cars into the river. Occupants from two of the cars were saved, their two vehicles managing to stay afloat as they were carried downstream. Rescue teams were on standby and had reached the cars as they had come to a stop in the middle of the river, held in place by an accumulation of river waste that had collected to form a barrier. Unfortunately, the third car had travelled further downstream and it was more than two hours before the two elderly couples inside were pulled from the car. They had not been so lucky and had died from exposure to the cold and wet conditions.

They were found huddled together as if they had known their fate and had accepted it.

The news had just been reported that the three people who were saved had reached the local hospital and indications were good for a full recovery.

The news went on to mention, that engineers were on site at the bridge, to find out the cause of the collapse and there was speculation that the bridge had suffered from the cutbacks by the local authority over the last few years. The bridge had been due to be replaced last year, but was deemed safe by local engineers under the guidance of the council and the replacement bridge was put back indefinitely. The reporter had tried to get a statement from the mayor's office to substantiate the gossip, but was told that they could not comment on why the bridge had collapsed until an engineering team had fully investigated the collapse and that until any enquiry is concluded, it would be irresponsible to speculate in view of the recent tragedy.

Steve hits the off button on the radio, shaking his head at hearing the bad news, knowing full well that this sort of thing would go on for years. The public would lose interest and the court case would lose the direction for the real reason of the tragedy, until finally a settlement would be made of which only the lawyers would be winners.

Tina is sat at home, her mother upstairs getting ready for bed and is thinking to herself about the week she has had. She has called the police station several times to find out if Keel had been found. Other than his car, sightings have been reported to the police in neighbouring towns, but most of them have been people similar in description.

One unlucky person was reported by some kids and the police had raided the person's home, finding the man tied to his bedpost with another man in a rubber outfit flogging him. The man, it turned out, is the local head teacher and it would appear that the kids had played a prank on him to the delight of the crowd that had gathered outside his house, as both men were taken to the local police station and later released without charge. Unfortunately, as the police at the time did not allow the two men to dress, both were paraded in front of the onlookers as they were escorted in handcuffs. The other man seemed to be enjoying his ordeal with so many police officers about, unfortunately the head teacher would probably find that he may have to move away.

That brought little comfort to Tina, as the man who had raped her was still out there. Little did she know that Keel would never be assaulting teenagers again.

Her mother comes back in the room, dressing gown on and a face pack that brings a smile to Tina as she thinks, life still goes on. Elena smiles back, thinking that her daughter is strong and that she would get past this and move on with her life. She had to for the sake of the kids. She remembers back to the years with her late husband, life had been much more difficult. Life now, has been a little easier with bringing the children up on her own. She has had to work harder and it has been difficult over the last few years with the recession, but there is work out there.

She has never told her daughter of the times working as a chamber maid. Several times she had found herself caught cleaning the hotel room and men quietly returning to the room and grabbing her ass and other areas of her body as if they owned her. She knew she had to keep quiet about it, as any complaints against customers would usually get them thrown out of the hotel. It would embarrass the owners and she would be paid a few dollars to keep quiet and made to quit her job with a quiet word about never talking about what had happened or to expect never to work in any other hotel in town. She had seen this happen to many a new girl as well as a friend of hers who now worked in the local laundry, cleaning.

She has worked in some of the bigger hotels and rich men away from their wives on business tended to be the worse. One man, she remembers, had recently been on the news for such an incident with a local chambermaid and has been asked to stand down from his role on the board of a very big company. His wife is now suing him for divorce and he is set to lose half of his wealth. The chambermaid no longer works for the hotel but a bunch of lawyers have surrounded her, hoping to win some of his money. Good luck to her if she wins, she thinks.

They both sit together, enjoying each other's company and trying to take their minds of the last few days. Tina has told her mother about the funeral on Sunday and although Elena thinks it is not a good idea to go, she will escort her daughter out of respect for the family. She is still not quite sure why her daughter seems to worry more about this Mr O'Neil, than her own ordeal. Maybe it is her way of dealing with things by allowing herself to worry about others. At least she hopes it is, as she cannot believe that her own daughter would be involved in what happened to Mrs O'Neil.

Chapter 16

Steve is woken by his alarm clock. It's five in the morning and he wants to get an early start in the lab before the rest of the team turn up.

He had recently handed his ID tag back in when he had quit several weeks ago and Nigel had called around the previous night with his new ID. Security was fundamental with the work they were carrying out and it was important to Steve. After all, it's all the teams' research over the years and nobody wants another company or country to steal their work. Espionage is big business and Nigel has set himself up as security chief, making sure nothing leaves the lab without going via him. Steve's fine with this, as it means that he can concentrate on the important aspects of the project and leave all the protocol and politics to Nigel.

After grabbing a quick shower and downing two cups of coffee, Steve heads out. The weather is still gloomy outside but the rain has eased off a little. Water pools are forming everywhere and he remembers last evening after taking George for a walk. The dog had not been enjoying the walk, much to the amusement of Steve, until a car driving too close to the curb drove through a pool of water, soaking Steve and missing George. Steve, soaked through, could swear George was smiling up at him, his eyes asking Steve, who's the smart one now?

Steve has left George in the house, having phoned Tina the previous day to see if she would look after George. She had been delighted and would be getting around to his place early. He had placed the door key in a safe place and had left money for Tina. Tina had

146

initially refused the offer but Steve had insisted, as they both knew she would not be going back to work at the pharmacy. He had told her that he may be late and that she could use the spare room if she was tired. He did not know if that was the right thing to offer under the circumstances, but she has been fine with that. He had promised her that he would run her back home when he got in.

Steve had a thirty minute drive to the engineering lab on campus. MIT was founded in the mid nineteen century and was now one of the most prestigious universities in the world, with a net income running into the billions from its many adventures over the years producing many of today's finest scholars, some of whom had gone on to win Nobel prizes . Many learned students had ventured into government and had become the inspiration for today's new talent.

Steve was one of those gifted students and it is down to his ability to think outside the box, that has lead him to come up with the design that may very well change the course of energy throughout the world.

Fusion power has been sought after since the turn of the last century and it wasn't until the sixties that scientists began to come to grips with the ability of taking the theory from a dream and turning it into reality. Steve had gotten interested in fusion after visiting an industrial estate in Oxfordshire, England when he worked in the nuclear industry. One of the businesses on that estate was looking into new forms of energy, in particular a new form of rocket fuel. The company was CCFE, the Culham Centre for Fusion Energy, going by the name JET, short for Joint European Torus. It is their research and use of Tokomak, a fusion designed experiment using magnetics to contain plasma, that had got Steve thinking along the lines of containment.

His chance to take his theory further was granted when he got a call from Kenneth to join his team. As with many scientists in the field, the stumbling block was not in how to produce the amount of fusion needed to sustain itself but in how to produce more energy coming out than was needed going in.

Magnets were used to control the plasma inside a chamber. The problem was stopping the plasma escaping from the chamber. For an experiment like this to work, a large enough chamber would have to be built using two types of known metals, beryllium and tungsten. These were the strongest metals known to man that could withstand the amount of heat needed to generate fusion energy, the same source of power that was only found in the solar system, in the stars.

The problem was containment. If you cannot stop the plasma from escaping, then you cannot keep the temperature from dissipating. Many different designs have been tried to produce the plasma and the closest to come to succeed has been the Tokomak design, using enormous magnets that assert force on the plasma, with positive and negative balance increasing the mass in the centre of the chamber and keeping the plasma in place. A temperature of one hundred million degrees is needed to sustain fusion.

The sun produces solar flares and this is plasma escaping from the surface into space. Inside the chamber, the same forces are at play and plasma shoots out, hitting the chamber walls, known as periodic plasma edge disturbance, eroding the chamber and decreasing the ability to contain the heat. Experiments have been carried out using frozen hydrogen isotopes, 10mm in diamater, that are shot into the chamber to control the plasma escaping. The outer walls of the chamber are constantly kept cool using cryogenics. It was this material that had killed Steve's friend and mentor, Kenneth Mitchell, an accident that should never have happened. All the safety features for the design had failed and to this day, the outcome of the inquest had not been reached.

Steve thinks there is a better way to contain plasma and sustain the required energy for fusion and over the course of five years, working in private, away from his team, with other engineers and scientists sworn to secrecy, he had come up with a design to contain fusion. This is the design the team are excited to see work and they need to use the facilities at Fermilab in Batavia, Illinois, forty five miles from Chicago. Most the team will fly into O'Hare Airport and Steve is planning to drive up the day before as he has no intention of leaving George behind. It will be bad enough when he has to fly to Switzerland.

The lab has gone through some amazing changes since the 70's and, until CERT was built, was the largest collider in the world.

In 2011, Fermilab found its funding slashed by congress. It was a great blow to the people working there and many jobs were lost. The Senate had recently restored some of the funding but, like many science facilities in the States, Fermilab is operating on a shoestring budget.

MIT stepped in with an offer that could not be refused and Fermilab has allowed the use of its collider for a week. The funding will be a great boost and provide for the continuation of important projects.

The facilities in Fermilab village will house the team and they have use of the two collider detectors, known as CDF and D Zero. Both these will collect data on the banks of computers that will store upwards of twenty five megabytes of data per second.

If all goes well, in a few weeks, they will have the use of a much more powerful data storage facility at CERT. Data there is processed at a rate of 300 megabytes per second.

The collider at Fermilab is four miles in circumference and thirty feet below ground. The site sits on 6,800 acres of prime real estate with woodlands and nature on the door step.

Steve can see George enjoying the stay with many different animals to interact with, even a herd of bison to play round up with.

He checks his watch as he enters the lab. He has at least an hour before the first team members show up. He makes for his personal computer in his office. He notices his name plate is still on the door. Not a new one. Nigel, he thinks, was sure he would be back to work. At his desk sits his personal computer. One he had personally built from scratch with the help of the tech boys in IT. Opening to the main page, he programmes his code into the system. The system is one he knows and is confident cannot be broken into. Steve has the ability to recall memories from years ago, his capacity to store information being massive. He has trained his brain this way and many of his achievements are not on file but instead are still stored within him. This is how he has managed to stay one step ahead of the competition. With industrial espionage on the up, even MIT has had its systems broken into and Steve has been approached by various companies offering him large amounts of money to join their groups. But once Steve signed up with Kenneth at MIT, he could never allow himself to be swayed by money. He was loyal and though he had recently resigned, he would eventually have given over his results to MIT, but only after safety measures he could accept were in place.

His code was in the same league as Fort Knox. After opening up the pages, he checks his results from weeks ago and adds to these the new data he had gathered since the last time he was in.

Lab coat on, he enters the main lab and opens up the main A frame and begins his transfer of data, his memories downloading into the system, his fingers tapping on the keys, without so much as a break, for the next hour, never once slowing.

Hearing a noise behind him, he turns and sees, smiling from ear to ear, one of the team members, Lucy Li Lu, an American born nationalist and a great friend. She is two years younger than Steve and very much the character on the team, with a wicked sense of humour and a dress sense that give Goth's a run for their money. An intelligent lady, with a love for data. She loves figures and could outsmart most of the team with her ability to digest new information and make sense of it. She is invaluable to the team and is one of two data analysts, who will be going through all the material stored by the detectors in CDF and D Zero, after their experiment in Fermilab. The other analyst is Carl Mass, in his early forties, with a pony tail and a love of the Harley Davidson motorbikes. No matter the weather, he would always turn up on his bike. The man would not have been put off by the last few days' monsoon conditions and normally is the next to arrive.

Lucy had picked up two coffees on route and presents one to Steve. This is something Steve and Lucy had done over the years as the two early birds on the team. You would have to, on occasion, prise Lucy away from her computers. Her babies she called them. She and Steve worked well together and their friendship worked as they both enjoyed flirting, to the amusement of the other team members, knowing fully well that Steve was in love with his wife and Lucy, loyal to her girlfriend. Although she had told Steve she had a thing for his wife and any time that she fancied being adventurous, to give her a call. She had left Steve to think about that with a wink that said "Am I joking or not?" That brought a smile to Steve that passed as quickly as it came, as it caused him to think again about Karen. Lucy had already contacted Steve, sending him her condolences and letting him know he could always call on her for support.

Lucy reads the look on Steve's face, women's intuition coming out, and, reaching out, carefully hugs him, trying not to spill their coffees. Steve appreciates the gesture.

Looking past Steve at the main frame, coffee forgotten, she hands hers over to Steve, her mind now focusing on the screen, looking back at Steve, she asks him if he had now put in the required data to run the show.

Steve nods to the delight of Lucy, who immediately starts hitting keys, all else forgotten. Steve shrugs, both cups of coffee in hand, one already to his lips. The other he places beside Lucy who would drink it eventually, after several trips to the microwave to re-heat.

Throughout the morning and into the afternoon, the team are at work, collecting the data and putting the new research through simulation. Everyone is excited about Steve's research, some envious that they had not thought of it themselves.

The engineers are on standby waiting their chance to put this new information to the test. Steve had already worked out how to implement the designs and had been busy with two of the engineers, working out any final flaws with the designs. Both Denji Tanaka and Misa Susan Bishop are of Japanese and American parentage. Misa is the only other female working on the team.

Together, they go through several different configurations, working out the best way to sustain the plasma levels and maintain fusion in the chamber. Steve had several weeks ago simulated the best way for his research to work and he had thought that his tests could not be bettered. Misa had put paid to that with an improvement in performance, reducing the need for a greater infusion of the material by introducing smaller quantities over a greater area, rather than allowing the material to disperse around the chamber as it comes in contact with the plasma.

At the end of the day, Lucy and Carl had run through much of the new data and processed it so that others could put it to test in their own fields.

It was almost nine thirty in the evening and Nigel had spent much of the day on the phone relaying the new information to the team already in place over at Fermilab, getting them to reconfigure the chamber. Steve, with the engineers, had already designed it to work with modifications in mind and over the course of the week, they would be busy getting the new designs in place.

Nigel comes out of his office, grabbing everyone's attention, "Everyone, please down tools. It's late. Tomorrow is Sunday and I think I speak for everyone here when I say that this is a great start on Steve's great idea and we are thankful that he has allowed us to go forward with the work. God willing, in less than one month, we will be the team that helps the world move forward with clean and sustainable energy.

But this is also a sad moment and I feel I speak for all of us when I say, we all feel with you Steve, the pain of your loss and we will be beside you over the course over the next few weeks, our combined strengths together to support you in your time of need."

Everyone nods in agreement, going over to Steve and hugging and giving his shoulder a reassuring rub. Steve, again lost for words, has tears forming in his eyes; he is thankful for these people he works with, for their support and compassion.

Arriving home he finds Tina fast asleep on the couch, George beside her, his head on her lap, also asleep. He makes a slight movement to acknowledge Steve's presence but is content to stay put. Steve pulls a cover out from the bottom drawer in the cabinet and places it over Tina, careful not to wake her. After watching the pair of them together, he heads upstairs to his bedroom, looking across at his bed, wandering if he will be able to sleep. Walking over to the side of the bed, he sits down and closes his eyes. He sits, not stirring, trying to hold it together, still unable to come to terms with losing his family. The air is still in the room, a strand of hair has fallen down across his face and for no reason the lose strand lifts back up in place as if an invisible hand has moved it back.

Chapter 17

Steve is woken by the smell of coffee under his nose. Slowly opening his eyes he sees Tina looking down at him. She feels embarrassed having been found out, remembering her time at college sneaking a peek in the boy's locker room. To stop the blush she knew was forming on her face, she quickly holds out the coffee to Steve who sits up, a hand out to receive the cup.

"Sorry, I thought you may have been awake."

Steve, looking down at himself, sees he is still wearing the same clothes he had worn the day before.. He rubs his eyes, at the same time keeping one eye on his watch. Just after six in the morning. He cannot remember falling asleep and this was the first uninterrupted sleep he has had since the accident. No waking up with bad memories in the middle of the night.

"Thanks you. If you give me five minutes, I'll run you back to your mom's."

"You don't have to. I called my mom ten minutes ago. She's making her way over with a change of clothes for me. I figured it will save time. I hope you don't mind if when she gets here, I grab a shower. "

Steve again looks at his watch, wondering why he had fallen asleep so quickly without getting ready for bed. He expected to be tired after a long day at work. He was surprised to feel almost rejuvenated. He thought that once home, it would all come rushing back and he would again get his usual restless sleep. But he felt like he had slept for a week.

Smiling at Tina, he apologises for his dress sense in bed and drinks back the coffee in one go before passing back the cup.

"Thanks again. I'll grab a shower first and thanks for waking me. I have a feeling I would have slept all morning. Good thinking about your mom as we need to get going soon. I take it your mom is still coming with us. Are you sure you want to go?"

Tina nods, "Yes if you're OK with it. I didn't know your father and sister but I would have liked to."

Steve nods, telling Tina that he should grab a shower. Tina stands there before it sinks in. It would not look good, him undressing in front of her. Embarrassed, Tina shuffles out, a small smile forming on her face and a giggle about to break lose.

Down in the kitchen, George is finishing the last of his meal. Tina looks at him and thinks that maybe Steve could do with a bite. Her mother has told her that you can't go wrong with rustling up some eggs and she checks out the larder. Sure enough there are eggs and they are still in date. She had noticed that Steve had shed some pounds, though no surprise there. Grabbing the eggs she gets to work after finding all the needed implements. Ten minutes later Steve has joined her in the kitchen and having smelt the cooking on his way down, realising how hungry he is. Tina has put another brew on and she points at him, telling him to go sit at the breakfast bar. Steve obeys after giving George some affection, making a bit of fuss over him after leaving him the day before. George is back beside Tina, his head tilted with a begging expression on his face.

Tina looks down, "George, you're a pig," George replies with a shake of his head followed by a bark, his tail wagging.

They both laugh at this, Tina knowing full well that she will give him some egg. The doorbell goes and Steve has his hand out to stop Tina.

"I'll get that. It's going to be your mom."

Elena brushes her clothes down as the door opens. She looks up at Steve, her eyes giving way to a mother's distrust of a man who has recently come into their lives unexpectedly and in her mind, unwanted. She thinks he is trouble and would prefer if her daughter would cut ties with this man. She also thinks her daughter's assault is linked in someway to this man but cannot explain it, a mother's intuition. But her daughter is very protective of him, so she will be civil and give him the benefit of the doubt. It has not started out well with her daughter not returning home last night. Her call to say she will be staying the night and not to worry, meant as a mother, she would do just that. This man was in court a few days ago on trial for the murder of his wife. Now he has her daughter staying the night.

"Mrs McElroy. Please come in" Steve looks up at the weather, clouds still heavy in the air but at least it was not raining. Bringing Elena into the lounge, Steve asks to take her coat and disappears around the corner, placing it on a hook, returning to find Tina hugging her mother. Looking around at Steve, Tina tells him the eggs are done and to go and eat. Steve salutes and exits, leaving Tina to grab the bag her mother has brought. Inside were her clothes, shoes and a make-up bag. Giving Elena a shove towards the kitchen, she tells her she won't be long and heads upstairs. Elena makes her way to the kitchen to find a dog over a plate on the floor. Steve looks at Elena and introduces her to George, who quickly looks up for a second at her, before plunging his head back down to the plate.

"Sorry about that. No manners." Steve gets up and offers Elena a coffee. She accepts, telling him she takes it white, no sugar. With a fresh cup in front of Elena, Steve returns to his stool.

"Your daughter makes good eggs. I think George agrees, though I think he would pretty much eat about anything." Steve was trying to make light conversation as he could tell Elena was uncomfortable being there. After all, the first time they met was in a police station with him being booked for murder and now they were going off to a funeral for a family she had never met. What must she be thinking of him?

Elena waits a while before she says anything. She thinks it is best to be civil, but this man should know that her daughter is important to her. "Mr O'Neil, I'm sure you can tell that I am having trouble coming to terms with my daughter's relationship with you. I don't know you and I am very sorry that we have met under these circumstances. I know you have helped my daughter at her work, but a week ago, both of you were just two people who met only at her work place. Now she has been assaulted by her boss and you have lost your family. God knows how you must be coping with all this and I feel for you, but Tina is my daughter and she is half your age."

Steve puts his hands up to stop Elena as he knows where this is going. "Before you go any further, I have no interest in your daughter other than as a friend and I can understand that you are protecting her and I think you are right. Tina needs to be with you and under your protection. I can assume with circumstances like this and with my wife gone, that you may feel things will develop. I enjoy talking to Tina but my priority is for my baby and you are right, she is half my age. I think what is going on here is two people trying to heal, if that makes sense and in time your daughter will eventually find the right person for her but for now, the two of us are coming to terms with what has been inflicted on us. If you are unhappy with Tina knowing me, then please, when she comes down, go home. I would not like you to worry about your daughter being in my company."

Elena thinks this through and eventually tells Steve that although she is concerned, she would not like to intervene at this time, but if Tina looked as though she was developing feelings for Steve, then that would be the time to part company. Her daughter is intelligent and is no fool when it comes to men, but if there is any sign of something other than friendship, she asks Steve to stop seeing her. Steve agrees and asks her if he could call her Elena instead of Mrs McElroy. Elena smiles for the first time, seeing why her daughter likes this man. After all, she thinks, she would have turned around to check his dario out if she had not known him. Dario was a word she now used thanks to her younger female colleagues. Elena covers her small smile as she blushes, leaving Steve to wonder what that was about.

They carry on making small talk about his work. Elena is amazed about the type of work he is involved in and Steve shrugs as if to say, anyone can do it. Ten minutes later, Tina is down with them.

Steve is thankful for the company as it takes his mind off the coming morning. He eventually thinks about time and tells them that they can travel in his car. George can come, but will stay in the car. He tells them that arrangements have been made after the service at his father's house. A catering team had been hired by Nigel and a key has been left with his father's neighbour, Frederick Klein, for the caterers. Frederick had already called to say that he will be coming to the service. His wife, though, was still too ill to attend, but she sent her love and condolences. Steve makes a mental note to send her some flowers.

They have about a two hour journey. Traffic was quiet, it being a Sunday and many people were keeping indoors due to some of the heaviest rain to hit the area in over fifty years.

Steve's father had been living in Greenwich, in Hampshire, just over a hundred miles away. Steve's mother is buried in St Joseph's Catholic cemetery just west of Greenwich. This is where his father and sister will also be buried. His father had already purchased the plot after Steve's mother was buried and there was a place for his sister next to her mother.

The mood in the car is sombre and there is very little talk on the drive. George is in the rear of the car, his head on the seat rest between Tina and Elena. Dogs, he thinks, as he catches the look from George, in the rear view mirror, his face full of character watching the back of Steve's head. Steve thinks dogs have a finer sense than humans when it comes to moments like this, picking up on the melancholy vibe being generated by all. What can you tell us George? Is there life after death? Steve thinks to himself.

Two hours and five minutes later, they are parked at St Joseph's. There are about forty cars parked in the lot. Steve thinks many of these will be normal daily visitors.

Looking around, he remembers the time he was here last, for his mother's funeral. The fountain made from tempered stone still sits in front of the entrance to the chapel. He remembers a large picture of Christ's resurrection on the wall inside the entrance and on either side of the entrance to the cemetery, there are two beautiful Angels standing on two large granite monuments.

It isn't until he meets Nigel at the door, shaking his hand and thanking him for his help, that he looks down through the chapel, and realises there are no visible empty seats. All the cars outside were for the people seated in here, he thought. Nigel looks at the shock on his face, "Your father was much respected, as you can see, and your sister also has friends here."

Many here were colleagues who had worked alongside Steve's father at Hampshire College, where he had taught Science. Some were students who attended his lectures and others were older students from years past. All of them were here out of respect for the man he had been.

Steve walks down the centre aisle, acknowledging people he knew and shaking hands with a few he had not seen for years. Some were friends he had grown up with when he went to the local school before his university days. Others he knew as he was just working with them the previous day. Lucy caught his attention as she had dressed down. He thought her normal wear would suit any funeral, but she had removed much of her makeup and looked quite pretty. Funny how people look when the war paint comes off, he thought.

A couple of places were left for Tina and Elena as Nigel showed them their seats.

Steve carried on to the front and sat on the left side.

For the next two hours, sermons were made and hymns sung and one by one people came to the front to say words on behalf of Steve's father and sister. Most services would normally last less than an hour, but there were many people who wanted to express their feelings and Steve was last to say his words.

He had thought long and hard about what he would say and in the end, he tells everyone that he did not just lose a father and sister whom he loved, but two friends who, it would seem, would be greatly missed. He goes on to say, that if there is any justice to their deaths, people here would remember what they stood for and that the world could do with more people like them, people to take forward the ideals his father had stood by and that people respected him for. He had believed in a united world where equality and decency and respect for nature were fundamental for the world to survive. This is what his father had bestowed on him and he had always believed that one person could make a difference and that now was a time to make that difference.

After the burial, those that could went to the house. Steve could never remember a time when he had shaken hands with so many people and was grateful for their kind words.

The catering team had put on a good spread. At least fifty people had come back. A couple of young men had cornered Tina and Elena had been taken to one side by a very large and overweight man whom Steve did not know and whom he was pretty much sure was one of those people who turn up at funerals looking for a free meal after the service.

Steve himself was pinned by two widow women who were pouring their souls out to him and constantly patting him, as if they were checking to see if he was real. Some people lived for funerals and these two he thought were in that league. Eventually Nigel dragged him away and Steve thanked him for getting his attention.

"If I don't get back soon, I'll not be able to get to the hospital for visiting time and we still have a lot of work to do tonight."

Nigel agrees with the amount of work to do. He looks around for the team, keeping an eye on a few of them that seem to be knocking the booze back. He decides that it is time to go. Most of them had come in a MIT minivan hired out to staff. A chauffer had been hired to drive them. Rounding the group up and turning to Steve he says, "We'll see you in, what… four hours."

Steve feels ok with that and once again, shakes his hand, thanking him for all his work arranging everything. Nigel was always the organiser and today, Steve was thankful for that. The team shook his hand one by one as they left, Lucy and Misa giving him a long hug, both still red eyed from the funeral.

Looking around, he spots Elena and decides to wade in; standing between the large man and Elena, he apologies while pointing at his wrist. Elena nods with a whispered, "Thank you" and tells the man she has to go. Tina was in the kitchen with two young lads and she also looked thankful when Steve said they had to go. He made his speech to the remaining guests, telling them to take their time and that he was sorry that he had to leave.

Before going, he locates the head of the catering team and hands an envelope over; extra money to share out between them and thanked them for their service. He had to see one more person before he left.

Frederick came straight to the door. He had made his excuse not to come around after the funeral as he had spent more time than he liked away from his wife, but he had asked to look after George until Steve came for him. Besides, George would have been under the table getting fat from all the food dropped on the floor. They shook hands promising to keep in touch.

Frederick's Wife was asleep still and Steve did not want to wake her, but again he made a mental note to get flowers the following day and have them sent.

Both Elena and Tina had asked to see the baby on the drive back and Steve could not refuse and it would save time, so he headed straight for the hospital. Both women were excited when they viewed the baby and were shocked that they were refused by a nurse to hold the baby, both of them instantly on Steve's side against the injustice of the social services.

When he drops off Elena and Tina, it is Elena who asks him to drop around whenever he needed to talk to someone and had to be pried away by Tina. As he leaves, Tina makes the gesture with hand to mouth movement, suggesting that Mom has had too much drink. The joke was her mother hardly ever touched alcohol and a glass of sherry was enough to leave her a little tipsy. Steve nods and thanks her for coming.

Steve was back in work inside the four hours Nigel had said, eager to get back to work. George was placed in one of the officers where he fell straight to sleep. Steve knew he had not given himself any time to really think about the day. He knew that if he did, he would fall into despair. People were relying on him and he was thankful to keep busy.

Sunday passes and it is not until two in the morning when time is called. Everyone is told by Nigel not to come in before ten. A finger is pointed at Lucy to comply. She curtsies to Nigel, which brings laughter from the others.

Steve is stretching, watching them file out as one by one, the computers are turned off. More information uploaded from the days labour. They were a step closer to achieving the dream. Turning, he leaves the lab with George in tow, walking out the entrance to his car, unaware that he is being watched.

Chapter 18

Moralis is at his desk, the time is just after seven am. He had arrived early to see if any emails have come in over the weekend from the insurance company as they have promised to send details on Mrs O'Neil's life policy. Nothing has arrived but he isn't surprised.

Looking across at his desk, he sees it is covered with more paperwork then when he had left it Friday night; he has always wondered who came in at the weekends to load up his desk with more work. It never seems to go down.

Hearing movement from the hallway, his partner Washington comes around the corner, also early. He wonders if she has a boyfriend. She was not one to talk much about her private life. He has noticed that one of the young guys in the office had taken a shine to her, Richards. He remembers the roster; Richards is on duty this morning from six. They had set up the roster on Friday between their precinct and Lowell, splitting the work load to watch over Scholfield in hospital. It meant they would have more hours on shift with the drive, but that's the way it was played out by his superiors. All about the budget he was told. Richards was on till two then his partner would take over, the new guy, Greggs, a transfer from Vegas or someplace five months ago. Not a young officer, but he seemed to know his job.

Washington is holding two coffees and a bag of donuts. Moralis hears his stomach rumble.

"Sounds like the donuts have arrived in the nick-of-time".

"Funny. Ha, ha, Washington, sounds like you got out on the right side of bed."

Washington smiles, not adding to the comment. She was pleased that another side of Moralis was showing, thinking, so he does have a sense of humour after all. They seemed to have bonded in the last week and that was good for them to properly work together. Moralis is interested in her theories.

Yeah! She's got a man, thinks Moralis.

Washington asks if Scholfield had come around and if forensics had come back on the car? Moralis shakes his head, also letting her know that news from the insurance company had not turned up; no doubt they are wondering why the police were questioning the policy and getting their lawyers to check things out before they got in touch.

Friday night, they had gone back to the accident scene and found that someone had already been and picked up the wreckage. They had scoured the area for missed pieces and found one piece embedded in a tree. Both of them concluded that if this was a normal accident, no normal recovery vehicle would have been so thorough. They knew they were on to something. That piece was now in forensics being matched up with the O'Neil's car accident.

Today, both of them are watching the clock. They are waiting to get their warrant signed by the judge. Their supervisor won't be in for another hour, giving them time to catch up on paperwork and they both grab the top folder of their desks.

Steve has not listened to Nigel and is back in the lab preparing more tests. Beside him is Lucy. She had actually made it in before him and he knew she would defy Nigel about coming in at ten, so he had brought the coffees. Lucy has her war paint back on and is busy punching the keyboard. Out of all of them, she would go through on average, three keyboards a year. Not a girl to piss off, he thought, as you ended up getting the

166

jabbing finger in the chest when she wanted to make a point. When eventually you conceded the argument, whether she was right or wrong, it all came down to how much pain you could take.

Right now, Steve was finalising the last of his experiments through simulation. Each one had been tested and re-tested over the last two days and other than a few hic-ups, most had panned out. Once they were happy with the simulation, it would be a matter of creating the product for their tests at Fermilab.

These designs of Steve's would be a more advanced composition superseding previous uses of the material.

He had taken his idea to Kenneth when he first came on the project and Kenneth had been instantly smitten. Some of the funds allocated to the project were signed over to Steve for him to experiment with. It was Kenneth's idea to keep this side of the design away from the others. The death of Kenneth put paid to the secrecy, but Nigel had the ear of the people funding the project and the experiments were allowed to continue. Most of the team did not resent Steve keeping his experiment secret as he had made many contributions to the designs on the chamber. Everyone was aware that others had tried to steal the designs and felt that if they were going to come out on top, then Steve's secret was their golden goose for them to succeed.

Now the team were aware of the designs needed for the plasma in the chamber to stay at maximum strength. Loss of heat will be controlled at a sub particle level. Steve had come up with the idea of using nanotechnology to help with keeping the plasma encased. Nanotechnology was a name coined in the 80's by K. Eric Drexler, who had a Ph.D. in researching protein engineering.

Steve had looked at the idea and thought he could improve on nanotechnology to work in the field of fusion. The idea was to take a protein at a molecular scale and engineer it to react differently with plasma. Each different type of Nano protein would be designed to either protect the chamber from the plasma or help increase the temperatures adding a boost of energy. Others would be used as miniature sensors designed to collect data. Every chamber would have a manufacturing base to reproduce the Nano proteins at an industrial level. This was needed to keep control over the plasma. Without it, things would either shut down or, worse, they would get out of control.

The two colliders in operation at Fermilab and CERN were designed to discover the origins of the universe, the hunt for the Higgs Boson, also known as the God particle. The idea to send two neutrons at near to light speed, smashing them into each other and generating a nuclei reaction attributed to what is known as the big bang.

These colliders will be reconfigured to send frozen pellets of deuterium and tritium around the chamber at great speed and smash them inside the chamber built inside the collider, creating a higher chain reaction as more and more fuse together into a plasma state, as particles bounce off the walls discharging higher particles of energy that are funnelled to a steam turbine and transferring the energy into electrical power. The heat inside the chamber would have to exceed the transfer heat by 200 to 330 times to create fusion and this power will be maintained by the constant barrage of Nano particles.

Every experiment simulated by Steve has shown different responses and it is one of these responses that had originally made up Steve's mind about slowing down the project until they could be certain that this particular response would never happen. Unfortunately, the people at the top had ploughed tens of millions into the project and they wanted results. Steve had resigned over their decision with a promise to his father and Karen not to compromise safety. The chances of it happening are part of the twelve per cent he is worried about. Fingers crossed, all will go well.

After a morning filing paperwork and making phone calls to various people, Moralis gets a call back from the company dealing with the life policy. They had made the checks to locate the source of the policy and found that it had originated from O'Neil's house almost two weeks prior to Mrs O'Neil's death. A time was given that they found unusual. The document was emailed at 2.15 in the morning. Not unheard of but still, why do it at that time, he thought.

A call breaks the spell. Moralis answers and relays the message to Washington. The warrant has been granted so they need to go to collect it. Moralis checks his watch. 14.25. The trouble with Monday was the increase in offences committed over the weekend meant that the judge has to deal with more arraignments. Two officers have been granted to help out with the search of the premises on the estate.

They arrive outside their building at 16.10. The roads were busy from the school runs. Many parents, driving too fast for their own good, no doubt wanting to get back home to catch the ending of whatever programme they were watching.

They are met by a locksmith also with skills in disabling alarm systems. The man had been requested that morning by Moralis as they were unable to track down either the owner or person renting the building. Moralis gives him the go-ahead to pick the lock. This takes around five minutes and once in, the man turns his attention to the key panel on the wall. It is a high security system that takes the man almost ten minutes to clear. The main bell outside had gone off and after two minutes listening to the wail, Moralis has one of the officers pull the cover off it and disable the wires by pulling them all out.

A call comes through at about the same time. Washington takes the call. She calls back to Moralis that Scholfield has come out of his coma. Moralis tells Washington to hang back and call the hospital and find out if he is talking.

Moralis with the two officers, torches in one hand, work their way down the corridor towards the back of the premises checking the rooms one by one as they searched. Most of the doors swing in revealing an empty shell of a room. With the weather outside still overcast, most of the light entering into the rooms is from their torches and the light bouncing off the walls, throwing ghost like shadows in every direction. Moralis takes the lead with one of the officers following behind, throwing the doors open on the either side of the corridor. The second officer is told to hang back and make a thorough search of the rooms. Moralis is now at the rear off the premises. Two doors feed into the room. An old sign at the top says "Storage." Storage for what, he thinks?

Washington put down the receiver after getting through to the floor Scholfield was on. She had managed to get a conversation with a doctor working the wards. Washington was put on hold whilst the doctor checked on the condition of the patient. He came back on line four minutes later, though it felt like an eternity to Washington as she wanted to get inside the building. She felt she was missing all the fun. The doctor told her the patient is awake but in and out of consciousness. He told her that they will know more in a few hours. She puts down the line after being told that there is no problem with them coming up, but speaking with the patient would have to be authorised by his doctor.

Leaving the vehicle, Washington is stopped by the locksmith, asking her who was going to sign his invoice? He goes on to tell her that he was just a working man and not one of the three lottery winners at the weekend that can live a life of luxury with over five hundred million to share between them. Washington is polite but impatient as she wants to get in the building. She informs the man that he needs to send his invoice into the station where it will be properly dealt with. From behind her comes an explosion that sends debris flying through the front doorway, taking the door with it. Glass in the windows around the building are almost vaporised with small razor sharp shards flying through the air. The roof at the rear of the building has completely exploded upwards and debris is raining down everywhere. Washington and the Locksmith are thrown of their feet and land almost ten feet away. The locksmith is unlucky and he slams into one of the vehicles. He is immediately knocked unconscious. Washington fares better but the wind is knocked out of her. Shards are hitting the ground around her, missing her by inches. It is a full thirty seconds before she is able to raise her head. The smell of smoke is in the air and the sky is raining light flakes of what once was the building's roof.

Still dazed, Washington, hearing muffled shouting, gets to her feet, trying carefully not to fall over. Shaking her head, she slowly looks around, finding people keeping their distance from the falling debris, shouting and pointing at her. She finds it hard to hear them and knows that the explosion has temporary deafened her. She starts to shout back, "Get help. Please get help!" Running to her vehicle, she picks up the mike and calls dispatch. Shaking her head, trying to get the buzzing sound out of her ears, she gets a voice on the line. Without waiting she tells the operator that officers are down and gives her location. Turning, she makes for the open doorway, one thing on her mind. Are they alive?

The man enters the room, keeping an eye on the door, he makes his way to the side of the bed where the drip feed is feeding into Scholfield's arm. There is a mixture of saline and morphine running into his arm. He is fast asleep, oblivious to everything and everyone around him. The man looks down at the person in the bed. He is not happy with what he has to do but he has got himself mixed up with some very powerful people and he owes them money. Sorry buddy, he thinks, it's you or me. Taking the drip feed, he replaces the bag with another one with the same colour liquid within it. Without waiting to see what will happen, he exits the room. Five minutes later, doctors and nurses are running into the room. Beside the bed, the monitor is heard through the commotion, the tell-tale sound of a flat line.

Chapter 19

"Can you hear me lady?"

Washington looks up at the paramedic attending her injuries. She is clearly in pain and the ringing in her ears is deafening, making it hard for her to hear his words. She has not said much to anyone. She looks around at the people running around her, watching as, in slow motion, her fellow police officers, fire crews and medics run in and out of the building. A stretcher appears, carried by two medics. One of the officers caught in the blast has survived.

She remembers finding him. He was badly burnt and Washington had come across him in one of the rooms. She had heard him crying out in pain, parts of his clothing on fire. She could see that he was badly burned. She assumed that he must have been blown back in the room, the door partially protecting him. Washington shivers as she recalls the stench of burning flesh. She had to douse the flames before she could administer first aid and had stayed with him until the paramedics had arrived and taken over. The officer was caught in the blast close to the exit. He might have fared better if he had not been coming out of one of the rooms when the fire had ripped through the corridor, catching the officer.

After the medics had arrived, she had made her way to the rear of the building. Crews were filing past her, some were trying to get her attention but she ignored them, her focus to look for her partner not knowing what she would find.

She knew Moralis was dead. There was no way he could have survived this, she thought, as she

173

approached what was left of the doorway to the last room. The fire had extinguished itself with the explosion. A few areas were smouldering and the walls were blackened, otherwise there was just the bad smell in the air. Most the people around her assumed she was called out with the rest of them and left her alone. Looking around what was once the store room, she could see gas bottles of different sizes, lying sprawled across the floor. There were ones that had clearly exploded and it would appear that the walls of the building were thick inside and had contained much of the blast. The furnace that they wanted to inspect had completely been ripped apart, as if most of the blast had been directed at it. It was a wonder that the chimney was still standing. There was no evidence of bodies, either Moralis or the other officer. Both must have been at the centre of the blast. Another officer had recognised her being the partner of Moralis and had escorted her out under protest.

She watches as one of the ambulances leaves, carrying the Locksmith who had suffered concussion and broken bones when he had flown through the air hitting a vehicle. She could not recall his name. Moralis had spoken with him on the phone and outside the building prior to going in. She had been engaged in other duties.

She could hear a lot more now as the paramedic had managed to gain her attention. She was more in shock with losing her partner than her own problems, thinking about his wife and family. She had briefly met the family a few months ago, at a police function to raise money for the families of injured soldiers serving at home and abroad. They were a nice family and she could tell Moralis was a proud father. His wife Claire was a lovely lady and they had talked mainly about how she coped being married to a police officer. Claire

174

had told her that if it was not for bringing up three children, she would have found it harder not to worry about her husband. The kids took much of her time up and she was grateful that they were all still at home. Claire had made a joke about the lines around her eyes being happy lines, not the other way round. Washington thinks, that will change now.

Washington had refused to go to the hospital in the ambulance and had told the paramedic just to patch her up and give her some pills for the pain. She suspected that the ringing in her ears was temporary and had promised to see a doctor later when things had calmed down.

Washington stays at the scene, giving a statement to two of her colleagues. The people who were working in the buildings on site, that had come out to investigate the explosion, eventually leave. There were only a few stragglers staying back, the ones hoping to get a last glimpse of something more gruesome.

Washington corners one of the fire officers, Clive Denials, an officer with Belmont's fire division with over twenty five years' experience. She asks him if he had any idea of what may have caused the explosion. He knew who she was and that it was her partner who had died. He is very sympathetic with her, not wanting to rush in with a conclusion. He tells her that from what he can identify from the destruction, it looked very much like an accident; some of the gas bottles had fallen over, possibly caught when the doors were opened and it looked like one had exploded, setting off a chain reaction. He tells her that is his first impression but more evaluations would need to be carried out before a decision can be reached. Washington has her own idea on the explosion but is keeping it to herself, for now that is.

It is dark and spotlights have been placed in the building as the electricity supply had been damaged in the explosion. A generator is working, supplying power to the lights. Tarpaulin had been erected across the roof area stopping water from washing away evidence. The weather has turned wet again, making it difficult to work outside and a heavy breeze has picked up.

Washington watches as the last vehicle leaves. She is allowed to stay on site to evaluate but not to interfere. An officer has been assigned to her and he is now patiently waiting for her, feeling sorry for her but at the same time wanting to get back. He is getting cold and he can see that nothing more is being done this night. He tries to catch her attention and she eventually turns to him, a sad look across her face that makes him feel a little guilty.

"Come on then. Let's go and thank you for driving me back." Washington slides in, wincing as she puts her seat belt on. The pills the paramedic had given her earlier have worn off and she can feel the bruising all over her body. She knows she will be very stiff in the morning and asks the officer to take her home. She needs a bath to ease her injuries and remove the grime. Also she knows that some of the falling debris is more than just layers of dust from the building but organic matter she does not want to think about. She needs a long soak and to focus her mind. She wants to get the people responsible for this atrocity. This was no accident, she thinks to herself. This was a set up. But she needs evidence and she needs to get all the evidence together before she can take it to her superiors.

After Washington is dropped off, she let herself in, turning off the security to her apartment. She stands in the hall for what seems like an eternity, thinking about the loss of lives. She shakes herself out of her almost catatonic state and proceeds through to the lounge; the kitchen was separated by a small central aisle. She again stands still, but this time she was aware of her surroundings. Something feels wrong but she cannot place what is making her nervous. Looking around, Washington can see nothing is out of place but she feels as though someone had been in her apartment. She inhales trying to get a whiff of a scent she is unfamiliar with lurking in the air. The gun is out of her holster in two seconds as she has a vision of someone in her apartment. Step by step, she stealthily goes through the rooms, checking the closets and under the bed, eventually working her way back to the centre of her lounge where she carries on circling around, looking for tell-tale signs for anything out of place. Nothing appears to have been moved and she eventually holsters her gun, giving herself a rebuke for being paranoid. Taking a deep breath she heads for the bathroom.

Washington checks the time. It is just after ten, Tuesday morning. She had a call from her supervisor the day before telling her not to come in early as she had already given a statement on site and it was more important that she get some quiet time before coming to the station in case she remembered something important to go in the report. This is standard procedure considering that it was her partner that was killed and she could easily forget small details that might make a difference to the investigation.

Washington had showered and is in her kitchen drinking coffee. She had already made a visit to the laundry room that morning to get her clothes cleaned. She is sure though that she would never wear them again. When she had collected them off the bathroom floor, the smell brought the visions back from the previous day, the officer on fire, the smell of his burnt body. An expensive top she had recently purchased was now heading for the trash, she thinks. She laughs a little at the abnormality of the thought. Thinking about a top when two men had died. She had heard people fixated on mundane things to cope with stress. Is she coping she thinks.

She rolls in to work just before one. Every one she passes looks at her as though she were an apparition. She keeps her head down and heads for her desk. She sits down slowly, her eyes locked on the empty chair opposite her, never to be sat on again by Moralis. She immediately turns her attention back to the unfinished paperwork on her desk. It appeared reduced. Someone had sorted through it, no doubt taking some cases off her that needed finishing or starting. Moralis had the O'Neil file in his desk drawer and she is loath to get it. With the file on her desk, she opens the contents, working from the back. Something is wrong. Things she had typed were not in the file. She is about to go back to the drawer when her phone rings, a call from the office secretary telling her that Captain Childs would like to speak with her in her office. Washington puts down the phone looking at the drawer. She turns away and heads for the office.

"Please take a seat, detective."

Washington sits in the chair opposite Childs. She knows why she has been called here. Her senior partner is dead and at some point she will be doubled up with another detective, someone senior to herself. She knows this won't happen immediately. People in her line of work are a bit skittish when it comes to being partnered with a detective whose partner was killed in the line of duty. She wants to hold onto the case with O'Neil as she feels it is the only chance of finding answers. Someone else looking at it would view it differently.

"Detective Washington, I am sorry we haven't had time to get acquainted over the last few months. Your partner Moralis was a good police officer and we shall all miss him. How are you coping?"

Washington shrugs, telling Childs that it was too early to say but she obviously feels saddened by the loss of her partner.

Childs nods, looking at Washington, trying to read her thoughts, "The funeral I have been told will be held this Sunday for both Detective Moralis and Officer Lynch. Mrs Moralis has asked that we keep the service simple. No parade. Officer Lynch was born here and his family has also asked for a quiet remembrance service."

"If you need to take any leave, I recommend you do it immediately. Your work load will be shared out. I won't talk now about a new partner, but when you get back, we should get you partnered up as soon as possible."

Washington flinches at the captains words. "I understand Captain, that I will be given a new partner and that I am still considered a rookie detective with only a few arrests under my belt, but I would be grateful, if you would allow me to finish up the work Moralis and I had started. There is too much here with all that has happened recently, not to feel that things are not as they seem."

Child looks at Washington, trying to decide if it would be a good idea to go chasing ghosts. It is too easy, she thinks, to lose your way in a case and she knows Moralis had his teeth in this one and look where it had got him. "I am sorry Detective, I don't see anything here and unfortunately your witness is dead."

Washington jumps up, stammering, raising her voice. "Who is dead?" Childs tells her that their man, Scholfield, had passed away in hospital yesterday.

Another accident; it would appear that one of the nurses had given an overdose of morphine to him and he had gone into a seizure. He was already weak from his condition and unfortunately the drugs were too much for his body to accept. A nurse is presently helping police with enquiries.

Washington is pacing, agitated with more disturbing news from Captain Childs. She stops, her eyes fixed on Childs, wondering why this woman cannot see that something more is going on. Things stink!

"Captain, don't you think there are too many accidents? Keel has gone missing. Scholfield sends a message telling us that he has seen a body and now he's also dead. Now Moralis and Lynch are dead. Men involved cannot be traced but we have evidence of these persons. Mrs O'Neil's life policy sent on an email around two in the morning. Things do not add up."

Childs stands up, leaning across her desk, "Washington. What you are telling me does not add up to a conspiracy. You have no evidence, though I believe you are waiting for a report back from forensics on two cars. Unfortunately, again I have some bad news for you and someone is going to get his rank busted down if we ever find out who lost the evidence bag. These are all just coincidences Washington and unless you have anything more for me, I am dropping your line of enquiries. I cannot justify putting more time into this. I should never have allowed Moralis to go to court with O'Neil in the first place and we are too busy to spend more time on this. If anything turns up in the future, then we will look into it. We are burying two good police officers at the weekend. I do not intend to chase any more ghosts. I am sorry, but that's final. Go and write your report, then grab some R&R and that's an order."

Childs sits back down, shaking her head, thinking she was being harsh on Washington. Moralis had told her good things about this detective and she thinks that if she is strong, then she will put this behind her and move on.

Washington is too stunned to say anything. She turns and leaves the office, making her way back to her desk and plopping herself down on her chair. She sits a while, thinking things through. She stands and goes to the drawer the file was in. No paperwork had fallen out, from the folder. She makes her way to the evidence cage and signs in. Going into the cage, she looks for the USB flash drive that was put into evidence last week, the one found on Scholfield's apartment floor is also gone!

She next walks down to transportation. Her's and Moralis's vehicle had been brought back last evening as she had not been allowed to drive herself back. Finding the vehicle, she finds the laptop on the back seat and turns it on. Opening up, she finds file after file have been deleted. She sits back resting her head. She has to think clearly and put everything in order. One thing is certain, one of her own is a bad cop.

Chapter 20

Steve checks the time. Just after eight in the evening.

He has been working since six that morning and realises that he has not eaten much all day. After grabbing a coffee and sandwich from the vending machine, he takes a seat in the canteen. News is on TV in the background, primarily reporting about the weather.

Giving himself five minutes, he takes his cell phone out of his pocket and checks last night's message. It was from Detective Washington, asking to meet him after work in private. The message was short. "This is Detective Washington. I need to talk to you in private, tomorrow night at ten. Meet me at Whitney's Café. Don't tell anyone."

At first he had wondered how Washington had got his number. It was the one Nigel had given him but then he recalled handing his possessions over to the police when he was charged. The number would have been checked then. He was intrigued. Why is she contacting him in secrecy? Whitney's café he knew, a bar on Harvard square, just fifteen minutes from work. If he recalled right, Wednesday was a popular night. After putting his cell phone away, he finishes off the last of his sandwich.

Steve's attention is drawn to the news breaking on the TV about a young mother and her child, who were crushed under a runnaway truck in Cambridge. He turns to the screen, an attractive woman is talking to the camera, her hand is holding a mike and she is having difficulty reporting the news as rain is being blown into her face by strong winds. Behind her in the distance sits a large truck. It looks like it had collided with a wall as the front end is damaged; the wall in front has been turned into rubble. The cameraman was obviously after shots of the bodies and was veering in on two shapes on the ground. Both had been covered over. Police, fire and ambulance crews were at the scene, their vehicles surrounding the accident, lights whizzing around on top and sirens still blaring away. The police were keeping the crowds on either side from getting in close. A man was screaming in one of the crowds and he had managed to break free, running towards the scene. It was clear that he knew the persons who had died as he was calling out names. Two police officers had managed to catch up with him and were holding him back. It was clear that he was very distraught as he falls to his knees. Steve feels very sorry for the man; he could relate to the man's anguish. He hits the off button and leaves. He's had his share of tragedy and doesn't need any more.

Washington had made it to Whitney's café by 21.55. She had found herself a quiet area away from the juke box. The bar was surrounded by groups of drinkers, some who were clearly intoxicated. She felt eyes on her; an attractive women sitting alone in this type of establishment would draw attention. She looks at her watch. O'Neil is late, she thinks, and if he doesn't show soon, she will be rich pickings for the brave drunks.

Steve enters and spots Washington. He notices a man walking, or rather stumbling towards her. There are several men behind him encouraging him on. He watches as the man tries to engage Washington in conversation. The man is finding it hard to stay on his feet, swaying around like a puppet. The noise inside the bar makes it difficult to hear what is being said. Washington stands and moves to the guy, whispering something in his ear. At the same time she is reaching inside her waist jacket, a gun clearly visible. The man staggers back with a shocked expression on his face as he stumbles back to his friends. They are laughing at him, looking at the shock on his face. Turning from them he walks towards Steve and as he passes, he mumbles something about being tied up with a gun up his ass as he walks out the door.

Steve makes his way over to Washington, who is still standing as she watches him walk over, a small smile on his face that leaves as soon as she speaks.

"Thank you for coming. I wasn't sure if you would show."

They shake hands and she gestures for them to sit. A waitress had spotted Steve when he entered and comes over for his order. Steve orders a beer and asks Washington if she wants a refill. She had not touched her first one but accepts the offer and two beers are ordered. The waitress leans in and asks Steve to make sure he orders from her, giving him her name and following up with a big smile. He turns his attention back to Washington, who has seen the waitress clearly try to flirt with O'Neil, who had not even batted an eyelid at the interest.

Steve is curious as to why he has been asked to meet Washington, as it is clear that it is not on official business. Her partner is not visible or he is hiding somewhere and they are trying to play him. He will allow her to do all the talking.

"OK Detective Washington. You have asked me to meet you. What's all this about?"

"Do you mind calling me Carla? Washington sounds so formal."

"OK Carla. My name is Steve as you know. Now what's this all about? I am obviously curious to know why you have asked to meet on what I can only assume is unofficial business. I am sure your superiors would not take kindly to this meeting. So what is it you want or want to tell me?"

Washington ponders her response. She can tell that he is not overjoyed with being here and who can blame him. She wonders if this is a good idea. Lives have been lost and she now thinks that it all has something to do with this man; she needs to know why?

"Steve, since we last met, things have escalated. Before I explain, it is my opinion that you were not responsible for the death of your wife. We had the toxicology report back from forensics and it is still unclear why your wife died. You will be contacted soon about this and I believe you will be able to claim your wife's body. Since then other people have lost their lives. To be blunt, I think you hold the key to everything that has happened recently and one of the people now dead, is my partner."

Steve keeps quiet, listening to Washington, taking everything in that she is telling him, putting aside questions he wants to ask. He is shaken by all the deaths that have occurred but still not quite grasping what it has to do with him and why they are talking here about it and not at her station. He realises why they are here when she finishes, telling him about a police officer she thinks may be involved. He remembers the news from Monday evening about two officers losing their lives on the outskirts of Belmont but he had not heard who the two officers were. That news was obviously kept quiet until the family had been told and he had been too busy to follow local news. Moralis was one of the two that were killed. Washington finishes telling him about her investigation and asks him a question. Why would someone kill his family?

"You mean my wife?"

"No! I mean your family."

"I don't follow. My father and sister were killed in a road accident. Everything you have told me sounds like unfortunate accidents. Where is the evidence that all these deaths were anything but accidents?"

"Steve. I know what I have told you sounds like a person's over active imagination and believe me I wish it were. What makes me believe all this. Only someone who works on the force will have access to my work. Someone has gone to great trouble in erasing every bit of evidence we had collected. Paper work has gone missing. Evidence placed in a secure locker has gone missing. The paint to match the paint marks on your Father's car has been lost. My own laptop has had files deleted and Monday night when I had got back home after losing my partner, I thought someone had been in my apartment. It wasn't until yesterday that I checked the log from my keypad display. All entries and exits from my apartment over the last six months had been erased. All that information is held in the log for six months and then a new log starts. I have only had the security in place for a little over five months. So I know the display would still have over five months of entries.

"Why, are you telling me all this? Why are you not taking this up with your superiors? Do you know who this person is you suspect?"

"Yes, I think I do but without evidence, I cannot go accusing another fellow officer. Why am I'm telling you this? Because it all started with you and there were photos of two men breaking into your home last week taken by Scholfield. Those also have gone missing, and why would you send a life policy for your wife at two in the morning?"

Steve raises his voice, telling Washington that he never filled in a life policy, let alone sent it in at two in the morning. Who does that? He asks her what date he had supposedly sent this? Washington recalls the date and Steve leans back recalling where he was on that date, his expression turning angry.

"There is no way I had sent that policy on my computer from my house because I was never in my house on that date. We had both gone over to my father's as my sister had recently moved back there after a relationship of hers had gone south. Karen and Sis are," Steve stops himself, "were good friends. Do you realise if you had asked me that last week, I would not have been arrested or gone to court and I would not be fighting for jurisdiction over my child" Steve was seething, angry with this women and her ex –partner.

The waitress had returned with the two beers, hearing angry words from the man and seeing his angry stare turn from the women onto her as she places the beers on the table; assuming she is the cause of the argument with the couple, she walks away quickly. Carla keeps quiet for a minute, allowing Steve to calm down, watching him take a drink.

"Sorry Steve. We never had a time frame for the policy when we charged you. Moralis did some digging and the insurance company were a little hesitant about giving us any information. They were guarding their backs, especially with the aftermath of this thing with Keel, who by the way I think might be the body Scholfield saw being cremated. These people, whoever they are, seem to know our every move and to state a cliché, are one step ahead of us. My superiors want proof and I have nothing to show them. So why are you still alive? What is it they want from you?"

"What are you telling me? Everyone, including my wife was killed because I knew something. Do you know how ridiculous that sounds? This is crazy. Do you know how crazy you sound?"

Steve stops himself, shaking his head. No, he thinks. That's just too absurd. This can't have anything to do with my project. Companies, he knows, can be unscrupulous, but would they go to the extent of killing? Again he thinks. If you are capable of killing once, then why not twice or three times or, with what he has just been told, seven times. He shakes his head not wanting to believe that people have been killed so he would complete the project. He would have completed it eventually. Shaking his head again, Steve tries to think logically. He looks across at Carla, a frustrated expression on his face.

"Steve, are you OK. What have you remembered?"

"Before I tell you anything, I want your word, you are not setting me up."

Carla agrees and leans in.

"First of all, everything you have told me can be put down to pure coincidence, but if it's not, then there are people who are interested in my project with MIT. I say that lightly, particularly concerning the research I have been involved in. I have signed a contract with MIT never to reveal my work to anybody outside of my team. Even members of my team did not known what I was working on until recently. It has been kept a close guarded secret by a few people I know. My family I told, breaking the rule to a point, but keeping important work to myself. A few team members I told and obviously the people controlling the purse strings in MIT. They knew the work I was creating.

"A break-in had occurred a few years back and some of our data was stolen. My work was safe as I have the best security. Better than Fort Knox. My memory, important figures and data for my work are kept up here and if I need it, I can go straight to it. The work that was stolen hinted at what we were doing, and in less than two weeks, we will be putting it to the test. If it works, we will be the first and what we have to offer the world will mean a better future for all. If you

188

ask me if what I am working on is worth killing for. Then yes. I believe you when you say people have been killed. But my wife's death is a tragedy and I cannot believe she was killed because of my work. That does not make any sense. I think you need to go back over your evidence. You need to confront this officer you feel is corrupt. Then if you find evidence to back you up, come back to me. In the meantime, I'm left with having to make visits to see my own child because of you and as you so thoughtfully put it, I may be able to put my wife to rest. Thank you very much."

Steve stands, his hand removing some folded bills from his pocket, peeling a few off and dropping them on the table. He stands a while, looking down at Washington, then turns and walks out.

Washington takes her time to leave. She feels that she now has the reason why so many people have died, even if O'Neil can't see it or doesn't want to see it. Let's face it, she thinks, who wants to be told that they may have been indirectly responsible for their wife's death? Taking a last sip of beer and standing, she drops some more bills on the table and leaves.

Heads turn when she walks out. A few seconds later a man walks out after her, Cell phone in hand, he makes a call. The person on the other end had been waiting for the call and picks up. After listening to his man, he then informs him that something has to be done about Washington.

After putting the phone down he thinks about their man. The officer had been useful but if he's found out, things could turn sour. There is very little evidence tying him with the officer but if Washington goes digging and the officer talks... He leaves that thought open. All good things must come to an end and he starts planning his next move.

Chapter 21

A few days have gone by since Steve had his meeting with Carla Washington. What she had told him had upset him and he was finding it difficult to concentrate. Some engineering components needed fine-tuning and nothing could be left to chance; these were serious calculations that had very little room for error in the field of fusion.

Work colleagues had noticed he was distant and agitated. One time he had taken it out on Lucy for a small miscalculation that would have been picked up eventually, as they never left anything to chance, all calculations were covered at least five times before it was accepted.

Nigel had pulled him to one side, asking if he was ill or something, but Steve had told him that it was probably just lack of sleep and that he would catch up at the weekend with the drive over to Fermilab. Nigel seemed to accept this but Steve had noticed that Nigel was constantly checking up on him, which he put it down to him being overly concerned for the project.

Washington had travelled into work. She had taken time away from the station as requested by her captain and was there to get the attention of one of the officers. She had made an excuse about leaving some personal things in her locker that needed cleaning, as she wasn't due back to work until Monday. She had joked with the female desk sergeant about men not being the only species to stink out the locker room with their odour, women could also compete in that game after a workout in the gym and some of her kit needed picking up.

She talks to some of her colleagues, as the officer she is interested in is out on patrol. She is running out of reasons to be there, when she catches him returning. He looks a little confused as she gives him a smile that lingers longer than normal. Hopefully, he will take the bait and come over to talk to her. She wants him to think he has made the play. Turning around, she strolls to the canteen, certain he would follow as she is wearing the tightest pair of jeans teamed with a plunge line top to get his attention. She can tell that she is being checked out by other officers, whose eyes were following her movements. God, she thought, you're a slut, girl. Sure as shot, a couple minutes later he strolls in.

"Hello Detective Washington, thought you were taking time out. How come you're in work? Missing your work colleagues?"

"That must be it Officer Richards. I must be missing seeing your face around and I was getting withdrawal symptoms."

Carla smiles her best smile as she said this, telling herself not to overdo it. You will only confuse the man after the many times you have ignored his attentions, she thinks to herself.

"The trouble with taking time off with no notice, is not having anything to do. What's a single girl to do with her time? The weekend's coming up and I need to let my hair down. Sorry Richards, I'm just having a moan and it probably sounds like I'm being shallow considering I have just lost my partner. I just need to get my mind away from thinking about the funeral this weekend."

Washington hopes that Richards has taken the bait. Their difference in rank will mean that they cannot date as dating someone from the same force would be frowned upon. She hopes Richards has the balls to try his luck.

"I'm sorry to hear that Detective Washington, it's going to be hard on us all. If I can help in any way, just let me know, and I mean anything."

"Are you flirting with me Officer?" Washington replies with a stern face.

Richards stammers, as he thinks Washington is going to ball him out, just when he thought he was getting the come on. Now he's not so sure.

"Just joking with you. Look, I can't keep calling you Richards. How long have we known each other? Paul isn't it? Seems silly as we're out of ear shot, you can call me Carla. Just don't tell anyone. So what do you get up to when you're not working, boys' night out or you a ladies man, Paul?"

Washington was drawing him in, casting the bait. The guy probably had a hard-on right now, she thought, deciding not to look down and blow it by laughing; but she almost did as she registered her little pun.

"Friday night, I normally catch a movie. The weekends, I'm normally out with the lads, sometimes with a girl. Right now, just out with lads."

"God, I can't remember the last time I went to the movies. I might do that tonight. So maybe if you're out, I may see you around."

Washington checks her watch, telling Richards that she needs to be somewhere else. She gives him her best smile and a glint in her eye, one she normally reserves for the men she fancies. She makes sure she brushes past Richards as she leaves, giving him a smell of her fragrance. As she brushed past him she is certain that he was hooked. All she had to do now was check movie times and wait to see if he turned up.

Steve knocks on Nigel's door and leans in. Nigel looks up from a file he is reading.

"Nigel, just you and me left. I've just seen Lucy out the door; that woman would sleep here if you let her. What time are you planning to go, I thought it might be good to catch up over a beer?"

Nigel checks the time, "Thanks Steve, I could certainly do with one, but can I take a rain check? I still have some paperwork to get through and afterwards I have to speak with our sponsors about the coming week. Right now with the end so close, they want daily updates on everything. When we get over to FermiLab, let's grab a beer then. Whilst you're here though, I had a call from your attorney. You were busy so I took the call. They couldn't really tell me much, client confidentiality and all that. Said for you to call them Monday. They did give me a hint that it was good news for you, so hopefully that will cheer you up a little considering you have been a little off these last few days."

Steve nods, thankful for some good news. It's a little early, he thinks, for them to tell him he is winning. They have not yet been in front of a judge to plead his case. With the Switzerland trip to CERN coming up, It was thought best to wait until he was back.

"Thanks Nigel. Don't work too late. See you Sunday then and have a safe flight."

Steve grabs George on his way out. The dog is good company for him and they are going to spend time in the car together. Reservations had been made in a motel on route where dogs were kennelled. It was also an area of natural beauty, so a bonus for the ride up.

Steve made a detour on the way out, going via the loading bay. Boxes are stacked in several rows, waiting to be loaded. There are professionals who looked after the load, ensuring it all arrived in one piece. Steve just wants to be sure everything is in order before it left. All it would take is one important item to be left and that would cost them a day. After checking the inventory and counting the consignment, Steve eventually declares all is ready to go.

If all goes well at Fermilab, then they would be back here for a few days to iron out any glitches before flying out to Switzerland. Steve though, is concerned over the speed at which they are progressing; most of the planning had only been finalised months ago, just before he had given notice and it was just the last five per cent of the project that was being pushed. The part he had mused over was the part that would decide if it succeeds or fails. Secretly, he is proud of all their achievements, not just his own. It was a good team and for the most part, everyone had pulled together. He quietly says a thank you to his dead friend, Kenneth.

"Come on George. A treat, let's call on Tina."

On hearing "Tina," George's tail starts wagging.

Washington, watches the vehicle drive past her, parking several cars away. Richards steps out and locks the blue 85 Pontiac Firebird, a car he had re-built himself. At least that's what he keeps telling his fellow officers. What it is about men and their cars, she thinks.

Washington waits until he is around the corner, then follows. The cinema is three screened and she thought it best to arrive after him and not look like she was waiting. Also she does not know what type of movie he is interested in. She had checked the three movie on show, two of which were romantics, she could hazard a guess it was not going to be the chick flicks. But who knows, he may surprise her.

As she walks through the door, she spots him standing by himself, looking at a movie poster, making out that he's reading the print. She notes that his head flies straight to the door when she walks in. Got you, she thinks, as she makes out she had not seen him. She walks to the line of people waiting to buy their tickets. Seconds later, Richards is behind her.

"Hello Carla. I guess you decided to come out?"

Washington half turns smiling to herself.

"Hello, Officer Richards."

Richard's smile leaves his face, a look of confusion forming as his surname is used. Washington laughs at his discomfort.

"Sorry Paul, I couldn't help myself. You should see the look on your face. So what are you here to see? Can you suggest a movie?"

Richards face brightens and he recommends the action movie, telling her that it has a good write up with a good acting cast. Washington thanks him and tells him that she would prefer one of the other movies, again watching his face change. The smile gone again, she laughs, telling him she could actually do with watching something that does not need thinking about, a little violence, the usual car chases and the last bit she plays out as she looks him in the eyes, some sex.

Two hours later they exit the cinema. They had shared some popcorn in the movie and Washington had made sure to brush off some that had stuck to Richards's jacket. They talk about the movie outside as they walk back to their cars. Washington can tell he was nervous. He is plucking up the courage to ask her back to his. She has seen this played out in previous attempts to pick her up. Richards has to be a bit braver; after all, she is his superior.

"Don't get me wrong when I ask you this Carla, but any chance you want to come back to mine. Look, I realise it's dumb of me to ask, but really just a coffee."

Washington tells him that, yes it is dumb, and keeps quiet for a few seconds before telling him that she could do with company. She makes it clear that it will be coffee only and that he should not to get any ideas. No one is to know, she tells him, making sure that he doesn't see this as a boy's ego boost to go tell his colleagues.

She follows him back to his place. She had checked already where he lived and knew he was only ten minutes from hers. After they park, he escorts her up to the top floor of a four, one bedroom, apartment complex. The door opens onto a short corridor, with a door on either side leading to the bedroom and bathroom. She walks through to the main room with a fitted kitchen that looked of high quality. Everywhere she turns, the apartment reeks of expensive appliances. The flat screen on the wall is one of the biggest she has ever seen.

Richards takes her coat and places it on a hook, then heads for the kitchen, asking her how she takes her coffee. Walking around the room, she takes note of the high tech stereo, wondering how an officer of his ilk could afford all this equipment. She made a note of his PC. Turning her attention back to Richards, she starts asking personal questions, about where he comes from and how long he has been in the force. She takes a seat at the breakfast bar and Richards stays the other side as he passes over the coffee. More relaxed now, he leans over the table and asks her about her life.

She wants to make him feel comfortable and not let him suspect her motives for being in his apartment. If he is the bad apple, then he is dangerous and as she suspected, Scholfield did not die from an overdose of morphine accidently prescribed by a nurse. Richards, she had noted, had always been around her desk and was always keen on what she was working on. Looking around the apartment, she suspects that his toys were not paid for on an officer's wages.

Eventually she steers him back to work, asking him about the times he was working, trying to tie him down to events in the office and the hospital. As she asks away, her expression changes as the times he gives, do not add up. He makes a joke about her questions, telling her that it sounds like he is being interrogated. "No," he informs her, when he had finished the last shift watching out for Scholfield, he had gone straight home. He tells her he was called out late in the afternoon to attend the incident involving the explosion. He had briefly spoken to her, concerned she was not injured. He remembers seeing his partner take her and Moralis's car. He couldn't recall who had asked Greggs to drop it back at the station.

Washington stares at Richards. "Stupid - stupid!" She tells herself under her breath. Greggs is the bad apple, of course he is. Apologising to Richards, she makes an excuses to leave faking a yawn, telling him that she would see him at the service on Sunday. Leaving him with a kiss on the cheek, she tells him she will see herself out and grabs her coat. Before she leaves, she asks him how he can afford all the goodies in the apartment? He tells her he's from a wealthy family and he has a trust fund. He asks why, as he is taken back by her sudden departure. No reason, she tells him, just curious. She turns and leaves, feeling a little guilty for leading him on. He'll get over it, she tells herself.

Getting in her car, she backs out the drive and heads back to her place. She is not aware that she is being followed. The two men are the two from the picture taken by Scholfield. They follow at a distance. They have orders just to watch her, but that could change.

Chapter 22

Steve had enjoyed the drive over to Fermilab. George had been good company and they only had one eventful moment in an otherwise uneventful trip. Saturday they had been booked into a motel. George had been placed in the kennels but was unhappy about the experience and started to make a racket that kept awake other residents. Steve was given a choice, to either keep the dog quiet or leave. Taking the night time desk clerk to one side, he made a deal. George was a very happy dog that night, sleeping on top of Steve's bed, and Steve was fifty dollars lighter.

On arrival, Steve is given instructions to the village. The village is inside Fermilab's boundaries, containing housing and laboratories. Steve's instructions on arrival were to pick up his keys for the apartment and to get his ID. After handing over the appropriate forms concerning insurance and nationality, Steve is then issued a badge which allows him clearance to most of the facilities on site. The one thing you could not miss about this place was the structure in the middle, known as Wilson Hall, a high rise building that dominated the landscape. The main offices and labs were on the top floor with the cafeteria on the first floor. Most of the grounds were accessible to residents, although a few years back things had been different because of 9/11. Things today were a little more relaxed, but security was still tight in limited go areas.

Steve is impatient now that he is here and he wants to check that all the equipment had arrived. He is also keen to check out one of the two large detectors where they will be holding their tests; one is known as CDF, the other D Zero as both will be used to monitor the experiment. Their fusion chamber had been built under CDF which in itself stood four stories high. This had been incorporated into the Tevatron Collider and the new equipment should have arrived Saturday. Engineers working here, were not allowed anywhere near their equipment. It is part of the agreement and the dollars paid to keep a tight lid on the experiment.

There were three engineering teams working around the clock fitting all the new equipment in place. Nigel had flown up on Saturday to organise the work. Steve is going to take over on arrival to finish off the last leg and test the equipment. Steve knows that things were running smoothly as otherwise he would have had a call from Nigel letting him know something had gone wrong. Touch wood, he says to himself as he climbs down a flight of stairs with a wooden bannister. The underground chambers were a warren of tunnels that travelled for miles underground in every direction.

Arriving under CDF, Steve spots Nigel amongst the gang of engineers working. Steve knows all the engineers on the project and he is greeted by all those that had spotted him, shaking his hand and congratulating him on his idea. There is no time wasted when he approaches Nigel, quickly shaking his hand and getting straight to business. Nigel tells him Lucy had also arrived on Saturday and a good job too, as she had to work through the night reconfiguring some of the schematics as they did not correspond with their own system. Other than that, Nigel explains the order in which construction was progressing. Steve, happy with progress, lets Nigel go as he had a ton of work elsewhere to complete.

Steve works through the rest of Sunday, into the early hours of Monday morning. They are looking to test on Tuesday and fire the chamber up on

Wednesday. Thursday is their last day, and many engineers have to work through to Sunday, taking out their chamber and putting the structure back to its original design. The engineers left will get one day to themselves before they fly over to Switzerland to meet up with the engineers on site and repeat the same procedure, but on a grander scale.

Monday through to Tuesday came and went with a few problems that were eventually solved. Steve had called on Lucy and Carl with their team of data technicians. Lucy had been knocking back the Red bull and was hyper. Lucy was known for her highs and whenever people asked for her the whole team would start singing Lucy in the Sky with Diamonds to the unsuspecting person, leaving them thinking everyone on the team had more than a screw loose.

It was almost three in the morning on Wednesday when Steve and Nigel make their last inspections, every engineer and technician waiting on their approval. Eventually after ticking off the last check list, Nigel turns to Steve, asking him if he is satisfied. Steve just replies, she, being the chamber, was ready to be fired up. Everyone around erupts in applause and many backs are slapped. Nigel turns to Steve with two beers in his hands. Steve accepts his as they clink the bottles together, enjoying the liquid taste as they tilt their heads back enjoying the cold rush of amber.

Steve, unable to sleep, has been looking at a picture of his child; a nurse had taken for him. It is the one thing that is fuelling his energy levels. George had fallen asleep, cosy, tucked up on the bed. He looks across at George, thinking, he will have to get him out of this bad habit.

He had checked his messages when he got in; two messages from Tina asking how he was doing and a missed call from Carla Washington. She had not left a message, so he assumed it wasn't important. He continues going over the procedures for the test in his mind, working out all the kinks trying to see if there was anything he had missed. He still thinks that they have pushed too quickly on this and he knows where the competition was coming from and that every company had their leaks, so there was nothing new on the horizon about other known breakthroughs in fusion. That didn't mean there was no competition. Steve decides it is not his job to worry about such things; after all they are doing it for the world. Eventually every country out there will have its own fusion chambers. The next stage of development will be fusion rocket engines; clean jet travel, and the wider picture, the ability to travel in space, the ability to land on a planet and process rocket fuel from water sourced from the planet, enabling travel to the far reaches of space. His last thought, as he drifted off to sleep, is, would it happen in his life time?

Steve shakes hands with the MIT representative looking after the safety of the public with regard to leaked radiation. All types of reactors deal with radiation disposal and worse, leaks and most are under the guidance of the government, but universities like MIT have their own. Stuart Carmichael has been with MIT for many years as they have their own nuclear reactor on campus. Steve had a lot of respect for the man as it was his job to monitor leaks.

Gama rays are not science fiction, as many people thought, watching movies like *Fantastic Four*, but they are science fact and can still cause harm. This is the radiation that fusion creates, though as a rule it is less harmful than being out in the sun.

Everyone has their fingers crossed. All personnel had been removed from the tunnels as a safety procedure and only persons involved with the test were inside the control rooms, protected by thick concrete. The day of the burn, as everyone called it, was here.

The superconducting magnets were turned on, along the four miles of copper tubing, vacuum filled, to prevent energy loss. Copper is used as it is a good conductor of electricity. The magnets give off tremendous amounts of heat and would melt the copper if it was not for liquid nitrogen used to cool the walls.

Two pea size pellets of deuterium and tritium are set in place, ready to shoot around the tube in opposite directions at close to the speed of light. Once the required speed is reached, both the pellets are aligned to smash into each other in the fusion chamber creating an explosion igniting the hydrogen gases. The process is repeated at light speed with other pellets following behind as if all had been fired at the same time, each one increasing the heat, showering the chamber with particles of energy, turning hydrogen into a mass of plasma. Superconducting magnets are turned on around the chamber, keeping the mass in the centre as it builds. Each explosion helps the temperature to rise. The temperature needed to create fusion has to be six times hotter than the sun's core, with temperatures needing to reach one hundred million Kelvin. All this happens in a fraction of a second as the last pellet enters the chamber. Magnets on either side drop into place, enclosing the chamber. The chamber is helped from overheating by the liquid nitrogen pumped around the magnets.

All this has already been tried in the past and it is the containment shields that are under constant stress from heat and particle bombardment, causing the shield to fail and contaminating the plasma, allowing it to escape and preventing fusion occurring. For the first time, Nano machines are sent in, spreading around the chamber acting as shields as they block the heat, eventually burning up, forced to the centre by the magnets, to change composition, breaking down into hydrogen and then turning into plasma. These micro machines, if they work, will revolutionise the field of fusion bringing forward by nearly twenty years a breakthrough in clean energy with an abundance of raw material, the world's oceans.

With the size of the chamber at Fermilab, fusion will not be achieved. They need a larger design to make it work. This test was to find out if the Nano machines work and some are designed to harness the information, sending it back using microwaves to the super conducting computers where massive amounts of data are stored and accessed through disk caching software.

Steve thinks, Lucy is going to have a field day as he pushes the button.

It isn't until half an hour later, when all the applauding had died down and people had control again over their emotions, that it really sinks in.

The chamber was designed to run for twenty minutes, allowing data to be processed and tests carried out, with segments of the chamber known as cassettes to be removed and replaced with extra strong Nano machines put in place to hold the plasma. Each engineering process was tried and tested within those twenty minutes and it worked like a dream.

Lucy and Carl, upstairs, were ecstatic as petabytes of data started to arrive, filling up the tape storage system.

Analysts checked every instrument, looking for any loss of heat. Shields were analysed and the Nano machines were processed and analysed for performance. It was shown that almost ninety per cent worked. There was a contingency in place allowing the failure of thirty two per cent, so this was better than they had hoped.

Nigel ran back and forwards between each operator checking their work. Technicians and engineers had been at the ready in case things went wrong and the machines needed turning off. Every conceivable contingency was in place and, in the end, it all worked. All their efforts; years, months, hours, minutes and seconds of planning had paid off.

Steve had celebrated by taking George out for a long walk, both enjoying the surrounding countryside and to add to the occasion, the best weather they had seen in weeks, a glorious sunshine day. Could it get any better?

Chapter 23

"Detective Washington."

Carla, her back turned, looks around at the officer that had called her name. She had been busy looking through files and is startled by the man's voice. Officer Greggs is looking between her and the file she has in her hand. She carefully turns the file around so that it cannot be read and responds to Greggs.

"Officer Greggs, what can I do for you?"

"Nothing for me Detective, but you're wanted. Your new partner has arrived and he's waiting by your desk."

"Thank you Officer Greggs, I'll be in, in a minute."

Greggs stands there, not making a move to go, staring at the file in Carla's hand.

"Officer, is there something more? If not, can you go and tell the detective I will be with him shortly?"

Greggs finally acknowledges Carla and reluctantly walks away. Carla takes a deep breath and puts the file back. The file drawer she had been looking in was partially open; the two letters on the drawer front were for G and H. Had Greggs seen the file, she wondered. Even if he hadn't, he would be blind not to see the drawer open. Carla reminds herself to be more careful checking up on this man. He's a dangerous person and if he suspects you know... She did not want to think about the consequences.

Carla had spent the week working with two other detectives, Reilly and Koontz, both seasoned detectives with the force. They had taken her under their wings, making her feel relaxed in their company. Koontz had a daughter and he told her that she was about the same age, though after two kids her daughter did not have the same figure. "Takes after her old man," he joked as he rubbed his overfed stomach as though it was a friend. She enjoyed the banter that the two had with each other, always making jokes, but when it came to work, both were very professional. It was different working with these two officers. Moralis had been serious and all work, although he did start to mellow with her. She still missed him and had cried for the first time at his funeral. Moralis's wife, Clare, had sought her out after the service and they had talked, Carla promising to visit. She knew she was still coming to terms with Moralis's death and as she was his work partner, Claire was in need of talking to people who knew him.

She walks back in. Greggs is nowhere to be seen. Looking across at Moralis's desk and sitting in his chair is her new partner, Detective Ryan O'Conner, a thirty five year old detective, who had moved from Chicago. The rumour circulating was he had caught his wife in bed with the next door neighbour and had put the guy in hospital. The man had not pressed any charges against O'Conner and, when the job came up on the notice board for a detective in Belmont, his supervisor had more or less ordered him to take the position. His wife had already moved in with the neighbour. O'Conner knew his limitations and left.

Detective O'Conner stands and, smiling, shakes hands with Carla. O'Conner apologises for sitting in Moralis's chair but Carla just shrugs, telling him it was his now so he might as well get used to it. She had thought he was coming in on Friday and he tells her that he thought he would come in a day earlier. She introduces him to her fellow officers. Richards seems a bit put off shaking hands. He is still upset with her from last Friday night and he is curt with O'Conner when asked some questions. O'Conner takes note of this, watching Richards, as his eyes kept straying to

Washington. Carla quickly moves on, taking him out of the station and getting him acquainted with Belmont. They stop at a local coffee shop on Main Street, one she and Moralis used to drink in at least twice a week. She finds O'Conner easy to talk to and she thinks that he is also easy on the eyes. She stops herself from getting any romantic notions and makes an excuse that she had some business to attend to. O'Conner stands, apologising for keeping her, telling her that he wasn't officially starting until Monday, but he asked her if she was free at the weekend as he could do with seeing more of the town. He promises to pay for lunch. She tells him that if she has some free time, she would give him a call.

Carla has other things to think about, she had left a message with an old friend of hers she knew from the academy when they both were training to make detective. They had both worked hard at the academy and had to tolerate a lot of male chauvinism. Susan was a very pretty, young, redhead from California and when she had made detective sergeant, had applied for a precinct in Vegas. Carla had phoned her the previous night and asked her if she would get her some information on an officer who had worked there. She told Susan not to worry if she couldn't but her friend had told her that she recognised the name and had heard some rumours. She had told Carla to call her back the next day as she may have some information for her.

Cell phone in hand, Carla calls her friend, listening to what she has found out. Five minutes later, sitting in her car, she thinks about what her friend had said. Greggs, it seems, had run up a huge debt with one of the casinos. It was common knowledge he had a gambling problem and it was assumed that he would have lost his job and probably both his legs if someone had not come to his aid. It would seem that someone had and bought his debt. Susan had done some digging on this and found out that a law firm from Cambridge, Massachusetts were the new owners of his debt. It would appear that this firm had taken some clients out to Vegas and had asked around for information on police officers owing big money. Greggs' name had come up and, several weeks later, he had a new job, working here in Belmont. Carla recognises the law firm as she has come across them. Now she is sure who the big players are and what they are capable off. She has to watch her back and the one person she wants on her side that can help, has been wronged by her. What she is unaware off, is they already know about her and her digging. Greggs had made a call. He had panicked when he saw his name on the file, Washington was looking at. He had called his contact and he was told not to do anything stupid. Unfortunately he did just that by threatening them, saying that if he was found out, he would not be the only person to go down. He knew names and that he had protected himself against the time when they might think he was of no use to them. Unknown to him, they were aware of this information, which had been placed in a safety deposit box. They had opened the box and removed the evidence, thinking the officer was stupid not placing it in a bank vault. They were planning to use him a little longer, but now that had all changed with his call.

Washington had again tried to call O'Neil and the call again goes unanswered, going straight to voice mail. She decides again not to leave a message and hangs up. She's not slept easily in her apartment since someone had been through it. She had made several attempts to see if she was followed but never spotted anyone. She had decided to make a move and try and force Greggs to talk. She had an idea that if she didn't move soon, she would be the next target and had toyed with the idea of just walking away from it, but her conscience got the better of her.

Carla, had been sitting outside Greggs' place for half an hour. It was ten thirty at night and she had been watching the lights going on and off in the apartment on the third floor. She decides to make her move, leaving her car, she crosses the road, keeping an eye out for other interested parties. She rings the buzzers, one at a time. One of the tenant's answers and Carla lies about leaving her keys and not wanting to ring her apartment and wake up her kids. The release lock sounds, Carla pushes open the door, shaking her head about the story she had just told, thinking why she was not asked how she would get in her apartment if she wasn't going to buzz up.

Carla takes the stairs, eventually coming to the third floor. She stops outside Gregg's apartment and pulls out her gun, slipping the safety off. She thinks to herself, this is a bad idea and she should walk away. She doesn't and knocks. Seconds later, she hears movement from behind the door. She knows Greggs is looking through the viewer at her. She has to move quickly, he may also have a gun. Eventually she hears the sound of sliding metal and the door opens a crack, Greggs' head peering out. Carla doesn't hesitate and using her body, she throws herself at the door, catching Greggs off balance. He flies back, something clattering to the floor as he falls backwards. She rushes in, her gun pointing at his face as she kicks the door closed behind her. She sees the object that had fallen out of his hand, his gun. She shakes her head at him as they both look at the gun on the floor. She tells him not to think about it and to carefully crawl backwards into his apartment, telling him not to try and stand, as she likes him just fine on the floor. She bends down as she passes over his gun, picking it up carefully, not wanting to put her finger prints on it. As she watches him shuffle back, she gets a good look around his apartment. The place is a mess, like it had been trashed. Carla stops him when he is halfway into the room, telling him not to be stupid and make a move for her. Greggs has found his voice, telling Carla that she was in big trouble pointing a gun at him and that she can forget her job and the next ten years as she's heading for a one way ticket to jail. She makes a point asking why he had a gun on him, when he could see who was knocking at his door. She tells him that she knows everything about him and that he was already in trouble in Vegas, owing money to some nasty people and that a drug deal had gone wrong; people were busted and his name came up for passing on police information. Nothing was proved after a thorough investigation by internal affairs, but the report filed was still open on him. She then tells him about the company he is involved with, finishing off with the murder of Scholfield. She gives him a little time to grasp the consequences of what she knows. She hopes the bluff works as she has no evidence, but Greggs is not aware of this. Eventually she sees the change and from experience she knows she has him. She's been in enough interviews to see a person admit defeat just by their body language. He tries to make a deal with her, telling her all he knows. He knows cops who go to jail have a bad time. She's not stupid, wanting his confession down on paper. She had brought some with her, and throws the sheets down to him, feeling inside her jacket for a pen. Greggs looks past her, his eyes widening. She turns but it's too late, the hands grab her from behind and she struggles, kicking backwards at her assailant, but he's big and lifts her off the floor, as if she was a rag doll, slamming her straight down and knocking the wind out of her in the process, the gun flying out of her hand. She tries to rise and finds a boot on her back pushing her down. She tries lifting her head, seeing Greggs through a fog as she tries hard not to pass out. Greggs, his eyes pleading with her to help. His eyes turn, looking at something else, following the movements of another person in the room. Greggs scrambles back shouting at the person, begging him not to do it.

She hears the shot and is deafened by the noise. Blood starts seeping from a wound around Gregg's crotch. Carla chokes back bile as he starts screaming, clutching at his wound. His suffering is cut short with another bullet to the head. The last thing Carla remembers before she blacks out, is the voice of the man on top of her telling her, he's going to enjoy removing her clothes.

Carla slowly opens her eyes, drifting back into consciousness; a siren is wailing off in the distance but getting louder. She tries sitting up. Something happened. She is having trouble trying to focus and then she remembers and opens her eyes. She's on the floor in front of a bed. She doesn't recognise the room. The floor is sticky and she realises she naked. She looks around, seeing the room clearly. It is a mess. Greggs' room comes to mind and she rolls onto her knees, lifting herself up. Her watch is still on. It was just before eleven. Only twenty minutes had gone since she entered the apartment. She finds her jeans across the floor. She can't see her underwear. Her top is on the other side of the bed and she grabs for it and quickly dresses. She can't see any of her other clothes and slowly makes her way to the door, peering out. She catches site of a leg pushed out, the other tucked up. Looking around the half open door she sees Greggs. She remembers!   She looks around for her jacket.

Where is her jacket? Looking around, she spots it thrown down on the floor. She stumbles across the floor and picks it up, checking the pockets. She finds her cell phone and pushes the call button. A name crops up. A name she should not have on her phone. Greggs? Confused she finds quick dial for the station. The sirens sound like they are outside. She walks to the window and peers down. Two police cars have stopped and officers are getting out, rushing over. She spots her gun on the floor and gets a waft of the tell-tale sign of gun smoke. Bending down, she picks up her gun and smells it. Her gun had been fired. She looks across at Greggs, dead on the floor and back to her gun.

In the background, she can hear people running up the stairs. She knows how this will look. Her mind is starting to work and any second now the door will fly open. She has no time to waste and dials the number she had tried dialling before. Seconds go by and this time, it's answered.

"Steve. Please help me. It's Carla Washington and any moment now I'm going to be arrested for a murder I didn't commit. Please believe me, I need your help."

Chapter 24

Steve was shocked by the late call, "Is this a joke? What's going on and why are you calling me?"

In the background he could hear some banging, people were shouting. He could hear Carla calling out to someone, something like "wait a minute." The next thing he hears is a splintering sound and then people seemed to be shouting at Carla about putting down a gun. There is more commotion and Carla comes back on line. In the distance people were telling her to hang up.

"Find me a lawyer fast and please do not use your attorney. Whatever you do, don't go to them. I'll explain everything to you."

The phone is snatched from Carla's hand. A police officer comes on the phone and tries to get Steve to tell him who he is. Steve keeps silent, trying to listen to background noise. He eventually responds by telling the officer to tell the lady that he would find her someone.

It was late when Steve had received the call. He had been out walking George. Standing in the middle of the park, looking at his cell phone, he tries to figure out what the hell was going on. Why had Washington called him, of all people? If she was in trouble, surely her own police unit would make sure she had a good lawyer. He is stunned by the call and for the life of him, he is again sick to death with everything going on around him. He can still hear the desperate plea from Washington. What was that about not calling his attorney, why would she say that? She seemed almost desperate. How could he help her and why should he?

She has been nothing but trouble for him, both her and Moralis. Steve feels a pang of guilt, remembering Moralis was dead. Why, he thinks, why call me?

The following morning, Washington hears the latch to her cell open, the face in the opening telling her a lawyer had come in to see her. She had been processed the previous evening and had been interviewed by two officers that had been called in from a different district. She had refused to talk and had eventually been placed in a single cell. If she had not been an officer of the law, she would have been in a cell with several other women to pass the night away. No one had been down to see her from her own unit and she had wondered if O'Neil would find her a lawyer. She wonders why he had been the one she called. At the time, instinct had taken over; Illogical as it sounded she had thought he would help. She realises that the only other person she would have turned to, was dead. Who could she trust?

Things had moved quickly for Washington. Because of the seriousness of the crime and who was involved, it was considered that an arraignment should happen before the media got hold of the story. Both sides had agreed and a last minute slot was found later in that afternoon as it was Friday and the next opening wouldn't be until Monday. By then, the media would have picked up on the story. Looking around the court, she spots O'Neil near the back. The girl, Tina, is with him.

Washington is seated with her lawyer, Tanya Byron, a young twenty six year old up-and-coming lawyer. She had informed Washington that her company had received a call from Steve O'Neil that morning and that she was in the office when the call came through. She had recognised the name as she was once good friends with his wife, Karen and had asked to take the case. She was making a plea on her behalf. She had already

214

put in a plea of not guilty and was now fighting for bail. The prosecution, Sean Ryder, a forty year old veteran to this type of work, is trying to undermine her lawyer, detailing the evidence against her; Carla's gun, used as the murder weapon and the fact that she had been the only one found in the apartment with the victim. The prosecution is trying to make a point that the murder was a lover's quarrel that had gone terribly wrong, making a point of where one of the bullets had been fired and that her underwear had been found in his bed. He emphasises the point that her underwear was a pair of red G-string knickers. The judge pulls the prosecution up on this point, telling him not to use the courts time to make his case as this was just a plea for bail.

It doesn't look too good for Carla, but she feels she has a half decent lawyer. She is grateful O'Neil had found her and grateful to him for doing so. She turns around when she heard the doors at the back close. The person who had just walked in, is her new partner, Ryan O'Connor. She corrects herself as she thinks, not anymore. What an introduction to Belmont he is getting, she thinks. She stops herself from laughing at the situation. She remembers her father telling her, if the choice was to laugh or cry, always go for laughter. Now was not a good time to piss off the judge and she almost laughs at that.

Her thoughts are invaded by the banging of the judge's gavel. He has made a decision to allow Carla bail. Bail is set at $250,000. Where is she going to get the ten percent to put down? She has some money saved but not $25,000. Her lawyer is looking at her, smiling.

Tanya reaches out and shakes hands with Washington, telling her that it had been close and that her bail was being paid for this minute. She also lets her know that she will get a call to arrange a meeting to go over her defence prior to her trial date as she will need to know every detail if they are to succeed. Washington nods, still trying to figure out who paid her bail. Before she can ask, Tanya has left to talk with the prosecution.

She takes a deep breath, a little shell shocked since her ordeal. She looks around to see who was still in the court. O'Connor is coming down to the front. He has an uneasy smile on his face. She looks for O'Neil and Tina, but they are gone. She is wondering again who had paid her bail.

"You look like you could do with a drink. My turn to buy the coffee, or do you need a stiff one? I was going to be joining my new partner on Monday, but I don't think that's going to happen. We are both presently not working so I think it's allowed."

Carla half hears what Ryan was saying to her, her mind elsewhere, "Sorry! What's allowed? I'm a little confused, a drink. Why are you here O'Connor?"

"I had to check in with work. Sign on the dotted line, that sort of thing and then I am called in to see your Captain Childs, and she lets me know what's going on. If you are wondering why your work colleagues are not here, they were ordered not to be. That does not mean they have abandoned you. You have loyal people there, especially officer Richards. Funny, considering it was his partner that was killed, but then it seems no one really liked this Officer Greggs."

Their conversation is interrupted by Steve and Tina showing up. Carla shakes his hand, thanking him for getting the lawyer but still confused about her bail being paid. Steve immediately puts her mind at rest about that, as he had received a cheque through the post the previous day. It was the pay-out for his wife's death. It would appear that the insurance company had sent a letter of apology about the statement that was taken from Keel and that they were not aware that one of their employers had acquired the services of Shaver and Mills, the law company. They had asked him if he would drop the lawsuit against them and had added a bonus of $25,000 to the original pay-out of $200,000. Steve, when he had received the letter, was appalled by it, as he had never applied for a policy in the first place, as he kept telling people and he was even more confused about the lawsuit. He would have sent the cheque back, but when Tanya reminded him that she would be working to get bail for Washington, he realised what he could do with the money. Carla fills him in about the lawsuit. It is Moralis who had told the white lie to get them to send information on the policy. They were dragging their feet, so he had just persuaded them to move a little faster.

Ryan interrupts them, lost in their conversation, but pointing out the court attendant who was coming across to ask them to leave. Once outside, Carla introduces Ryan. Ryan shakes Steve and Tina's hands, telling everyone that they could carry on talking here or they could grab a late lunch as he was hungry and that it would seem he had a little catching up to do on events. Everyone agrees, but Carla tells him that it is a little complicated and it might be wise that he doesn't get involved; turning at the same time to Tina, she tells her, she should not be here either.

She believes that both she and Steve are being watched and that people had lost their lives, telling Tina not to get involved seemed like one less person to worry about. Tina makes it clear that she is already involved, reminding them of what Keel had done to her. Both women start arguing and Steve steps between them, getting their attention and telling everyone that nothing would be achieved by arguing and that he had left his dog alone at home, so they all might as well go back to his. Ryan offers to give Carla a lift, as she knows where Steve lives and she can also fill him in with the story. Tina grabs Steve's arm, giving Carla a hard stare as they head off.

Steve and Tina arrive back first. As they get out of the car, a woman runs up to him with a microphone in her hand, almost pushing it into his face after she tells him who she is, and immediately asks him about the tests he was involved in over at Fermilab. Steve is stunned and looks past the woman to a man running with a camera. He can just about read the network on the side of the camera, which looked like WSBK TV. Steve tells the woman that he cannot talk to her, telling her that she was on private property and that she and her cameraman should leave. He turns around, keys in hand and opens the door, calling out to Tina. Tina is still facing the camera. He calls again for her, before he finally grabs her arm, pulling her inside and closing the door. He walks around the condo closing all the shades, making sure no one can see inside and instantly gets on the phone to Nigel, telling him about the network outside his place. Nigel is furious, telling Steve that someone at Fermilab had blabbed and now the story was out. Nigel wants him on a plane that evening, as he was flying out himself. Steve tells him that it is too late for that now and that it was stupid to waste a flight, considering the price of the seat and that he would be flying out tomorrow at, 20.00hrs. With the six hour flight, the time difference would put him on the ground at, 08.00hrs. Sunday morning.

He cools Nigel's anger, telling him he will find a place to hide for twenty four hours and will board on schedule as planned. Nigel tells him to get out as soon as possible, as it won't just be the media on his doorstep. There will be the paranoid nut jobs who think the world will end with black holes. Steve tries to explain the theories about black holes being a fact to Nigel who immediately tells him not to go on about that mumbo jumbo stuff. Steve shakes his head at the phone and they quickly talk about meeting up Sunday. Just as he hangs up, there is a knock on the door.

Carla and Ryan had managed to get past the woman with the microphone and were standing, waiting to be let in. Steve explains to Carla why the media were there. "Great!" Carla tells him, explaining that as soon as her picture gets on the news, with her facing a murder charge, it will be media frenzy outside. She had managed to avoid them outside the courts by taking a different exit.

George had managed to slip inside the group as they were discussing tactics about getting out. He is moving from one person to the other, subconsciously they are all stroking his head as they carry on the conversation. Eventually it is decided that Tina will leave, taking Ryan's car in a hope, that she will be left alone. The rest of them will slip out the back. Steve has his bags packed already and Tina is going to look after George, staying to look after his place whilst he's away. She is still out of work and Steve had offered to pay for her services. She will have the use of the car and it is arranged for her to drop Steve off at the airport. They might as well make their way over towards Boston and find a lodge or hotel on route for the night.

Ryan is quite pleased with the idea of spending time with Carla, even if she is a murderer. She has managed to bring him up to speed on the last couple of weeks and he is still wondering if it is a good idea to get mixed up with this bunch as he was jumping over the back fence.

Tina had put George in the back of Ryan's car and had tried to get past the same reporter who had positioned herself at the end of the drive stopping Tina from leaving. She tells the reporter that she was just there to pick up the dog and she has no idea what she was on about and manages to drive around her almost, colliding with the cameraman. The reporter watches her go and then turns around, already putting Tina out of her mind. Five minutes later, Tina picks up the three of them, sitting on Steve's luggage and clearly out of breath after their run.

They had found a hotel, fifteen miles away from Boston airport. TV Networks were always hanging around airports and neither Steve, nor Carla, wish to run into any of them. They think it best not to draw any attention to themselves and the luggage would make it look like they were all travelling. George is no longer with them as they had dropped him off around at Elena's. Tina had told her Mother that she would be back tomorrow and not to worry about seeing her on the news. Elena was about to ask why her Daughter was on the news, when Tina kissed her and ran back to the car, leaving both Elena and George watching from the doorway as they left.

They had booked two doubles. Ryan winks at Carla and she smiles back, telling him that she hoped he didn't mind sharing a room with Steve. They decide to freshen up in their rooms first and then regroup in five minutes in Steve and Ryan's room. Steve still needs to hear what Carla knows and things are still dangerous for all of them.

Five minutes later, Steve and Ryan are sat on the two room chairs and Carla and Tina are on the edge of the bed. Carla then tells Steve about everything that had happened. The only thing she did not have was the name of the person who was calling the shots, though it had to be someone linked with Steve's project and someone who could command from a high position.

Steve sits back and this time he doesn't tell Carla she is mistaken. He had thought about things since their last meeting and had not wanted to believe what she was telling him, but now he had more to think about. He does not want to believe her story, but he has to face facts. He just needs to work out how he is going to find out the truth and when he does... would he be able to control himself? His father had brought him up to forgive people for their weaknesses but he was in no mood to forgive anyone for what they had done to his family.

They decide to order room service and then get an early night. Steve needs to take a walk by himself, and Ryan wants a little time with Carla. Tina has decided to go back to her room and watch the box.

The following day, they order room service. With nothing to pack, the bill is paid and they are away. They find a nice quiet place to hold up and eat before the drive to the airport. Steve does not want them to waste their time babysitting him and tells them that they should separate and he will get to the airport by himself. He still has a long wait before his flight and he needs time to think on his own. He promises to keep in touch and they say their goodbyes. He needs to replay everything that has happened to him in the last three weeks and possibly even further back. He wants the truth and he wonders if he was going to be the same person, when he came back.

Chapter 25

Stretching, Steve yawns. He had stayed awake during the whole flight as he was not a big fan of flying. When he was a kid, he had travelled with his Father on an internal flight which had been hit by turbulence. It had at one point knocked out the electricity, blacking out the plane and sending sirens blaring through the cabin and he remembers the look of fear in the eyes of one of the hostesses as she tried to calm the passengers. Ever since then, he's been a reluctant passenger. That was why he used George as his excuse not to fly when they travelled down to Fermilab. He also found it difficult to think about what he thought he knew and he kept playing it over and over in his mind trying to come up with a logical reason for all those deaths. Everything dictated that logic was pointing in one direction and if it was true, then he would make sure those involved would suffer.

It is just after 8.30 in the morning by the time Steve is cleared through customs. He is given directions to the buses running to CERN. He only has to wait a few minutes before his bus arrives and he enjoys the seventeen minute journey as he takes in the sights of Genève.

On arrival, he is directed to Building 33 where he is to pick up the key for his room in one of the hostels. After dropping his bags off, he reports to security to pick up his ID badge.

He had tried to get Nigel on his cell phone, unfortunately for some reason he was not picking up. He tries Lucy's and she picked up immediately. She had arrived with Nigel and the rest of the team the previous day and she was having a ball with the super computers they had at CERN. This time she has four powerful detectors to work with that are much more powerful than the ones at Fermilab and would produce data at a much faster rate. Steve has to stop her from rambling on as he has his own schedule to keep and Lucy was one of those people who could make you miss your own funeral.

He wants to inspect the work, the engineers are finishing off in tunnels 100 meters below him. The Nano generators used to reproduce the billions of Nano machines had arrived months ago and were stored on site in a warehouse waiting for the time they would be installed with the Plasma chamber. Engineers who had inspected the generators had, at the time, no knowledge of the purpose they were constructed for. On the outside they were just like any other engineering machine. It wasn't until you took the body of the container apart that all engineering feats designed before, were revealed to be child's play in comparison to these six Nano generators. All this had to be assembled in the tunnels after being lowered and directed into the optimal position for the tritium and deuterium pellets to collide at maximum velocity using the power of the Large Hadron Collider commonly known as LHC.

Steve is proud of the engineers picked for this project. Each one has his or her place, from making simple washers to designing innovative components. The LHC was designed to send beams of protons in different directions like the one they had used at Fermilab, but on a grander scale. They had to reconfigure the type of energy pulse that accelerated around the collider and were using miniature pellets of tritium and deuterium that were bigger than beams of protons. New firing chambers had to be designed and installed to meets the requirements of the twenty seven kilometre collider and they only had a six day window of opportunity to fit and test or, they would be out of time. The time frame had helped as it had fallen on holiday season. They then had to dismantle and insert all the original features back in place. MIT had paid millions for this opportunity and they would never have been given this amount of time without all their years of financial and technical support.

Before maximum speed could be reached, the pellets had to travel through four smaller accelerators whose job was to boost the pellets to maximum speed before reaching the LHC. The LHC would then provide further power, taking the pellets to almost light speed, accelerating the pellets through the collider at 11,000 cycles per second before directing them into each other. All this would be monitored from the main control room that had been designed for the LHC and completed in 2008, commonly known as the CCC, short for CERN Control Centre.

Monitoring stations, designed with laboratory conditions, were also designed for the Nano Generators. These stations were called shields and each one was given a letter from the main shield, to identify it. They were attached to each generator and viewed from within by two technicians whose job was to maintain the flow of Nano machines. Every design from MIT; was built for one purpose, to get a fusion reactor to work, to generate more energy than it required. They know their micro Nanos work, but can they perform at the rate required to get the plasma to maximum temperature and then sustain it without destroying the chamber? As he walks around the chamber that stands almost four stories high, Steve thinks that in two days' time they will know that answer. This time, size does matter with the heat needed to generate fusion. The chamber was designed to a size to allow plasma to build, increasing mass but controlling the size with the heavy superconducting magnets, each one protected by the Nano machines. The power of fusion is then converted to steam turbines, changing that energy to electricity and then sent back into the grid. Two turbines had been dropped down to accommodate the amount of energy the chamber was expected to produce. Every safety feature designed to protect the system was in place but it was that margin of error Steve always worried about.

Before long, Steve is out of his jacket with his sleeves rolled up, getting his hands dirty with the other engineers as they comb the miles of electrical wiring and cooling ducts surrounding the chamber. Other than the technicians in the monitors, no one else is allowed in the tunnels when the LHC is switched on. Liquid helium is pumped around the system to cool the 1,232 magnets that push and stabilise the pellets as they make their journey with Ramses, designed to monitor for radiation leaks. These were only two of the dangers the work force faced in the tunnels. There were always accidents when working on such a large project and Steve had seen many accidents that could have been avoided in his life and he was keen to keep these occurrences to a minimum.

It is late before he finishes up. Teams were set in shifts of eight hours and Steve had seen the early morning shift, followed by the afternoon shift and now he is heading back to get some rest after seeing in the overnight shift. Tired and dirty, he rolls into his room and crashes out on his bed.

Steve is brought out of his slumber by the ring tone of his cell phone's alarm. Trying to focus, he checks the time. He had put his watch forward when he had landed in Genève and the time is showing 6am.

Grudgingly he pulls himself up and drags his tired body into the shower, where he stands for ten minutes trying to invigorate his tired limbs.

Fifteen minutes later he is finding a seat in the cafeteria. It is a little chilly outside and most of the team are inside, already gorging on their breakfast. Steve had not eaten since getting off the plane the previous day and is famished. His tray is full to the brim with an unhealthy combination of junk food and coffee. He has managed to eat most of the food, drowning it with several cups of coffee, before he is joined by Lucy, Carl and the rest of the technicians that were working in the control room. They are there to detain Steve before he vanishes off to play with the engineers, as they need to consult him on the project, as Nigel had been delayed with some bureaucratic obstacle that needed a financial incentive. He had called to say he would be available later in the day. Steve is surprised about his absence, as they were testing later in the day and the following morning, ready for the full burn, as they called it tomorrow evening.

Lucy corners him on his walk to control. She is letting him know about the readings they had achieved at Fermilab and the feedback they were getting was nothing but positive. The one thing that is bothering her, are the readings produced after everything had shut down and cooled off. The sensors were still working and they were picking up a power source still operating in the centre of the chamber. It only lasted for a few seconds but it showed that the Nano's were being drawn to the energy source. Steve shrugs, saying it could be explained by residual energy coming from the magnets after they were shut down which was the most likely explanation. Lucy agrees with that assumption but says she would do some further testing. Steve tells her to keep him informed. In the back of his mind, he is considering one other plausible but highly unlikely scenario that would find him on a one way journey to the funny farm.

Steve and his team are used to working with the best equipment that MIT had to offer, but they are blown away by the state of the art technology in place, in the control centre. Thirty seven station monitors are set up to run all the accelerators and view all the combined data as well as providing the protection with the cryogenics and fail-safe of the apparatus.

The six Nano generators are the only engineering feature that is not commanded from the control room. They have their own built in fail-safe system and the twelve technicians in the monitoring stations, attached to the generators and any one of them could hit the red button to close down the supply of Nano machines. There is also further back up with CCTV inside each station.

The fusion chamber they were using here was four times the size of the one at Fermilab and was also monitored using the sensors within the chamber and from the sensors built into the Nano machines. CCTV was also set up inside the chamber and protected with a combination of liquid nitrogen and Nano clusters that insulate from the interference of the strong magnets.

The day moved quickly into the evening and before long, they were ready for their first tests. The technicians and engineers who did not need to be in the tunnels were ordered to leave. Every one of them was accounted for as they left. Two of them had foolishly decided to take a ride on the crane as it was removing a load out of the tunnel. The netting holding the load had given way sending both men falling. If they had been higher, both would have certainly died hitting the concrete floor. As it was they were less than ten metres in the air when they fell, leaving them with broken bones and internal injuries. Both were medevac'd out and the test was delayed for an hour.

Nigel had returned late in the afternoon and is busy checking all the monitors and having the equipment recalibrated, which sends a deep resentment throughout all the technicians. Steve had managed to have a few words with him, trying to find out why he was not around, but Nigel was being vague on his movements and told him he would talk to him afterwards when there was more time.

The first test is a simulation test where the procedure would be carried out as if it was the real burn. If this is successful, then they would proceed with a trial test and carry out the burn for thirty minutes, taking it close to fusion and to check all systems were working properly. If successful, they then would run a final check on all readings, the condition of the chamber and magnets, looking for signs of fracture. This would take up half the day, before they went for the final and last burn.

Everyone is in their places, their headsets on and there is a final head count before Nigel goes for the countdown, bringing to life the artificial simulation of the accelerators. As they go through the motions of accelerating, the two pellets in opposite directions, reach virtual high speeds, increasing as they move on to the next accelerator before transferring to the LHC, where they reach almost light speed. The final stage is the manoeuvre into position for the burn as both pellets collide; splitting apart, shattered into millions of particles, burning the nitrogen within the chamber and turning it into hydrogen as the temperature rises from more and more pellets colliding. In the time the first explosion occurs, the Nano machines are released in clusters, millions on millions performing their virtual tasks, the super magnets holding back the plasma as its mass increases and eventually reaching fusion, a ball of virtual molten helium kept in place by the equilibrium within the chamber. Fusion has been sustained. The power from this is transferred to the steam turbines as they convert this to electrical energy, passing it on to the virtual main grid. The simulation is a success.

Steve watches along with everyone, monitoring and registering the system working as it should. The tests are carried further as they implement scenarios in which problems might arise and for the next few hours they go through these, one by one, as they simulate all the challenges they would face as if this was the real burn. Eventually, by the early hours, they have their answers and they are ready for their next task, to put their collective knowledge to the test, the first real burn. The team has worked hard and a little rest is needed for people to recuperate. Most are heading straight to their rooms to sleep and recharge.

It is no time before everyone is back in the cafeteria having a hearty breakfast and discussing the tests, everyone excited for the coming day and what it will bring. Nigel has called to let Steve know that he will meet them in the control room. Steve lets everyone know that he will catch up with everyone before the tests as he wants to check things out in the tunnels.

On arriving at the lifts, he almost collides with a group wearing lab coats and temporary passes. Heads down, they move past him. Steve wonders which visiting group they were with, as his team had taken over the main use of CERN and only a handful of experiments working in different fields were going on inside the main complex. One of the young women, no older than eighteen he thought, had bright orange hair and Steve shakes his head, thinking about the youth of today, glad that Tina did not follow the trends set by the fashion industry.

He forgets about her and spends the next few hours in engineering. He need not have bothered. The engineers know their business, and he is only down here with them as he feels more at home in their company than with the scientists. He finally accepts that he isn't needed and makes his way back to control. Nigel is there with the rest of the team. Everything is ready. People are in place and the system is set to run. Nigel is the one to start the process and push the button and for the next half hour, they watch on, their expectations high and for good reason. The years of hard work finally pay off as all the elements come together and the fusion chamber performs with success, turning hydrogen into helium gas and taking it one step away from a plasma state and fusion. After everyone has celebrated and elations have died down, they are back to being professional and with just seven hours until the full burn, they check the data and start to prepare.

Every check is made and the information is collected and stored. Lucy bypasses some of the research from the test and concentrates on the residual data after the chamber has been cooled, the hydrogen has been vented and the chamber has been cleansed with nitrogen oxide. She is looking for a particular time frame and she is dumbstruck by what she reads and immediately seeks out Steve. On finding him, they both go through the information, looking at the calculations and finding that one thing keeps coming back. This time they have CCTV footage and they check the film. Both are convinced of one thing; the paranoid group of scientific nut cakes they had read about and laughed at may have been right all along and his father had been one of them. He never took his father's ideas lightly and it was because of something like this, that he had originally come away from the project. He tells Lucy to keep the information to herself until he has a word with Nigel. A decision needs to be made and further tests need to be carried out.

Steve won't take no for an answer as he corners Nigel, telling him that they need to talk immediately. Nigel resigns to the fact Steve won't take no for an answer and tells him that they will meet in the conference room in an hour.

They face each other across the table. Steve explains about the results, Lucy had found. "Look at the readings Nigel," Steve asks. Nigel is confused. He is expecting Steve to bring up something else. Steve tells him that it is possible that they will have to rewrite the books on what they thought they knew about stars and especially their mass. It had always been thought that, like the sun, which is deemed a dwarf star, when a star's time was up it would expand, weakened as its hydrogen escaped into space and that it would collapse in on itself. It was the giant stars that go Super Nova as they explode and then collapse in on themselves, taking everything back in with it, creating what is thought off as a black hole in space. According to their calculations from Fermilab and their recent test, this appears not to be the case. The images from the camera show thermal imaging of an object that should not be there. The figures shown on the data provide calculations that a mass object is in the chamber with a magnetic pull and yet there is nothing visible to be seen by normal imagery. Steve goes on to tell Nigel, that more needs to be known about this anomaly before they go to fusion. Nigel disagrees.

"The test goes ahead on schedule. Stars have been around since the beginning of time. I agree we will need to look into this, but it does not mean we have to postpone. You're overreacting; our fusion chamber is not even the size of a Nano particle of our sun. Think about it Steve. This is the foolish talk of a mad scientist. Don't act like one now."

Steve is not put out by Nigel's remark, telling him that they were in the business of facts and the facts here did not add up, reminding him that experiments that go wrong do so because things were ignored and that a reactor is something you cannot afford to ignore.

Before long, both of them are arguing. Nigel is bringing up financial costs and chances that their technology may find its way into other companies, leaving them with their own financial black hole and his reputation ruined. Steve eventually stands up, looking at Nigel, shaking his head as he finally sees the man for who he is.

"Sorry Nigel, but the final decision is mine."

"Sit down!"

Chapter 26

Steve can't believe what he is seeing. Nigel is holding a gun in his hand and pointing it in his direction. He thinks back to the conversation he was going to have with him and now realises that what he had been thinking about was true and that he now knew he was looking into the eyes of his wife's murderer. The coffee in the canteen, he thought, had been spiked by Nigel. His only question to Nigel, as he is pointing the gun at him, is "Why?"

"I am sorry it has come to this Steve. I consider you my friend but we couldn't take the chance that you would take your knowledge to other people. Too much money had been spent and though you may not think it, I am loyal to my country. I am sick that our country is failing and other countries we used to consider third world are now the market leaders. We are falling behind and I for one will not let that happen. Fusion is ours and we intend to keep it. We will sell the rights to use it to other countries, but it's ours and we intend to keep it. You're an idealist Steve, but we can't afford people like you. I admit things got out of hand after Karen's death. We needed leverage and your wife provided us with it. As for the others, it was unfortunate but they were medalling, your father especially. He would have had you looking at figures until your hair was grey, before you made any decision. That's why he was a teacher of science, he never took any chances. No one wanted this Steve but you gave us no choice."

"Was Kenneth's death to do with you? And what about Keel? Was he killed by you?"

233

"Keel was a rapist. We didn't know at the time. We just assumed he was just another greedy guy with no morals and then we found out he had raped your friend. We just needed the statement. It was just good business sense not to have him fall into the hands of the police or it may have confused things. The last thing we needed him doing with opening his trap. As for Kenneth, he wanted me off the team and he had the ears of some of the shareholders. We couldn't let that happen. You were our golden boy. Someone needed to keep an eye on you. Kenneth had nothing more to give. If it makes you feel any better, it was quick. He didn't feel a thing."

"My wife did. She suffered before she died and so did the others. They were all killed by you or your henchmen. I intend to make you suffer for what you did. Do you think I care if you shoot me? Go ahead, but I swear my hands will be around your throat before I die."

"We figured you may feel this way and you are right. You will die, but not just yet. I said we have leverage. Who do you think is looking after your child right now? Do you understand? You get us through the final test and I promise your child will not be harmed, but if you don't…"

Nigel never had chance to finish the sentence as Steve launches himself out of his seat across the table, pushing the gun away. Nigel is taken by surprise at the speed of the assault as Steve, both hands wrapped around Nigel's neck, was squeezing the life out of him. Nigel is about to bring the gun up and shoot, when Steve is clubbed across the back of his head. Still trying to hold on, his grip failing, he receives another blow to his head and passes out. Nigel pushes back, coughing, trying to regain his breath. The man who had clubbed

Steve was the same one who had stuck the needle into his wife.

Steve wakes up. His head hurts. It felt like someone had used it as a bowling ball. Slowly he opens his eyes. He is slouched backwards on a chair.

"Glad to see you're awake. Please do not try that again. You remember our friend here is a very capable man as you know."

Steve looks at the big man looming down on him, ready to put him to sleep again. He recognises him. He was one of the two from the hospital wearing orderly clothing the day his wife died. Nigel notices the look of recognition and uses it.

"You have seen him before. At the hospital, am I correct? Your memory is good Steve. Then you would remember the man he was with, who has been given orders that he will carry out in five minutes, unless he gets a call from me to stop. You have to make a decision now as time is ticking. You complete the final test or you lose the last of your family.

Nigel looks at his watch, placing four fingers in the air to symbolise four minutes remaining. Steve, with nowhere to go has only one option and hopes to God his decision does not result in the deaths of others, but he is left with no choice. He nods to Nigel.

"Is that a yes, Steve?"

"Yes, you bastard!"

"Just so that we can be certain you do not try anything stupid, our friend will stay with your child until this is over. Is that Clear? No one wants to hurt a child. I certainly don't. After all, I'm not a monster."

While Steve and Nigel are talking, the other man gets the nod from Nigel to make the call and stop his associate from carrying out his orders. Nigel tells him that his bodyguard will be joining them in the control room. If anyone asks, he is a nephew of one our sponsors. Steve remembers Nigel going on about "us" and not just him. Washington was right when she said people with money were involved. Maybe not all of them, but one or two for sure were supporting Nigel in his campaign to get them their fusion reactor. At the end of the day, it was always about power and money. Those with it always wanted more.

Steve was being closely followed around in the control room by Nigel's body guard. The man never said much, mostly grunts. That did not make him stupid. Steve was trying to figure out how he was going to get out of this with his life. His one thought, to bring Nigel to justice along with his associates, whoever they may be. Time felt like it was going slowly, but many hours had passed and it was coming to the point of firing up the reactor to maximum. He can't see any way out. If he gets it wrong, his child is dead. He is certain Nigel would see to that. He now knows him for what he is, a cold blooded killer with no conscience.

The room is quiet as the time ticks away. The seconds are watched as the hand moves around, the last ten seconds, counted down by everyone in the room and then the button is pushed. There is total silence for a fraction of a second and then the team go to work, delivering the package that would have them remembered in the science journals, to be read and reread in the future. Monitors are closely observed as they recall the numerous features being relayed back to them. The room is busy with fingers jumping across key boards, pulling up the next screen of information. They feel the accelerator beneath their feet, one hundred metres below kick to life, sending the pellets through the twenty seven kilometres of copper conducting tubing, ringed with giant magnets, until they finally smash together in the chamber.

The data is flowing in fast. No mere human can keep up with the download. The important information is being read as the heat in the chamber significantly rises as the pellets collide and Nano machines pump through in the millions to protect the wall of the chamber. So small, you would never know they were there, if not for the reading coming through, showing them working.

There is a time factor involved at the point when the plasma reaches fusion, when all the properties inside the chamber are balanced; that equilibrium has been reached and that time is approaching. Everyone can feel the vibrations and if you ask anyone who is there, they will swear they can feel the heat as they watch the needle climb. Everyone holds their breath as the readings they are waiting for start coming through as the steam turbines start to process the energy, building up steam and sending it out to the grid as electrical energy. The readings of electricity flowing through the grid are climbing. They watch as the power going out is recorded and compare it with the power being drawn into the reactor. Phone calls are coming in from Genève, complaining that people are unable to boil water as the drain on the grid from CERN is pulling all electricity to the LHC and the fusion reactor.

The tipping scale is almost there and then cheers go up as the power from the grid shows more power going into the grid than is being pulled. Eventually this will be cut off as the reactor becomes self-sustaining.

Steve sits down, the bodyguard beside him, waiting for the moment Nigel will give the order to dispatch him. Steve knows he is not going to win. He cannot fight them; another life was at stake and thank God, he thinks, that nothing had gone wrong with the reactor.

At the corner of his eyes, one of the Nano stations flashes up on screen, catching his attention. He can see commotion from inside. There are people inside the stations with masks on. He recognises one of them with orange hair, the young women he had seen earlier. He jumps up as he sees his technicians being pulled out the door. He flicks through the cameras checking all six stations. The same is happening to all of them. He is about to hit the fail-safe button, when the bodyguard grabs him, covering him and pulling him away so that none of the others can see what is happening. He has his hand in his jacket, indicating his gun. Steve looks confused and is wondering what Nigel is now planning. He grits his teeth, telling his guard the Nano's will keep pumping and that they need to be monitored by those technicians as that they can't control them from here. The man peers back to look at the monitors. He looks a little confused. Steve hears him mumble something about it not being part of the plan.

"What are you on about, part of the plan? What is Nigel planning?"

Steve is thinking. What has Nigel got planned? Why has he allowed people to disrupt this? It doesn't make any sense. If he wants fusion, then why put a spanner in the works? He is going through what would happen if things are allowed to carry on and then all hell breaks loose, as more people in masks come running into the control room, threatening and attacking the technicians, demanding everyone get away from the monitors. They are brandishing weapons, some have guns and others have clubs. People start to scream and some of the technicians stand up to the intruders but are beaten to the ground. Steve looks around for Nigel. He spots him working his way to the exit. He looks confused. Something he planned has gone wrong, Steve thinks. These people are not following his plan or so it would seem. One of the masked intruders makes the mistake of telling the man holding Steve to get down on the floor. He instantly lets go of Steve, grabbing the intruder and head-butting him. The intruder immediately collapses to the floor unconscious. Steve makes use of his freedom and runs, hitting buttons as he crosses consoles, sending a fail-safe through the system.

It is too late. Some idiot has cut the power from the two steam turbines to the main grid. Temperature in the reactor is still climbing. The turbines outside are screaming as there is no outlet for the power. The cryogenics refrigeration plant had been broken into and the power had been cut.

In the control room, alarm bells start ringing and red lights are flashing at every exit point. A voice message comes over the system telling personnel to leave immediately. Steve is running around trying to shut down the system. Some of the intruders look confused and start to back towards the exits. One of them, the leader, is trying to give orders, but he is losing his authority with the group. Steve eventually shouts to everyone in the room, saying that below them is a reactor that needs to be shut off and if it can't - then they can forget about getting up in the morning because there will be no tomorrow for them. This gets their attention and the intruders start panicking, some throw their weapons down and are running out the room. Others stand frozen, looking to their leader. He has thrown his mask off and is pulling a technician back to one of the consoles, ordering the frightened technician to turn the reactor off.

Lucy runs over to Steve, after her captor releases her, panic in her eyes. Steve tells her to round up those that can still work as they need to shut things down. He is going to the reactor to try and turn things off from there. Lucy begs him not to go. He tells her that if it keeps rising, to get everybody out and get some distance. He also whispers in her ear about what Nigel has done. As he looks around the room, he sees that Nigel and his bodyguard have both left, and he wonders again what the man's plans were.

He makes it to the tunnels, passing some of the intruders as they are running in the opposite direction. He reaches the reactor, exhausted from his run and out of breath; he can feel the heat coming off of surface. Something is seriously wrong as he should not be able to feel the heat. Something is wrong with the cooling system. His first plan of action is kill the power in the Nano stations. Entering the first one, he hits the fail-safe and then quickly moves onto the next one until he's turned them all off. Time is not on his side and he runs back down the tunnel, finding one of the tunnel transport buggies. He jumps in and drives the remainder of the way to the cryogenic refrigeration unit. He finds the main power turned off. Thank God they had not damaged the system, he thinks, and he switches it back on. It immediately hums into life, pumping the liquid hydrogen through the tubes and back towards the reactor. His thoughts now are on getting back to the reactor and trying to restart the turbines. They need to bleed the helium out.

On arrival, he finds the power lines are disconnected from the turbines. The cables need to be plugged back in, in order to release the energy. He thinks, will the turbines still work? There is only one way to find out and he reconnects the couplings for the power to the grid and without thinking, hits the "on" button. The turbines jump to life. Steve's realises that things are still getting hot. The heat inside the chamber must be phenomenal, why it hadn't failed is anybody's guess as the inside walls of the chamber must be breaking down under the strain. The Nanos must have protected the chamber and had worked overtime to cool the surface.

At least that had helped stop the meltdown. There is nothing more he can do but go back to the control room and work from there. He is just about to use the tunnel phone to speak to the control room, when he crumples to the floor. He does not even hear the gun go off as the bullet tears through his back into his chest.

Nigel walks over to Steve, stopping and bending down to his knees, deciding whether to put another bullet in his old friend. Steve looks up at him, blood pouring out of his wound. He is coughing and spluttering, trying to push himself up on his elbow.

"You see Steve. Not only are you smart. You have managed by the looks of it to stop the meltdown. It's a shame. I will now need to add a little incentive for the reactor to go. I will tell them how you risked your own life to save people. You will be a hero. It's the least I can do for you. It's a pity after all your efforts that I will have to reverse it. Those idiots upstairs went a little too far but in the end, it's the same result. After all, we do not want anyone else copying your idea and using the facilities. My friend over there is leaving a little package. A back up for if things did not go to plan."

Steve looks past Nigel, seeing his body guard with a large container on a trolley.

Nigel notices the look, telling Steve that the people who had broken in tonight would be blamed for this. "The idea came to me when you told me a leak had come out of Fermilab. A leak there sparks a leak over here and hey-presto we have an international incident. I should think MIT will be able to seek compensation, don't you?" Before he walks away, Nigel remembers something, "Some good news, I'm thinking of adopting," he laughs as he pulls out the phone, disabling contact to the control room, and walks over to the turbines, hitting the "off" button. Both Nigel and his bodyguard leave.

Steve is unable to utter a word. His world is slowly slipping away from him as he tries to drag himself up, his last thoughts of his child in the company of Nigel and that justice never did come for him.

He has no recollection of when the end came. It could have been minutes. It could have been hours. But when it did, it was spectacular.

For some reason he is looking down from a height at himself, lying on the ground, the eyes closed, his body covered in blood, no movement. Yet here he is, separate from the body on the ground. He feels confused and yet, here he is; his arms in front of him, moving with the rest of his body, only he is floating. He can think and he feel no pain. He feels free, like a weight has been lifted of him. He has a strange feeling, as if something is searching for him. He can feel it and he wants it to find him. He looks up. Something is in the distance and it is the most beautiful spectacle he has ever seen. A shimmering brilliant white light, more radiant and captivating than anything he has ever felt before and he is drawn to it, almost as if he couldn't survive without it. He reaches out to it as he feels the presence of others like him and one in particular. He feels Karen's presence within the light and somehow she is calling out to him. And then something else happens, another light flashes below him.

Greater in intensity than his white light but much different, Steve has a feeling that this light is wrong, as everything around him seems to vanish before his eyes in the split of a second. Everything below him is eaten up as the light spreads out, destroying everything in its path. He watches the destruction below him as something close by takes shape, only it has no substance, just a dark shimmering entity. Finally the destruction stops and immediately objects that were destroyed start to fly back, whirling around through the air, sucked up like a tornado and all heading back towards the black invisible mass. He looks back at his light, only it seems to be getting further away. He can no longer feel Karen's presence and he panics as this light fades into the distance. The loss of losing Karen again... the despair overwhelms him and then something happens. He is also moving closer to the black mass as if something is pulling him to it. Unlike the objects flying about, pulled towards the mass of invisible darkness and crushed as they are sucked in, Steve only feels the pull as he enters through what scientist's refer to as the event horizon, the mouth of a black hole.

Chapter 27

Drinking his coffee, Steve is alone in one of the adjoining rooms. He has been given an office close to the control room and he has taken a break from looking at some schematics he was going over prior to their first test with the simulator; checking his watch, the time is 22.15hrs. Then the air temperature in the room appeared to climb.

He feels the hairs on the back of his neck prickle up. Holding his arms out, his sleeves rolled up, he can see the same happening with the hairs along his arms. Steve looks around for something electrical that might be on, like an ionizer, as this would account for the condition in the room, but there was nothing near him. Confused, he looks under the table just as something manifests twenty feet away, above him and close to the wall. He hears what sounds like thunder above him and immediately comes out from under the table to see a shadow appear near the wall. He is mesmerised by the sight, looking around him for something that might be throwing a shadow across the wall; but it is getting darker as it shimmered in front of him and it is also getting larger. It is at least a foot in width. The most amazing thing starts to happen as small objects in the room begin to rattle and move about as if an invisible force is pushing them. Then one by one, they start jumping up and down. Steve grabs for his pen as it tries to fly off the table; other items bounce across the table towards the shadow and vanished.

To Steve it looks as though time had slowed down as everything is moving now in slow motion and he looks at his watch, noticing that the second hand is moving slower around the clock face. Then something happens to Steve to force him to lose consciousness and he blacks out. A few seconds later, he opens his eyes. The room is normal again. Only Steve doesn't feel normal and he almost loses his balance. He grabs a chair and sits down hard.

His eyes closed, he opens them, looking around the room. Something is wrong. He recognises the room, only this is not where he was. He has to think, trying to recall what was wrong. Why can't he remember? Then memories start flooding back. He can't believe his mind because the memories he is recalling can't be real. Something is seriously wrong or he fell asleep here and had the worst nightmare of his life. That is the only explanation he can think off, because what is going through his mind is too crazy to contemplate. He has visions of himself in a strait jacket being wheeled off.

A knock on the door almost has him hitting the ceiling. Lucy pokes her head around the door, asking him if he had finished with the work she had asked him to look over. Steve stands up, a look of surprise across his face as he recalls this moment. She asks again, walking into the room, concern on her face seeing Steve with a look as if he had seen a ghost. He silently points down at the paperwork on the desk and she walks over to grab it. Looking back at Steve, she asks him if he is feeling OK. He looks at her for a second before he responds, telling her he is fine and that he will be with them shortly. Lucy tells him he should be no more than five minutes or he's going to miss the show. He asks her what show, not sure what she means. She tells him, with a frown, that the simulation is about ready to go ahead and then she laughs, thinking that he is pulling her leg. She points at him, telling him he is messing with her and leaves.

Steve sits back down even more confused, wondering if he was still dreaming. It was one thing to wake up from a dream, another to still be awake in one. Shaking his head at the thought of deja' vu, Steve stands and checks the date on his cell phone. It shows Tuesday. Tomorrow they will be going for the full burn. It is just a bad dream. He tells himself to get a hold of himself and get his act together. This is not a good time to have a breakdown and he exits the room, making his way back to control.

He enters the room and slowly looks around at everybody. He makes his way over to Lucy. Nigel has his back to him and was standing behind a few of the technicians. When he turns, Steve immediately stops, a look of shock across his face as he stares at Nigel.

"What's wrong buddy, you look like you have seen a ghost."

Lucy looks up after hearing Nigel's comment, a look of concern across her face again as she looks at Steve. Steve catches her staring at him and forces a smile. Turning back around, he finds Nigel has moved away. Steve watches him for a while. Lucy looks from Steve to Nigel, wondering what is wrong? Steve looks back at her and again shakes his head, telling her that, like all of them, he is just a little tired and that she need not worry. Listening to the conversation going on around the room, Steve is more and more feeling confused by what he is hearing. It is one thing to have deja' vu, it is another to keep having it. In the background, he can hear the order going out to clear the tunnels. He immediately runs across to the phone and calls through to the tunnels. A few of the technicians, including Lucy, have stopped and are staring at him.

"Hi Richard, Steve here, is everybody leaving?"

He listens to the reply and tells him to stop both David and Clive from climbing on the crane lift.

Richard asks him to repeat himself and he tells him to quickly run to the crane lift and have it stop as they can't from here. A minute later, Richard is back on the line asking Steve how he knew those two were getting a lift to the top. He lies, telling him he saw them walking in the wrong direction on the camera and had overheard them earlier talking about it. He just put two and two together. That is all. Steve asks him to check the pallet rope for damage as it is better be safe than sorry and hangs up before Richard can ask him more.

He looks around at the people looking at him and smiles. Lucy looks at the monitor and frowns. A minute later, a call comes through from Richard. The technician listens and looks across at Steve shaking his head. He shouts across to Steve, telling him that Richard had called and said that it was a good call about the crane as one of the ropes was damaged. The weight they were going to pull up, would have easily broken free.

Steve is feeling less sure of himself. He thinks about the possibilities of something but it is too unrealistic to be contemplated. He worriedly chuckles to himself, again thinking about putting a straitjacket on himself right now.

For the next hour the simulation runs and everyone in the room is excited by the process that they would deliver tomorrow night. Steve tells Lucy that he was feeling a little under the weather and she could catch him in his office. Nigel watches him go out. He had been watching him all night, wondering when he could corner him for that conversation. He wanted to get through tomorrow for his plan to work and he needed Steve to cooperate one way or the other. He knows that Steve had been told things by that meddling officer, Washington. He had thought he had stopped her with the murder charge against her, only the bitch was a little too smart and had managed to talk to Steve. He knows Steve is suspicious of him but suspicion alone, proves nothing. Steve won't stop the programme unless there is good reason. If for some reason he tries to stop the reactor from ignition, then he will use the ace he has up his sleeve, his child.

Steve is back, seated in his office, looking at the phone, trying to decide if he is nuts but knowing that if he doesn't make the call, then he has allowed things to carry on as normal and tomorrow if what he thinks has happened still goes ahead, then nothing will have changed and he will be responsible. What he can't explain is how he knows what will happen tomorrow. He just does, but how do you tell someone that you know the future? Perhaps he should say just one day, tomorrow's future; but it is possibly the most important day for the world because tomorrow, one way or another, life for everyone will be different.

Steve picks up the phone and calls the outside line. Ryan picks up. The call had been transferred to him. Steve immediately asks how things are going with Carla. He tells him that it doesn't look good for her as all the evidence points towards her killing Greggs. Steve stops him when he tells him, she is innocent and that he knows who the real murderer is. Ryan sits up straight, asking Steve how he knows. Steve tells him that he has no evidence at present but he knows why Greggs was killed and why they framed Carla. He also tells him that he knows her partner's death was murder and had been committed by the same people who had killed his wife and family. Ryan thinks Steve has lost it, but Steve tells him that he can prove it, but to do so Ryan will need to immediately protect his child as the child is in danger. Ryan asks him how he knows this, but Steve tells him, if he goes to the hospital, he might see a person hanging around and describes the man, telling Ryan that he is dangerous. Ryan tells him that this is his first week on the job and he can't just go over to Newton on a whim. He would be out of a job before he knew it. Steve tells him if he doesn't, then some bastard by the name of Nigel Shanks will be raising his kid as he will be dead and Washington will be marking the walls of her prison cell for at least twenty years. It was his call. Ryan tells him that it was true about scientists, they're all nuts, and tells him he will do it, but only because it will be difficult to date Carla if she's behind bars.

Arriving at the hospital, Ryan finds a place to park. He goes to reception and finds where Steve's child is. Walking into the ward, he speaks with one of the nurses. She directs him to the head nurse and he finds her going through what looks like a ton of paperwork. He tells her that he is there on behalf of, Steve O'Neil and she tells him to sit down, letting him know that she is aware that he'd be coming as O'Neil had called ahead to clear him. The badge helped as well. He asks her if anyone has been acting suspiciously in or near the ward or if one of her nurses has ever been approached and questioned. She tells him that she has not come across the person he has described but she will keep vigilant if someone of his description comes asking around.

Walking around the hospital to get his bearings, he runs into one of the hospital guards, a Marcus White, who had spotted him looking suspicious. After Ryan had identified himself as a detective, he asks if he had come across his man. Marcus hadn't but says he would keep an eye out. He asks Marcus for directions to where they monitored the cameras.

Ryan introduces himself to the guard monitoring the hospital cameras and eventually he is watching film footage. A large man is captured on camera, on the 2nd

floor, as he walks out of view, showing him from behind. Ryan can't see what he looks like but he is shown hanging around for a while at the end of the corridor and then he vanishes. Ryan looks at the other cameras to see if he can see the man, but the guy had vanished. With no luck on the cameras, he goes back out, walking from floor to floor trying to spot his man. After an hour of walking around he decides that he has looked enough for his invisible guy and that O'Neil was wrong. He stops on the 2nd floor again, an idea in his head and searches where he had last seen the man. There is a cupboard he had passed earlier that was locked and is now open with one of the cleaning crew inside. Ryan asks to see inside as he flashes his badge. Nothing seems out of place. It is just a cleaning cupboard. Next to the cupboard are lockers and Ryan gets an idea, asking the cleaner if there are any big guys working on the team. The man's English is poor, but Ryan eventually gets it out of him that someone built like a wrestler had started a few days ago.

Ryan doesn't waste any time and calls security to keep a look out for one of the cleaning crew and not to approach but contact him first. Marcus, the guard he had met earlier, doesn't take heed of Ryan's warning as he spots a cleaner who fitted the description. That is the last mistake he was ever going to make and two shots are heard, fired on the 1st floor. Ryan hears the shots and takes off at a run. He is at the scene in under a minute and has to barge his way through hospital staff, eventually spotting the guard he had met earlier. Marcus is sitting upright against the wall. Two wounds could clearly be seen in his chest. There is a pool of blood spread across the floor. A doctor is checking his pulse but it is clear he is dead. One shot had punctured his lungs and the other had stopped his heart. Ryan finds it hard to take his eyes of Marcus, feeling guilty for involving him and then looks around at the hospital staff who had gathered. He asks if anyone had seen a large man walk past. One of the nurses tells him that she had seen a man fit that description, walking down the stairs and she points to the stairway in the distance. Ryan turns and runs to the stairs in pursuit, taking three steps at a time as he runs down. At the bottom, he looks for the exit sign and runs past reception. Shouting at the receptionist as he runs past to call the police as a man had been shot, he hits the swinging door, pushing aside two people coming in. They shout at his back as he takes off across the car park. He hopes the man has stayed calm and has walked out, as this will allow him time to catch up. He thinks the guy will be going for his car and he runs to the exit looking for cars leaving. He catches his breath as he waits, trying not to look suspicious. If the man is still in the car park, then he will be vigilant. Watching carefully the few cars leaving, he notices one driven by a man wearing a t-shirt. Other people including himself had either jumpers or jackets on as the weather is a little cold. He knows this is his man as the vehicle gets closer. He has his gun out and down at his side trying to hide it from view. Ryan tries to look inconspicuous, but the driver isn't fooled and guns the engine, aiming the vehicle at Ryan and missing him by a fraction of a whisker as Ryan jumps sideways, landing on his back in the flower bed. He's up immediately and giving chase. As he runs after the vehicle, jumping over hedges, he is almost hit by another vehicle, driven by an old lady who panics, seeing Ryan waving a gun and presses down on her accelerator. Ryan throws himself across the bonnet, sliding to the other side and lands back on his feet without breaking stride. The vehicle is ahead of him by twenty yards and doesn't stop as it hits the main road, just missing the first vehicle as it swerves but not as lucky with the second as it also has to swerve to miss the car it is following, crossing directly into the path of the assailant. The force of the impact pushes the assailant's car onto its side as it spins across the road. Ryan breaks stride as he runs onto the road and other cars start braking, swerving in different directions, some hitting one another as they try to control their cars. The car he was chasing has come to rest in the middle. Cars are now stopped all around and horns are blaring as people are frustrated and angry at the chaos. He slowly makes his way over, both hands together, pointing downwards, between them, his gun, ready to swing up and fire. He watches as the car door swings open. With the car on its side, the occupant has to climb up to get out. Ryan is up with his gun, pointing at the man's head as it comes into view. Ryan tells him to come out slowly and to keep his hands visible. The man looks at him with a blank stare, one that said he was not going to cooperate. Ryan repeats his request and a gun appears in the man's hand, aimed at Ryan's head. Two shots are fired, one into the neck and the other taking the top of the assailant's head. He is thrown backwards by the force of the bullets, before sliding back down into the vehicle. Immediately, people start screaming. Ryan takes out his badge to show that he is police and thinks that, with only two days on the job, he is going to have a lot of explaining to do to his superiors about why two men had been shot, when he doesn't quite know the answer himself.

Chapter 28

Steve had received a call back from Ryan. He had waited in the office and had fallen asleep when the phone started ringing, bringing him out of his nightmare about black holes.

Ryan is desperate for information after telling Steve what has happened. He explains that no-one is going to place a twenty four hour protection, without evidence that his child was the intended target. All they have are two bodies in the morgue and his job on the line if he doesn't come up with a plausible explanation. Steve tells him to write his report, stating that he is following a lead from Washington and that the man lying in the morgue fits the description of a person photographed breaking into his condo. "Even if those photos have gone missing, they still have Washington's word they existed and I'm guessing they have had forensics go over Gregg's apartment with a fine tooth comb. If our man in the morgue was one of them, he may have left trace evidence. If this is the case, then Washington has evidence to support her." Steve goes on to tell him, if evidence is discovered, then they should go back over the other deaths. Something links them all and that's Nigel Shanks and who he actually works for. He tells Ryan that Nigel Shanks is a man interested in power and the dollar. His salary should be around $100,000 a year. If he is getting more, then where is it coming from? Ryan makes a crack that he should have been a detective. They talk a while longer, Steve trying to explain things without coming across as a mad scientist. Steve tells him he will be back in a couple of days if all goes well and tells Ryan to keep him out of the report as he is not sure who else works for Nigel.

Steve reflects on his recent travels and wonder what is going to happen next. He is to find out soon enough as Nigel, bursts through the door just as Steve puts the phone down. He has a gun in his hand and a very confused look on his face. Coming in behind him is his bodyguard. Nigel tells Steve to sit back down, as he had jumped up when they had burst through the door. Steve looks frustrated as he wonders what the point of travelling back in time was if he was just going to end up in the same position, only a day earlier with Nigel pointing a gun at him.

Nigel had listened to the conversation outside the door. Everyone else has gone and they are not due back until the morning to test the reactor. It is sometime after four in the morning and Nigel looks at Steve, wondering how he has managed to find out about him. Steve refuses to answer and the bodyguard comes over and backhands him across the nose, instantly breaking it. Blood gushes out and Steve throws his hands up to protect his face. He grits his teeth as he looks up at Nigel, telling him that he has been found out and he will have nowhere to run when it comes out about all the murders and that he knew that he had been the one to have Karen killed. Steve has resigned to the knowledge that Nigel will kill him again for the second time but he wants to have his say and tells him that there is no way he would be considered to be a loyal American. He is just a cold blooded killer and nothing more.

Nigel has no choice but to kill Steve. It may delay things but if they can make it look like a suicide, they may get away with it. After all, the man had been acting funny all night and the death of his wife and family obviously were too much for him so he had jumped to his death from this very room. Nigel smiles back at Steve. They know the police officer who was talking with Steve and with luck, they may sort that problem out. His two men who had been injured would have the chance to make up for their incompetence. Between them they should have no problem making sure the police officer has an accident.

Turning to his bodyguard, Nigel tells him to open a window. The gun still pointing at Steve, he tells him that he is going to have a little accident. The bodyguard comes around and grabs Steve, almost lifting him off the floor and half carries him to the window. Steve tries to break free but the man is just too strong for him. As the bodyguard struggles to lift Steve into the window, the door opens and Lucy walks in, head down, muttering about not being able to sleep and seeing the light on. She looks up at this point and sees Steve being lifted through a window and Nigel holding a gun.

Steve screams at Lucy to run but she is too late to act as Nigel shoots her, catching her in her throat. She staggers backwards, her hands to her throat, blood pouring between her fingers, her mouth wide open, her scream cut short as the life spills out of her. Steve's strength returns as he pushes backwards, catching the bodyguard on the bridge of his nose, forcing him to loosen his grip. He drops straight down, ducking as the man tries to push forward, missing him as Steve pushes up, lifting him off his feet and propelling him through the same window he himself was supposed to fall from. He can hear the man scream as he falls.

Nigel quickly turns the gun back around. Steve has sunk to the floor and is looking under the table to where Lucy had fallen. Her eyes are open but he knows she is dead, another innocent victim to add to all the other deaths. He looks back at Nigel, pure hate and adrenalin pumping through him, his energy returning as he prepared himself to tackle this murderer, thinking he can share the same fate as his body guard, even if it cost Steve his life.

"It's not the same is it, when you have to pull the trigger yourself? You're a mass murderer, Nigel. How are you going to dig yourself out of this one? What are you going to tell them, I killed Lucy and your man, and then I jumped out of the window? How many more people are going to die for you to admit you have lost?"

Nigel looks scared. He is corned, but he is still dangerous. He is trying to think clearly but Steve is making it difficult for him. He screams at Steve to shut up and tries to think. He can get money. He could hide anywhere in the world. He knows things that people would not want disclosed. He could use that to get him money. He makes the mistake of looking down and before he knows what hit him, Steve was all over him, knocking the gun from his grasp and raining down blow after blow against Nigel.

Eventually Steve stops, his knuckles bloodied from the constant blows. He looks down at the man he knew, all bloodied and barely conscious. Someone he had thought was his friend. Nigel is barely conscious as Steve stands not wanting any further contact with this person as he wipes the blood from his hands as he survey's the room, his eyes stopping to where the gun had fallen. Walking slowly over, he thinks about what he is about to do. Picking up the gun, he turns and walks back, the gun pointing forward as he finds his target. Nigel is a little more aware and has opened his left eye to stare at Steve, his right one being too swollen. Looking at the gun pointed at him, he tries to speak and plead for his life, his true colours showing who he is.

Steve's finger tightens on the trigger, his arm shaking. The gun never gets to fire as once again a dark shadow appears in the room and Steve's attention is drawn to it, his hairs standing up again as he feels the room shake and grow hotter. He knows what is about to happen, but he cannot understand why it is happening a second time; how can he travel this time? He is alive, all tissue and bone, pure matter. He braces himself but he's wrong and before he can complete the thought, he blacks out as something leaves his body.

Face down and in a small cramped space, Steve is reattaching the ends of connectors together after diagnosing a breakdown in the feed to the drive motors, feeding the Nano machines from the generator through to the chamber of the reactor.

He has been in the tunnel since he arrived directly from the airport and has not stopped since arriving as they were pushed for time if they were going to get things up and running for the first test on Tuesday. It is after ten at night and sweat is dripping off of him as he tries to crawl backwards.

That is when he hears the sound like thunder and the vibration of the generator; he thinks someone must have plugged in something incorrectly creating a feedback and he is dripping with sweat, a perfect conductor for electricity, he thinks, one fried engineer. A shadow forms over him but he is unable to turn to see it. Then it hits him and he blacks out for a second.

Slowly opening his eyes, unaware of his surroundings, he immediately starts to panic as he cannot recall where he is. His reality is lost for a second, then the memories explode back with a vengeance as he realises what has happened. He pushes himself backwards out from between the generators and lifts himself up, trying to get his bearings. Others had come over as they had heard the noise but had not been able to see anything other than some sort of shadow. Others had seen small objects dancing on the floor and

Steve quickly tells them that the polarities must have crossed, creating a magnetic pull. Some are left scratching their heads as they contemplate Steve's explanation as he walks away.

Steve quickly walks over to the phone and dials the control room. A technician comes on the line and Steve immediately asks to speak to Lucy. He can hear her name being called and ten seconds later she's on the phone.

"Lucy here, this had better be important as I'm busy here."

Steve sucks in, deeply overwhelmed at hearing her voice. Lucy asks who the heavy breather is as it does not work for her on the phone. Steve smiles at her joke and then answers her, asking her to make time as he needs a word in private and he tells her to bring those figures she has on Fermilab, not the ones of the experiment but of the residual data. Lucy is the one that is quiet now as she was going to bring it up later for Steve to see. Before she can say a word, he tells her not to think about how he knows, but just to meet him in fifteen minutes in the office that has been set aside for him.

Fifteen minutes later, they are both sat at the table and Steve is quiet as he needs to compose his thoughts before he tells her. He starts off with telling her that less than an hour ago he was sat in this office looking at her dead, on the floor. He lets that sink in before he carries on telling her that her death will happen tomorrow but not to worry as it won't happen now unless the same conditions are in place and explains that things in the past can be changed. Before she starts to challenge his findings, he gives her the results of the fusion reactor and the name of the man that she and everyone should be afraid off, Nigel!

When he finishes, he waits a few seconds for Lucy to absorb his story. He doesn't expect her to believe everything but hopes they respect each other enough to at least look at the possibilities. What he wants is for her is to explain to him how it is possible as she has the data in front of her. "What I do know" he says "is the time period. And if time continues backwards we will…" Steve does not get chance to finish the sentence as Lucy finishes it for him: "We will have to have the same conversation as if we had never had it."

Smart girl, Steve thinks.

She goes on to tell him, aside from the fact he may be nuts as she had always thought, the reason he keeps travelling backwards is the time loop. He asks her to run that by him again, after all, he is just a practical man with a science and engineering degree and a few other things thrown in just to keep his IQ ticking over, on the right side of 180, she has lost him. Lucy explains that if what he says is true, then they have not opened just one black hole, but two in the same spot but at different times, reminding him of the first test prior to total fusion. Steve thinks about this, letting it sink in. They had the results from Fermilab about the invisible mass and the same would have occurred with the test here. Steve is surprised how easy she accepts the possibility of black holes here on earth, but again she reminds him that they happen millions of times around the universe. She is really getting excited about all the possibilities, but he has to stop her as he needs to know what is happening. She tells him her theory is, the first black hole opened up and that down the line the second one did the same, only it was stronger. As they are on the same spot, they push at each other like two opposing magnets; only the second one is stronger and is pulling closer. "With you going backwards, you will find that each time, your time line shrinks, destabilising as it gets closer and if my theory is correct, then the first one will be devoured by the second and stronger one. It will carry on getting bigger, destroying everything in its path." Lucy finishes off with, "but that's just my theory, it might not happen that way." She smiles because in the back of her head she cannot believe what Steve has told her or she does not want to believe it because of the consequences.

She looks at him and thinks of telling him something that she has just thought about, the only way to possibly stop the process from repeating itself, only if she is right, then it would be unthinkable and she leaves it. Steve blinks, remembering the principles of time and space laid down by the greatest physicist of the twentieth century, Einstein's own theories of relativity, when time and space and gravitation have no separate existence from matter. He remembers the basics of time travel, about the fold in time. For time to carry on as normal, he will have to find a way to straighten time. Lucy has one more observation to make. She tells him that for some reason it is linked to him and the clue to stopping it lies with him, though he won't like the answer if he wants it to stop.

He looks at her, stunned with her analysis, wondering how she came up with her theory. She tells him that at weekends a group of them get around a couple of bottles of wine and come up with the scientific plausibilities. She remembers having one recently about a similar scenario. What he really wants to know is how he is moving back. Matter, as they know, cannot travel backwards; it would be crushed as soon as it entered the event horizon.

She looks at him, deciding if she should tell him. Taking a deep breath, she asks him if he really wants to know what she thinks is happening and that she feels stupid telling him this. Steve tells her just to go with the flow and he jokingly promises never to divulge that she has obviously had more than a couple of bottles of wine to drink. Lucy starts from the point of his death. He had told her he had had a feeling of looking down at himself and of seeing a brilliant white light. She tells him what he was seeing was an entity born of the fourth dimension and not from this world. This entity is well known around the world and has been researched many times. It is the white light that we see when we die. The entity or parasite or whatever you want to call it is energy. But we know it as the soul. Only our souls are singular entities that join us when we are born. They are attracted to our life force and stay with us until we die, when they move back to their matrix or their collective. Similar to deja' vu and people who believe that they have lived before, your memories never die and when there is a new born, a part of the collective breaks off and joins with the new life and it may bring with it other past memories. She looks at him, asking if he is following her. He nods for her to carry on. "It is believed that we had help when we left the trees and started to walk upright and that the soul gives us the ability to focus our emotions. Remember when you think of something and decide not to do it and then you wish you had. This is the turmoil that goes on inside us as we constantly fight a battle of control with the entity inside, the soul as many will call it. As our brains grow, the more we are able to control our own thoughts. "Remember I said that when you were looking down and could see your body, you were dead and your soul had left you and would have joined the collective, only something stopped it going to the white light. The only thing that would stop your soul from moving on is you not being dead and you aren't, at least not in your present time. Before your soul was allowed to travel, the black hole occurred and you can thank Nigel for

261

that. When he destroyed the reactor he started the chain of events and your soul was dragged through time to the day before and now you and the black hole are linked and you will both continue travelling back unless it can be stopped."

"Why just my soul? I should think that when the reactor exploded, others would have been caught in the blast. Other souls would have been released and absorbed through the hole. Why only mine?" "That's the easy part," Lucy tells him. "You were already dead and your soul was ready to move on. Other people who may have died, their souls would have moved on after the hole had closed down. It is only your life energy in your soul that is connected to the black hole. If I had time, I could work out a theory on this. There are different energies in the universe. It is possible that the energy of our souls is linked to the energy exerted by the black hole and this is just a theory Steve, but you could be the catalyst for why the hole is still opening up." Steve asks her what her theory is to stop it, but she shakes her head.

Steve just looks at her, absorbing everything she has just told him and thinking that if he ever survived this, he would seriously consider joining her party of theology retards and get drunk too. Lucy tells him that she needs to work and has asked that they meet back here in under five hours as she wants to see that, which he has told her, will occur. He tells her that in case he speaks to her again in the past he should know something about her that she has never told anyone. She thinks for a while and goes up to Steve and kisses him on the mouth. Then she stands back and tells him that she has always wanted to do that as she is in love with his mind, though it could never work as she loves women and she would cheat on him. He blushes and laughs, telling her that if anyone had to tell him a secret, it could never top this one.

Less than five hours later, they are back and Lucy, her eyes wide in amazement as she sees for the first time and realising the truth as the black hole materialises. Why had she not told Steve her theory on stopping the hole from opening up again? Steve would have to sacrifice himself.

Chapter 29

The noise is deafening in the enclosed space towards the back of the court house. Everyone looks to see where it is coming from. There is very little light and they do not notice the dark shadow at first, but feel the pull of some invisible force. The building feels like it is shaking as they stare, trying to make out a dark shimmering shape. Something is pulling them forward and they hold brace themselves. Carla tries to look for an open door, thinking that strong winds had come back. Something flies out of the top pocket of Ryan's coat and he curses as he tries to grab his pen and misses. Then it all dies down and Steve is picking himself off the floor, shaking his head from side to side when he suddenly becomes alert and looks at his surroundings. He finds that when he jumped, as he now refers to it, the time difference between locations was taken into effect. Instead of jumping around ten at night, he was back on American soil at the same time it would have been in Switzerland, only with six hours difference.

He had already travelled back to Saturday, causing a little panic in an internet café he had stopped in prior to going to the airport. For him it seemed a lifetime ago and one thing he was noticing was that his black hole was getting noticed as it grew stronger and he was checking the time as soon as he emerged. He had stayed in the café and had done some research on local news.

Turning around to everyone and smiling, he wonders how he is going to break the news to them, at the same time checking his watch, it is 16.09hrs.

Telling a person like Lucy is one thing but here are three people that live in the normal world where they expect their lives to follow a simple rule of logic, unfortunately it wasn't the normal world anymore and he would need their help.

They are a little freaked out by what they had just witnessed and he is going to give his friends more to freak out about. There is no such thing as a simple plan, he thinks, just come out with it; after all, yesterday is another day for him.

"Hello Tina, Carla and Ryan, I hope you all will stay calm, but I need personal information from each of you , that you have never told anyone, because what I am about to tell you will leave you wondering if I should be locked away. Something I did a few days from now caused that to happen and I have to stop it. If you haven't seen one before, you just witnessed a black hole and we can't go to my place as there is a reporter waiting to interview me about what I did at Fermilab."

He watched their reactions, all staring at him, speechless. Carla is first to speak, asking him if this was his way of making them feel better after her arrest, because it wasn't working. Steve just looks at her, telling her that she is innocent and that he knows who had killed her partner and others. He turns to Ryan and recites his phone number and some of his life story that he had picked up from him when they had shared a hotel room, following it up with the revelation that he had a big crush on Carla. Tina he just asks to trust him. He tells them that if they are a little sceptical, they should follow him and he will show them a future that hasn't happened for them and information he had googled from the internet. He asks them to have a little faith and also asks Ryan if he is carrying as he is going to need his weapon.

For the next two hours, he takes them through two incidents. The first is a student who has been drinking late and is about to be knocked over by a passing vehicle. The driver never stops. They travel to Cambridge where both occurrences happen. Steve asks them to travel in his vehicle as it would save time and Tina is asked to drive. He makes a couple of calls to people he has never met and passes on information about their lives and either, what was going to happen to them or someone they knew. He has no choice but to do it this way and hope they would take action.

The first incident with the student has them all stunned, as Steve, when they arrive asks them to be patient and wait a short while. Sure enough, he spots a young man staggering towards them and guesses that this is the person and rushes across the road, grabbing the student and pulling him out of harm's way, as a vehicle narrowly misses both of them. Ryan is asked by Steve to get the number plate from the car as the driver never stops to report the incident. He could contact the driver and have words and hopefully stop the person from speeding in the future.

Steve knows this will not prove anything as it could have been staged, but the next incident is a different matter. A corner shop is about to be robbed in broad daylight and a police officer is going to be hurt, shot by one of the two thieves, themselves shot down by the officer's partner. Both officers are by chance going into the store where the incident takes place, catching the thieves in the process and the rest, as Steve puts it, is history, though not for him. They wait for the two men before they enter the shop. Carla is asked to wait for the two officers to show and to help with the arrest as she is no longer able to carry a weapon. The two men are about to get their weapons out as Ryan, casually walks past and turning quickly before they are able to remove their weapons, kicks the legs out from under the larger of the two, knocking him down to the ground. He points his gun at the head of the other one and grabs his gun from inside his waist and points it down at the man nursing his leg. Carla is impressed with the way Ryan handles the situation and rushes over with the two officers, both of whom have their weapons out.

Ryan is asked by Steve to hand over his arrests to the two officers as he could not afford for him to be tied down to this. Ryan reluctantly agrees and the two officers arrest the two men for attempting to commit a felony. They ask Ryan how he found out and he tells them that it was just a case of two people acting suspiciously.

Ryan is still unhappy about handing the two men over until Carla comments on his quick reactions. She is looking at him impressed and he soon forgets about the two men.

They are all looking now at Steve as if he is some sort of Merlin magician.

They had found a quiet coffee bar and were all still a little mesmerised by what Steve has told them. He has less than two hours before he jumps and he needs some time on the internet to see what had happened the previous day. He also tells Carla that he will be seeing her before she makes her mistake with going to Greggs and he needs her to give him something private that no-one else knows about her. They are all still stunned and eventually Carla takes him to one side and tells him; her embarrassment leaves him smiling. She warns him if he tells anyone, he will be wearing his balls around his neck.

It is getting close to jump time and they have all gathered in a field between Cambridge and Belmont. Ryan pulls Steve to one side and tells him that, as he was jumping, which he is still having trouble believing in, then he might never meet Carla as Moralis might not be dead. Steve grins and tells him he should expect a call each day and now he knows his secret, he would now try to give him information on incidents in Boston. It was up to him to act on them. He tells Steve, that all he needs to do is send a picture of Carla and he would not think twice. He has been separated for over three months now and there is no getting back with his wife.

Steve also explains to him that he would be stopping someone from making a purchase that would get the person killed, but he does not let Ryan know what the purchase was as he knew people would start asking him to help. This is something he intends to deal with at the right time. He takes Tina to one side and asks her to believe in him, because at some point he is going to be back on the day she was raped. He tells her that the future will be different and she cries, not quite understanding and wishing that what he was telling her was true. He turns to Carla, telling her he would see her soon. It isn't long to wait before the ground starts to shake and all eyes fix on Steve, all of them having trouble believing what they were seeing. Steve, before he leaves, asks Carla a question. He is thinking about her answer when he arrives back to Thursday. He quickly remembers to check the time: 16.00, a couple of minutes different to Friday's jump. He is with George and they have recently arrived back after leaving Fermilab yesterday, he remembers. They had driven all night and he had fallen asleep on the couch when he got in. He takes George for a walk, passing a public box where he stops and calls the station, asking for Carla. He is put through and asks her to meet him and they arrange a time.

Carla is cautious when she arrives at the coffee bar. Steve walks in several minutes later, having watched her arrive and checked to see if she is being followed. He spotted the vehicle pull in several cars behind her. They had not immediately stopped and had waited before parking.

She does not immediately recognise Steve until he speaks. He is sitting at another table as they can be viewed from where the two people were in their vehicle.

"Don't look at me, Carla, or try to speak to me."

He goes on to tell her about the vehicle outside that was following her. She carefully glances around, making it look like she is stretching before taking a look. Turning back she retrieves her cell phone and pretends to talk to someone on it, while really talking to Steve. The reason she had not tagged him when he came in was the way he is dressed. The weather is still a little cold for the time of year. It is still a good month away from summer and the winds have died down from two weeks ago. Steve has on a waterproof mac and cap and was keeping his head down. He also has on a false moustache he had kept from a fancy dress outfit he had worn months ago at a party, thrown by colleagues of Karen's, when she had given up work.

"Who are those two and why are they watching me and why are you dressed like that?"

Steve goes on to recap what he has already told the Carla of the future, only this time he leaves out his travelling. He decides to lie and tells her that Officer Greggs is under surveillance, that they know Moralis was murdered and that Greggs had been used to kill Scholfield. They are also the ones who had murdered his family. She asks him who they were and he tells her that he cannot divulge that information and asks her to trust him or the operation would be compromised. He cannot really talk to her as it might draw suspicion on them. He tells her that there will be justice for the murders, but there are more people in the pot and going after Greggs will not get those people. He promises that when the time is right, he will contact her so she is able to make the arrests.

Steve hates to lie but he has no idea what will happen after today and if for some reason he cannot change the past from here, then at least Carla has a better chance to see justice done. She tells him that she can't promise anything as she is police and that if the people want to see justice done he had better contact her soon.

Steve has no idea if Carla's phone is bugged or not and he tells her to get another and to not use the one she has. He wants her to feel that she will not be able to do anything reckless as she is being watched by both sides. He hopes that, this will be enough to keep her out of trouble. He whispers to her that he will contact her soon; not a lie this time, just a little angle on the truth.

After they part, he is back on his cell phone, one he had purchased recently as he knows he cannot trust the one Nigel gave him. He thinks that there were many advantages to moving backwards, not just saving lives. He can also spend up to his limit on his card and use it again and again without going over the limit. He makes the calls to various people around the country telling them about things that are going to happen, again hoping that at least some of them would take his advice. He then heads to the library to use the internet. He has time before he jumps again to check the news.

For the next several jumps, Steve is tied to Fermilab. He has spent hours over the days going backwards, talking with Lucy, shocking her sometimes but telling her about her secret and eventually winning her over. He is lucky with saving a few people who were going to have accidents and he was by chance just in the right place to help people. Every day he goes out and purchases a new cell phone to make calls on and every time he jumps, he checks the time difference. His jumps are getting earlier and his time between the jumps is getting shorter. One of his jumps had almost cost him a broken leg as he had been half way up a gantry. It was lucky that his belt had caught when he fell, otherwise he would have had a broken leg for at least six hours. It had happened when he was with George as he was driving up to Illinois on Saturday. George was barking like mad and thrashing about, having jumped into the back seats. Steve had almost lost control of the car and had to pull over. It took a while to calm George down. Eventually he started the engine and turned the car around and headed back to the motel he had stayed in. He needed the internet. There were more people to try and save.

He wonders, does it really matter? After the jumps he has made and the conversations he has had with Lucy, it didn't take a scientist to work out how to stop the hole from opening up. Steve is the catalyst and to stop it, Steve, must die before his soul is trapped by the black hole.

Another theory from Lucy about the hole opening up is that when it eventually joined to the weaker one, it would carry on getting larger as it destroyed all matter within its reach. The world would not stand a chance. Life would be destroyed. Lucy took her theory one stage further. With the gravity pull exerted by the black hole, it would be strong enough to pull other planets towards it. Unlike a super nova when a star dies, this black hole was created differently and as it devoured the planets closest, eventually its energy force would be strong enough to take down the sun. The pull on it would be so great that the closest stars would also be trapped in its gravitational pull and be sucked in, as it grows stronger. More stars and planets that may contain life would be destroyed by it. Take it one step further. It could be strong enough to stop the universe from expanding and when and if that happened, the universe would be reversed as it is pulled back and she asks Steve, what would happen if the universe collapses down on itself? When there is nothing else to pull in? Steve shakes his head. "Try the Big Bang!"

Chapter 30

Nigel is witness this time to the noise and sees the dark form materialise outside his office as he holds onto his desk, not sure if he is trying to stop it shaking or himself. He notices Steve also looking at the shimmering spectre as it was closer to him. Small objects are flying around and disappearing as they fly up towards the strange dark shadow. He has to shake his head a few times at what he is witnessing. Then it stops and he slowly stands, taking his eyes away from where the malign manifestation had occurred. He looks back to Steve, finding him staring back and with, he could swear, anger in his eyes, before he turned around and walked away.

Steve, head down, is having trouble controlling his emotions every time he is in the company of Nigel. He just wants to throttle the man and he has to walk away and get himself under control. He has things to do today and he needs to move fast. He needs to know who the players Nigel works for, are. It is time to play him at his own game, Steve thinks, as he enters one of the IT wings at MIT.

He remembers that Nigel had spent a lot of time in his office the first time round and Steve has a feeling that he would have spoken to the people he worked for. It was time to find out their little plan. When he gets back to the point he is intending to stop at, he thinks it best that evidence should be compiled. He would then load it on a disc at some point, knowing he would lose a few hours of the day, and send it to the appropriate authorities. He also has one other important thing to do. He is going to kill Nigel. He cannot take the chance

273

that this man will continue inflicting pain on others. He has to be stopped. Steve hates the idea, but he can see no alternative because he will not be around to see the future.

Did he have time, he thinks to himself as he found himself dodging heavy traffic. It is Wednesday. Only a few minutes ago, he was in the company of Carla and that was on Thursday. Now he is running, weaving in and out of vehicles, their horns blaring at him. Steve is running hard and he knows it will be close. Thank God he is still healthy as he again narrowly misses the bumper of a taxi, driving in the opposite direction; the driver leans out the window looking back and cursing him. He hears the squeal of breaks as the taxi is struck going through a red light. The photo taken from the speed camera would show later that the driver was not looking forward. His cursing continues as a police cruiser appears from nowhere with two officers witness to the event.

Steve had jumped only ten minutes earlier, again creating chaos for the colleagues in the lab with him. He can see his target in the distance. Thank God, he thinks to himself, they are still alive. Out of his peripheral vision he sees a truck, the very same one he had watched on the news. It seems to be all over the road. He screams at the top of his lungs to the woman walking with a young girl, her daughter, both oblivious to what is about to happen to them. It is going to be close and this time there might be three bodies lying under blankets for the news, he thinks, as he shakes his head and from somewhere deep inside, pushes harder, knowing that time is about to run out. He does not hesitate as he scoops the mother and child up off the pavement, both screaming at the top of their lungs, frightened by his sudden appearance. He carries them forward, not once slowing as all three of them go flying off to the side, missing the pavement by inches as all three of them tumbled along the ground. Behind them, the truck has not tried to brake as it smashes into the wall and then rebounding backwards, gently rolling to a stop. Bricks were scattered all around and it is a few seconds before the dust settles.

Steve pushes himself up. He is coughing, trying to draw air back into his lungs. He can hear a young girl crying behind him and as he turns, he is hit full in the face by a handbag. He tries to protect his head as the woman carries on hitting him again and again, screaming at him and calling for police that she was being attacked. Someone arrives at this point, someone who had witnessed the whole occurrence. The man grabs hold of the lady's bag, stopping her hitting Steve and shouting at her that the man she was hitting had just saved her and the girl's life. He points over his shoulder at the truck, the driver passed out behind the wheel, drunk, not a scratch on him. The man leaves the woman and checks on the girl as she is crying, nursing a cut to her knees. The woman looks back at Steve and lunges at him, her arms flying around the back of his head as she hugs him, telling him she is sorry for hitting him and starting to cry again.

People have started to crowd around, some had seen the accident happen and are helping them to their feet, while Steve is getting slapped on his back and praised for his heroic deed. A young girl comes running up, telling everyone that she had caught the whole thing on her cell phone. It was just by luck, she had pushed the wrong button and the video was set to play. She had hit the wrong button because Steve had run past her and she had wondered why he was in such a hurry, when she witnessed him scoop the two people up, just before the truck smashed into the wall and caught it on her phone. Everyone is around her as she showed the footage. Steve quietly moves backwards and around the side of the building, before turning to run.

Wednesday moves into Tuesday as Steve finds himself with less and less time, a few minutes each day taken away as the black hole is moving closer to the weaker one and still growing stronger, decreasing the time Steve has each day. Each time it occurs, the forces around the hole are more destructive. People are getting pulled towards it as it grows in size.

Monday comes and Steve knows he has his work cut out for him. There are three lives to save in two different locations. Carla and Moralis are driving to a building outside of town and Scholfield is injured in hospital. Steve has no time to get a new cell phone. He has to make the call to Carla. She isn't picking up. He has no choice and as he runs past his team, leaving them speechless by his sudden departure. Nigel is straight on the phone as he witnessed Steve leave. He calls his two henchmen who are outside; both are still recovering from last week's spat with Scholfield. They answer just as the outer door flies open and watch as Steve runs out and jumps in his car, roaring off, tyres screaming. Throwing down the phone, they leave in pursuit.

Steve tries to call several times on route to where Carla and Moralis have gone. Here he goes again, he thinks, as he leaves a message for Carla to pick up. He knows he is not going to make it. He knows when Moralis will die and that he will be late by at least five minutes. He floors the engine trying to get more speed out of the motor. He has to try. His phone goes and he answers, "Carla!"

"How did you get my number and what were you jabbering on about, O'Neil? It's a bad area for signals. What were you trying to tell me?"

Seconds later Carla is running into the building, screaming down the corridor at Moralis as he is about to open the last door. He turns with his hand on the handle, hearing Carla shouting something at him. He continues to turn and push the door forward when a hand shoots out, stopping him. The younger officer he was with had stopped him from pushing in on the door. He had heard what Carla was shouting. Carla gets to them, out of breath, telling them that she had just received a somewhat unusual call from O'Neil telling her that they were walking into a trap and that the room that Moralis was about to step into was booby trapped. They all step back, looking at the door; and then Moralis tells them to get out fast.

They are all waiting outside when Steve arrives. He looks at the group, relieved to see everybody still alive. Now, he thinks, how you are going to explain this one? As he steps out of his car, a lie forms on the tip of his tongue. Moralis walks over, suspicious of him and asks him how he knew, wondering if he was clairvoyant. Maybe he wanted to hide something and Moralis was wrong about this man being innocent. Steve tells them his lie, that he had accidentally deleted a message from Scholfield about seeing a body and the people inside were going to blow it up when he ran. He had also found out that one of their own, an officer Greggs, was on the payroll of these people. Moralis and Carla both look at each other and Carla runs to their car and calls dispatch, telling them to contact Officer Richards, that he needs to go back to the hospital and watch Scholfield. She also tells them that Officer Greggs should be placed under arrest. Thinking quickly, she tells them to phone the hospital to get their security involved as quickly as possible.

All of this is witnessed by the two men who have followed Steve. They are talking with Nigel. He panics and tells them that they have to kill them all. Leave no witnesses. Get them back in the building and destroy it. Nigel, slouched over his chair, is furious. He needs Steve but now he has no choice after his two men had relayed back what they had heard when listening in on Steve's phone. How the hell, he thinks, did he find out?

They are all gathered around listening to Steve and do not hear the footsteps behind them. What they hear is: "Don't anybody move. Keep your hands down by your sides."

They all turn and freeze as they take in two guns pointing at them, held by two very tall men. Moralis and Carla recognise them from the photos on the flash drive. Steve has known them for longer and he is kicking himself, remembering that he had used the cell phone Nigel had given him.

Moralis tries to use his authority but one of the men comes up to him and without warning, hits him over the head with the butt of his gun. Moralis collapses and both Steve and Carla grab for him as he falls. Moralis rubs his head, trying to shake the pain away. The locksmith stands petrified, shocked into silence, the thoughts about winning a big chunk of the lottery, forgotten. The two men close in, telling the two officers and both Carla and Moralis to carefully remove their weapons and throw them on the ground. They watch as the guns are thrown to the floor, and then, they are ordered to make their way back inside the building. They are taken to the back and into a room. One of the men stays with them, two guns now in his hand as his partner has passed his over and then disappeared out of the room. The one watching them tells them not to try anything stupid as he tells them the first person to be shot would be the woman. The other man returns five minutes later and whispers to his partner. They are again asked to move and they proceed out, one man walking backwards, gun pointing at them and the other one, guarding the rear. They enter the end room, the one Moralis was stopped from going through, and spot all the gas bottles. There must be fifty of them. In the middle of the floor is an object with a timer on top and it is ticking. Steve has been quiet from the time the men had captured them. He has been trying to work out how to get out of this. He has noticed one of the men limping and that the other seems to be touching a spot on his head. He has to act fast as they are out of time and turning quickly, he kicks the one with the injured leg, across his knee. The man goes down instantly, knocking his partner's gun as a bullet is fired. Steve does not stop there as he carries on forward, head down, taking the man in the stomach and pushing him backwards as his head collides with the back wall. Both men down, he screams at the others to run. They do not think twice as they run out the door. Steve knows they will not get far down the corridor before bullets start coming their way and improvising, he grabs a small canister off the floor. Still moving, he runs through the doorway; turning quickly, he sees the man with the head injury raise his arm to fire. Steve slams the door on him as a bullet strikes the door frame. He had noticed the doors on this room were especially robust, made from hard wood and he raises the canister above his head and brings it down on the handle, totally shearing it off, and grabs out the latch pin. Throwing down the canister, he turns and runs. He can hear more shots behind him hitting the door. Seconds later he is outside. The others have recovered their weapons and he can see people in other buildings have come out to see what all the commotion is about. Moralis and the two officers are about to go back inside and Steve shouts at them, "No!" get back. He has seen the timer and he knows things are going to get very loud as he forces them to retreat, grabbing Carla in the process as she was on the car radio, calling for back up. Not letting go, he spins her around and they run, shouting at everyone else to find cover. People look on oblivious to what is about to happen. They stop a couple of hundred yards away and turn. Nothing is happening and there is a deathly silence as they look back at the building. Moralis turns to Steve to tell him they need to go back as nothing was going to happen. Then the building's roof blows up and they all throw themselves on the ground as debris comes falling down around them.

Turning to Carla on the floor, Steve smiles and asks her if he could borrow her phone. She's a little stunned and finds it in her pocket. He opens it up and points it at Carla telling her to say cheese and then taps in some numbers and sends it. He smiles again and tells her he had promised someone that and hands the phone back. She is even more confused.

Ryan hears the messaging service on his cell phone go off. He thinks it's another message from his estranged wife, giving him more bad news. Opening up the message, he sees a woman's face, dirty and she seems to be lying on a road. He thinks she looks beautiful.

Chapter 31

People start to pick themselves up off the ground, looking at each other, asking if that was an earthquake and confused by what they had just seen. They look over to where the black shimmering formation has materialised over their heads. Purses have been snatched away and headstones nearby have fallen over. Steve looks around him, checking to see no one was hurt. He has helped Tina up and between them had picked up Elena. Nigel is nearby and has grabbed Steve's arm to lift himself. Steve cringes when he sees who it is and pushes his hand away. He turns back around to check on his friends. Everybody seems shocked but otherwise there are no injuries. He wonders how bad it will be in another week. He checks the time: it is showing 15.43. He looks back at the graves of his father and sister and quietly whispers that he will see them soon.

He feels it is wrong to run off this time and when they have returned to his father's place, he pops over to Frederick and Elsa's to ask them if he could use their PC. He hopes he will not be missed as he checks through previous news footage and then makes his usual calls on his friend's phone.

He had jumped through Saturday, again scaring the hell out of his team and again running out of the building, purchasing another cell phone and making calls to numbers he had remembered from the previous day when he had researched news items over at the Klein's. It is now Friday, the day Scholfield had been found. There is little he can do as he has no idea where he was, only that he will be picked up, floating down the Concorde River. He has to let this one go, as he has another river to get to and he only has an hour in this weather.

Fifty five minutes later he stops at a bridge, looking across to the other side. Stupid, he tells himself, which side had they crossed on? The rain is heavy and he is having trouble seeing across the bridge when he hears the sound of an engine, though he cannot tell where it is coming from. He listens and then he sees what look like lights in the distance. Only they are on the other side and he jumps back in, finding that his car won't start; he had flooded the engine. With no time to waste, he jumps out and starts running across the bridge. He is wearing a dark rain jacket and knows he will be hard to spot, but he has to try. He is almost across to the middle and both cars have made it to the bridge and are starting to cross. The first car is being driven by the old couple and they are taking it slow. The car behind is close and it is clear that the driver is impatient, trying to make the first car go a little faster. It is this that had caused them to be on the bridge the first time. The old man spots Steve running towards him, his arms waving in the air and jams on the brakes. The car starts to slide before coming to a stop. Unfortunately, the car behind was not as fortunate and hits the rear end of the front car pushing it forward. It immediately starts to aquaplane towards the middle. Steve has nowhere to go but up onto the bonnet and he squats down, taking all his weight, then jumps up off the bridge, coming face to face with the driver as he lands on the bonnet. The driver has a look of shock on his face as he stares back, hands gripped on the steering wheel. With no time to waste, Steve slides off the bumper and opens the driver's door, telling the driver that he needs to back up. The old man looks at him and Steve can tell he isn't going to move. With no time to spare he jumps in, pushing the man along the seat and squashing him up against his wife. He locates reverse and floors it. The tyres rotate, the engine screaming, but they find no traction from the wheels. From outside, they hear wood snapping as the bridge starts to break up. Taking his foot off the gas, Steve slowly presses down on the accelerator and the car starts to move slowly backwards as he applies more pressure to the peddle, pushing further down and looks behind him, seeing the other car also moving backwards. The two cars make it off the bridge and he looks forward again, seeing the bridge falling into the river. Then the bridge collapses under them, just as the back wheels make it off the bridge and they grind to a halt as the underside of the car catches on what is left of the end of the bridge. The front wheels and half the vehicle are hanging over the edge. No time to waste, Steve jumps out and goes around the car. The other driver has stopped and has come forward, just as Steve pulls open the passenger door and pulls the old lady out, apologising at the same time as he hands her to the other driver and goes back in for the old man. He is petrified but Steve has no time to be patient and tugs on his arm, pulling him towards him. The car starts to tilt as more of the bridge gives way and with a last pull, the old man leaves the car just as it falls over the edge and into the river. Steve is on his back and on top of him is the old man.

Exhausted, Steve stays down on his back, the wet ground feeding into his clothes. Another person in the other car has come forward and lifted the old man off Steve, escorting him back to their car where his wife was being looked after. Steve sits up and thinks that going back in time will kill him and he laughs.

The days pass backwards, each time, the tremors were growing and each time he has a little less time. This day is important for Steve as he heads out. This time he drives and five minutes later he arrives at the pharmacy. He spots Tina reading some paperwork and knocks on the window. He watches her shake her head as she looks around and displays a lovely set of teeth as she smiles, at the same time walking over to the door. Steve throws his arms around her and tells her that it will not happen now. She looks at him confused, a lopsided smile and a questioning look.

He asks to use her cell phone and she hands it to him. Carla picks up and Steve tells her about Keel and who he really is and that they can catch him in the act if they were interested. He tells her about the secret she has never told anyone and if she doesn't act on it, he will post it on Facebook. Before she can curse him, he says he knows he will be wearing his balls around his neck, leaving her stunned as those were the words she was going to say to him. He tells her a time and where to meet. All she has to do is check on his information. He then turns to a stunned Tina and tells her she has just quit but they have to pop back later as she has a destiny with Keel. Right now, he is hungry and he has a dog in the car that needs a walk. Tina looks at him as if he had lost his marbles and he laughs, telling her everything as far as he knows will be fine and looking at her feet thinks that his credit card is going to take a pounding. He asks her after they had some lunch what type of clothes she would need for university.

Keel opens the door and staggers forward, one arm held out, hand against the frame. Tina is in the store cupboard. She had actually only been back ten minutes. Even though she knows what is going to happen and still has no idea how Steve knew this was going to happen, she looks at Keel and feels the panic rise in her

284

as he moves forward closing the door behind him and grabbing for Tina. Only she moves to the side and he falls forward, cursing her. As he pushes up, two feet appear in front of him. Steve looks down, disgusted with what he sees and the door opens again and both Moralis and Carla are stood there. Moralis moves forward and grabs Keel's wrists, pinning them behind him. He tries to struggle and ends up dislocating his shoulder as Moralis hangs on and cuffs his wrists, at the same time pulling him up and pushing him through the door, reading him his rights as he walks Keel out. Both Carla and Tina are looking at Steve.

"Don't worry Carla. Your secret is safe with me, I promise."

"Why do you keep calling me Carla? You talk to me as if you know me. My name is Washington, Detective Washington."

Steve shakes his head. There was no help, he thought, to understanding women and he turns to Tina, asking her if she was OK. She nods, still trying to work out what had just happened, he tells her, "Though our detective here is trying to work me out, secretly she is pleased because they have just taken down a serial rapist who had been wanted by the police and had been on the run under an assumed name. This is a good arrest for them and as Carla; I mean Washington is a young detective with a few months on the job, she knows that she and Moralis will probably get a commendation for the arrest. She's also, like you, a little confused about me."

He turns to Carla, a serious look on his face, and tells her that they will not find anything wrong with the pills that Karen had taken and those are the only ones that Tina passed to him last Saturday. Steve asks if they have detained the lawyer who dropped Keel back. He has in his possession a letter signed by Keel relating to last Saturday. They may find that Keel has been paid by this man and though it will appear that he and his company were taken on by the insurance company, behind all that is one man. His name is Nigel Shanks. Someone, Steve tells them, he used to call a friend and he is the one that is responsible for all the deaths, his friend Kenneth, many years ago and the deaths of Karen, his father and sister. He produces his cell phone and asks they check it out as well as his house as they are both bugged. He finds Moralis outside talking to one of his offices and asks him to look into a man who has been following him. He asks him to keep an eye on Scholfield. Moralis on hearing the name, smiles, thinking it was time to make a visit and if the man was being his usual interfering self, then he could share a night with other low-lifes, in a cell. He turns to Carla and Tina.

"There is so much I would like to tell you all, only you will find it very hard to believe and very soon I hope that all the pain and suffering will be gone and life will carry on as normal for everyone."

Carla looks at him and feels goose bumps down her back and asks Steve why he feels that he knows her. Steve smiles and asks for a pen and writes down a number and name on a piece of paper; handing it to her. He asks her to call as he had promised the person that he would make sure that at least one of them knew about the other and tells her to call as it won't do any harm. Tina laughs at the look on Carla's face and makes a joke about Steve setting up a blind date. Carla tells them both, that this was ridiculous and walks away pocketing the note.

Chapter 32

Tuesday he was by himself. He had arrived in his condo and this time he was not scaring George as he was still with the Klein's. This was his time to put the final plan in action. He would not be travelling around saving lives but he had gone out earlier to buy a cell phone and whilst out, had made several calls and left a message on both Carla's and Ryan's numbers to call each other. Then he had sat down to finalise things, ignoring the knocks on his door and waiting to make the next jump.

He thought his condo had taken a battering on Tuesday, but today many of his and Karen's ornaments disappear and alarms on cars outside, including his, are going off as they were triggered by ground shaking. He checks the time. Just before 15.24. Time is really catching up and looking around him, he jokes that Karen would have to buy some new items for the Condo. No problem, he thinks, she will be able to buy those and still have a few dollars left in the account.

He waits for the person to turn up. He has to do it today as he thinks he will not have the time on Sunday. It has to be today. The knock comes and he answers the door, shaking hands with Nigel as he walks in.

Coffees in hand, Nigel sipping his and Steve watching, he asks Nigel if he is enjoying his coffee and Nigel nods that he is.

"Good. I'm so glad. It probably doesn't have the same ingredients yours did when you handed it to me yesterday at the hospital, but then I never put sleeping pills in the ones I make for my guests."

The gun is out and pointed at Nigel. His jaw has dropped at the same time spilling coffee on his lap, burning him as he jumps up stunned,the cup falling from his hand and smashing on the floor, the contents spilling out. Steve asks him if he has anything to say as he had plenty and gives him a lecture accounting for all the deaths he had caused and would cause in the future and he tells him about the experiment and how it was a success except for one small detail. He explains how it created a black hole in time and all the nasty deeds he had done which Steve had reversed as he passed back through time, through the worm hole, inside the black hole. He adds that the reason why he was telling him this is, when he jumps again into Sunday, he intends to kill him and then himself before the hole can open up again and God willing, it will end the fracture in time as he is the key to stopping it. He tells Nigel, the reason why they test, was to establish where problems lie. Nigel had been brutal in his blindness to succeed. Now there's a chance to put things right. He will leave information for the police and others on Sunday to act on, as he won't be around and he hopes that someone will be smart enough to help all the people in the future or at least for the next four weeks.

Steve looks at his watch. It is getting close and he stands, telling Nigel that the next time they meet will be their last. What Steve does not know is that Nigel's henchman is outside in the car and that Nigel has placed his hand in his pocket and opened up his cell phone. Their conversation is going out and before he knows what is happening he is hit from behind. Steve manages to deflect the blow as he spotted the shadow on the wall cast in front of him. He had moved his head enough to stop a direct blow, but still hard enough as the blow glances off the side of his head, dropping him to the floor, but not before his gun fires by accident.

Still pointing at Nigel, the bullet goes through his chest and out the other side. The couch he is sat on pushes back as Nigel is forced into it and then topples forward; wheezing, Nigel clutches his chest, blood pumping out through the wound.

His bodyguard takes one look at what he has done and points his gun down at Steve and starts to pull the trigger back. Nothing happens and he tries again. He looks at his gun and notices that the safety is on. It must have pushed up when he tried to hit Steve over the head. Before he can push it down, Steve has recovered enough and has pointed his gun at the man and fired, putting a hole in his shoulder. The gun falls from bodyguards hand and he shudders as the pain rips through his shoulder. He looks down at Steve on the floor about to take another shot at him and decides it was too hot for him to be there. He turns and runs as the gun fires, the bullet missing him by inches as it strikes the wall.

Both Steve and Nigel are sat on the floor, both injured; Nigel's is fatal and they stare at each other. Steve watches as Nigel's eyes start to close. He is close to death and Steve does not like the sight of the man dying like this. It makes him sick and he realises he will have trouble killing him on Sunday.

The last breath expels from Nigel and Steve feels sorry for the man and then it starts. The shaking and before him, the dark shimmering beast of a black hole materialises and he waits, the last time he will jump through time and as his soul leaves his body to go back through the worm hole to Sunday, something else is also travelling with him and he realises a fraction of a second before he is dragged through that another soul is with him.

In a different spot but in the same room, the TV is on with the Big Bang series blaring out; Steve sits up. Someone is calling in the distance. A voice he has not heard in almost four weeks. Karen is shouting up to him about the racket he is making as she is complaining that he must have the TV on too loud as it is shaking the foundations of their condo. Steve jumps up and runs to the basement and down the stairs, stopping at the bottom to look at the most beautiful sight for him in the world. Karen turns, asking him if he's turned it down and Steve runs over and wraps his arms around her and cries.

Upstairs, he sits Karen down as he needs to tell her things and also that soon her water will break and they need to get out of there as two thugs are outside and if he is correct, all his planning has just gone to waste as he knows that someone else had jumped with him and it will not be long before those two outside get a call. He has to be careful with what he tells her as he knows that someone is listening in on their conversation and he goes around turning things up under the surprised, watchful eyes of Karen.

Keeping things short and not wanting to freak his wife out, he gives her a story he had rehearsed and hopes she believes him as the real story would be hard to grasp for anyone. He keeps an eye on the window for movement and tells her that they have to go now as he wants her in the car with them heading to his father's.

"You're not making sense and I am not going anywhere until you explain," Karen was not happy.

Steve uses the only ammo he has and asks her if she loves him to trust him right now and get in the car. Then he would explain, but they had to do it now, not later. Shaking her head, she lifts herself off the couch holding the weight of the baby and the both of them leave. After belting her in, he climbs behind the wheel and starts the car at the same time as looking for two people sat in a vehicle. He spots them and he carefully drives out and watches as they pull out. He has to time things right and as he approaches the crossroads with lights, he waits for the lights to turn green and waits some more. The horns behind him start blairing and he ignores both the horns and Karen telling him to move. He does move, just as the lights turn red and guns the engine, the car shoots forward and is narrowly missed by a car coming from the side. Three cars behind, the driver pulls out, around the two cars and tries to cross through the red light and is hit by an oncoming truck, completely obliterating the rear end as the vehicle is forced sideways into another large vehicle coming in the opposite direction. Neither passenger stands a chance as the larger vehicle is forced up and over what is left of the car, and through the front drivers and passengers compartment, killing both occupants instantly.

Karen is looking behind her at the mayhem and she is screaming at Steve to stop. Steve looks down at the puddle forming on the floor and decides now is not the time and points down. Karen looks down and starts to panic. Steve has seen the accident in his mirrors and takes no pity on the two in the car. As he drives, he looks out for the shop he wants to buy from and stops to the amazement of Karen as he opens the door, runs into a phone store and back inside of three minutes. Karen has calmed down and is controlling her breathing. She looks at what he has purchased and asks sarcastically was he getting another cell phone for the baby and that was how so sweet. He ignores her sarcasm and asks her for her phone. She hands it to him and he throws it out the window and calls his father on the new set.

His father picks up and Steve wants just to talk but he has to keep it short and he tells his father to go to the window and look for two people sat near his house. He tells him not be obvious and not reply to him until he's back. Steve hopes it is only his house and phones that are bugged.

Christopher has to grab his mail and he goes outside and picks it up from the mailbox, casually looking around as he pretends to read it. He spots the vehicle, black with sliding side doors and two people sat in the front. He walks back in the house and picks up the phone. Steve doesn't give him much time to ask questions and he tells him to go over to Frederick's and ask him if he could borrow his car but to drive it around the back where he will meet you. "Tell Frederick you will explain everything later." Steve tells his father to get Carrie and leave by the back door and meet up with Frederick. He tells him to bring the laptop and some discs. He tells him to also take his number and call to get directions for them to meet but, to keep one eye in the mirror. They do not want to be followed. Steve asks his dad if he is clear with the instructions and he adds that Karen's water has broken and to get his ass moving.

Ten minutes later Carrie is on the phone, asking him what the hell is going on. He asks her if dad can hear and Christopher, driving, answers yes. Then Steve tells them a story about Nigel and the people he works for adding that he found out by accident. He never mentions time travel but Christopher can tell he is holding something back, though he decides not to push it. Karen is asking why they are not going to the hospital and Steve tells her not to worry because he thinks she will take her time about having the baby and tells her not to ask any more questions as he needs to concentrate on the drive, telling her to chew on a carrot as he had packed some. She tells him where he can stick his carrot and starts to sulk for real. He looks at her pouting and he places a hand on her, just so he is close as he does not have much time left. Just short of five hours.

They meet half way at a restaurant that they all go to from time to time and Carrie rushes up to Karen, still sat in the car and George jumps out, his tail wagging even though Steve had told his Dad to leave him with the Klein's. Steve hugs his Dad as if he hadn't seen him in years and takes him to one side and tells him that they need to talk but that the main priority is to get Karen taken care off and that it was his father's job to make sure they were safe. Christopher knows an old friend with experience he could call and they can book in there as there are a couple of rooms to rent for people who drink to much with their meals. Steve agrees and they book two rooms and drive over. Karen is helped out and taken inside. She doesn't care where she has the baby as long as she can yell at Steve for the next couple of years. Steve grabs Carrie's laptop and starts putting in, information. Most of what he has on the Nano's are hidden away on his own laptop with an almost unbreakable code he had put in himself. He had retrieved the files and is just adding to it. One hour later, he is finished and has made the last copy that he gives to his father to post as soon possible. Everything Steve knows about fusion sent to respected scientists.

Then he takes his father to one side and tells him about his four weeks of hell, two people with a science degree and one listening to an amazing story about the impossible. Steve leaves out about the part he has to play to save the world and simply says that he now has to do something. A few hours ago he thought he could not carry it out, now he has to find Nigel and kill him, as he is also a jumper and he is not the type of person that will kill himself to save the world. Steve needs to find him before the next hole opens up and they are now down to less than three and a half hours. Before he goes, he hands over a letter for his father to read. He tells him he has to sneak off or he won't be able to leave Karen and he hugs his father for the last time and jumps in the car.

Chapter 33

As he drives, Steve calls a number and hopes the person picks up. Nigel answers as if he knew the caller would be Steve.

"I was wondering when you would call. So it's true what you had told me. I am like you now, destined to travel back through time. Tell me Steve because you forgot to mention it, when was that, oh yes, tomorrow when you shot me. So tell me, how do I stop travelling?"

Steve has expected this question and he lies to him, telling him that the black hole is tied to him as it only opens up with him but if he is dead it will stop. He hopes Nigel will bite. Nigel does but he has someone he wants to put on the line and Steve hears the voice of his friend Tina, crying for him to help them. Nigel is back on and Steve starts throwing threats about what he will do if he hurts her. Nigel tells him to shut up as that was just movie cliché crap and he should listen to him as he wants him to meet him and to add to the cliché, to come alone.

One hour later, he is parked outside the tallest building at MIT. He looks up and makes his way inside and heads for the lift. He steps out of the lift and climbs the several stairs to the roof. Nigel had told him to meet him on the roof. Opening the door, he walks out. Nigel is there and so is Tina with her mother, Elena. Steve recalls Tina screaming asking him to help them. There is also one of Nigel's henchmen, possibly one of those watching his father's place. He wonders where the other one is and on cue, he walks in behind him, shaking his head. He ignores Nigel and asks Tina and her mother if they have been harmed. They shake their heads, petrified. He realises they won't say anything to antagonise their abductor but he can tell they have endured some form of abuse. Nigel is sadistic as he himself has found out.

"Enough talking Steve, our friend behind you tells me you are alone. Very noble of you and I am sure the ladies here think the same, unfortunately it won't help them."

Steve had expected this and had the sense to have a bargaining chip. He needs to play it now, and tells Nigel to let them go or the world will know about Nigel and all his work on the project will be mailed out to a dozen companies and MIT will get nothing. "All the money spent by them, gone and who do you think they will blame?"

Nigel had wondered what he had up his sleeve and suspected as much, asking him what his terms are. Steve tells him to let the ladies go and he will make the call to destroy the discs. Nigel shakes his head, telling Steve that he must think he is stupid and offers him an alternative. The ladies will go with his men and Steve makes the call. If all is ok, he will let the women go but only after he has made sure they will never tell anyone about this. Steve asks him how he proposes to do that.

"There are certain drugs at my disposal that can make people forget things. A few days in the company of my men and then I will release them. In fact they can go now with my men. That is my deal. Take it or don't and I take my chance with, what did you call it, jumping and the world for everyone will come to an end."

Steve sighs and a look of defeat comes over him and he asks Nigel to have the women taken away and he will make the call. Nigel smiles and tells his men to take the women and he would meet them later. He removes a gun from inside his jacket and points it at Steve and asks him to make the call. Steve dials the number and tells the person to destroy the discs and shuts the phone off. Nigel asks him how he would like to do it. Steve knew he meant how he would like to die. He checks his watch. He calculated the next time shift would be in roughly ten minutes and he knows he has to die before it opens up but he intends not to go alone.

Nigel is standing close to the edge of the building as he has his own idea how Steve will die. A bullet in the head will not do. It has to look like suicide and he beckons Steve over to the edge and they both stare down. Steve recalls the night his henchman back in CERN died. A fall to his death, only today he is alive and well and hopefully, he thinks, in good company by now. He looks back up at Nigel who is waiting for him to jump. Nigel makes a bad joke about this being a different type of jump than he is used too and this one will be his final and he laughs. Steve is out of time. It is now or never and he prepares to take them both over the edge. Just then, the door opens and his father is there. Nigel, caught off guard turns, his gun swinging around and fires, just as Steve tackles him to the ground. The bullet catches Christopher in the ear, taking a chunk of skin with it as it passes, hitting the wall behind him.

Instincts had told him to duck and Christopher lifts his head to find he is alone on the roof. His heart lurches as he realises what has happened. He had followed his son to try and help him and all he has done is get him killed. With a heavy heart he walks to the edge, afraid to look over and see his son dead, on the concrete below. He looks down and sees Steve hooked by his trouser belt on a flag pole bracket. Lucky for them, there was no flag in position. Steve is unconscious, blood seeping out of a wound on his head. Below him, his arms wrapped around Steve's legs and holding on for dear life, is Nigel, fear spread across his face as he looks up to Christopher and begs him to save him.

Steve's belt is taking the strain of almost four hundred pounds and the weight is becoming too great for the belt to hold. Christopher can see this and he reaches over to grasp Steve as he tells Nigel to start climbing. He knows if the belt gave way he will not be able to hold them, but he will never let go of his son and so they will all die. Nigel tries to climb but Steve's trousers start ripping apart at the seams. Nigel hears the tear of clothing and panics as he sees the trouser leg pull apart, as the trouser leg starts to unravel. Nigel tries to climb, only he makes it worse as the trouser leg comes free, sliding down and catching on Steve's shoe. It snags for a second before it unravels at the same time pulling the shoe off and Steve's trouser leg, shoe and Nigel fall the twelve stories to the ground, Nigel screaming all the way.

Even with Nigel gone, the buckle on Steve's belt is still distorting and it will not be long before it breaks and Steve falls. A hand appears over the side. Christopher looks up at the stranger. Moralis tells him that they both need to pull together. Between them they heave and Steve starts lifting just as the buckle breaks and they both take the weight as slowly they pull him up, hands grabbing a hold under Steve's arms until his head and shoulder appear and Carla comes forward and helps. Between them, they manage to pull him up and lay him down. Then they all collapse, exhausted.

Tina comes through the door, having seen the display from below but is kept from running into the building by a police officer. She had kicked him and he let go of her and tried to grab for her but Elena had tripped him. Tina cries, seeing Steve unconscious and thinks the worse as she runs to him, dropping down and placing his head on her lap.

When Steve had made the call, it was not to a person to destroy the discs but to Moralis and Carla. He knew they were working that weekend as Carla had previously told him they were working a weekend shift when he had seen her several days ago in the future and he had explained to them about the kidnaping and that they should be ready to pick up the women and whoever they were with. They had no idea who he was but they were shocked when he told them things about themselves. Carla was very shocked when he mentioned her secret. He would not give them any more details other than details of what the guards looked like and Tina. He hoped it was enough and he told them he would ring and that would be the signal and to ignore what he said to them. That was his call when he made the deal with Nigel. He knew Nigel would kill them. At least this way, they had a chance.

He was starting to come around as he looked up, seeing Tina's face and then looked around at the group of people he knew, until his eyes fell on his father. He looked at his ear and his father said he would live, which brought Steve back to his senses telling them that he should not be alive. Tina misunderstood what he meant, telling him he was lucky and that his belt had saved his life. She tells him that Nigel is dead and he looks at his watch ready to push her off and jump over the side. His father reads his actions and screams at him not to do it and then it happens, Steve realising he has failed as the roof starts to shake and Steve in despair cries out, that it is too late. People are finding it difficult to stand and they all scream in shock as the black hole opens up in front of them. They feel the pull and grab onto each other, thinking the structure under them would give way and they would all die. Steve waits, knowing what is coming, and prepares for his soul to jump.

Then it stops. The roof stops shaking and the dark shape above their heads had gone. They all look at each other, amazed that they had survived. Tina turns to Steve to ask him if he is alright and he nods. He is numb from shock as he is still there. He had not jumped and he knew this because each time he felt himself lifting away and this time, nothing. It is Sunday not Saturday where he should be. What is different he thought. Why had he not travelled back? It made no sense; he should have jumped.

Tina hugs him again, telling him he was lucky twice in two days.

"Steve you almost died twice. You must have a cat's life. First yesterday and now saved from falling off a building, you must be lucky. What was that man talking about, jumping and the end of the world? What was he talking about?"

Steve ignores her last question and asks her what she meant about being saved yesterday as he felt confused by her statement? She looks at him as if he is joking with her until she sees he's being serious with her and tells her he has no idea what she's on about and she thinks that maybe the bump on his head has played with his memory.

"Seriously, you can't remember?"

Steve looks at his father and asks him if he knows why he is still around. His father is just getting over the shock that his son had been telling the truth about travelling back through time as he really could not believe it when Steve had told him earlier. He could not explain why his son was still with them and displayed his arms in a gesture to say he had no idea either.

He looks back at Tina and lies to her, asking her to explain as the bump on his head must have given him some mild form of amnesia.

Tina goes on to explain. "Yesterday, do you remember you came in the shop? No of course you don't. I'm being stupid…"

"You went to the back of the shop and that's when it happened. Don't you remember any of this?" Steve shakes his head, a dumbfounded expression across his face as he waits for her to explain.

Tina goes on to explain the occurrence, reminding Steve of his visit, explaining how he went to the back of the pharmacy and that's when that thing they all had just now encountered, only it appeared yesterday as well, near him, only it seemed scarier in a small area. It caught all of us by surprise and she explains to him, that's when he had stepped in the water at the same time the light fell down, you lit up the shop for a second and then everything went dark. But that thing was still there only much darker. She tells him, she didn't think twice and ran over expecting to find him dead and you were. The thing over head was still there and just like now, it disappeared. "If you think about it," Tina tries to explain, "you saved your own life as it was you that persuaded me to go on the first aid course. If I hadn't," she tells him, "you could forget about being here now as I would not have known how to give the correct treatment to get your heart pumping again." Tina finishes by telling him that he had scared her as it took almost five minutes before she felt his heartbeat. She was exhausted after their ordeal and she was not allowed to travel with him in the ambulance as she was not family and that was the last time she had seen him until now.

Steve shakes his head and laughs. Of course he thinks to himself. My soul could not react with the hole as he was for a brief time dead in the past from being electrocuted. The hole closed before Tina could revive him. It's gone for good, he is sure of it. He is certain that the hold it had on him is permanently broken. It has no vessel to keep coming back. His soul is safe and back with him for good. His soul has survived and so has the world. He grabs Tina and gives her a big hug, telling her, she doesn't know it but she has saved his life again and he will always be indebted to her.

He turns to his father and asks that they get back to Karen as there is a baby on the way. Christopher smiles and helps him up. Moralis steps in, telling them that they need to come to the station and make a statement. Steve tells him that he must be kidding as his wife is about to give birth. Carla steps in and takes Moralis to one side. They come back and tell him that they will take him to his wife and afterwards he will make a statement. He agrees and then everyone wants to go and Moralis shakes his head and tells them that he will get the officer who was supposed to be keeping hold of her to drive them. It was the least they could do. As they walk, Steve looks back at Carla and with the camera on his phone, takes her picture. He then sends it and tell her he has promised someone that and she looks at him as if he was nuts.

Chapter 34

Karen can hear sirens and wonders who is being chased and then they grow louder until she can see flashing lights through her window. She was propped up in bed and her first thoughts are that Steve is hurt and she panics, waiting for the knock. She has no idea where he had gone and then Christopher had vanished as well.

Karen lifts herself up higher just as the door flies open and Steve comes running into the room. He looks a mess and one leg of his trousers is missing. Steve stops as he looks down at his wife. She is beautiful he thinks and in her arms was a small bundle wrapped in a sheet. Everyone working in the restaurant had been in to see the baby when they had heard the news.

Steve stands there with a stupid grin and Karen, with a smug grin on her face, asks him if he is interested in knowing the babies sex? Steve nods but he already knows the sex of his baby daughter. He has been watching over her for almost four weeks but he keeps that to himself. From behind him comes Tina, her mother and Carla. Moralis waits outside but is dragged in by Christopher. A short while later, Carrie walks in, after taking George for a walk, she is mad with both of them for leaving but then folds after seeing their injuries.

Before Moralis and Carla left, Steve had given them his statement playing a little on the truth and told them he would see them tomorrow. He also let them know to look into one of their officers, a Sean Greggs as he was on the payroll of people inside MIT. He expects the people at the top would be investigated but like many powerful people, they probably will get away with it. He also asks them to send a message to the CIA and ask them to look into the person the President's daughter is seeing and tell them that the boyfriend has contacts in Columbia. "That's all you have to tell them, they will do the rest." They both look at him, wondering who this person is and how did he know so much about them" Before they go , Steve gives them one last bit of information about one of their own citizens, Tina's boss, Keel. Steve explains to them about his memory and that he recalls reading about a man by the name of Keel who is wanted in connection with assaults on teenage girls and that Tina's pharmacist turned up a short time afterwards and he fits the description. Moralis was about to dismiss this as coincidence but Carla tells him that it won't hurt to look into it as she looks at Steve, still baffled by what he's told them and wondering about what he hasn't told them.

Steve and Karen are sharing some quiet time with their little baby girl. Christopher and Carrie remain in the next room with George. Steve remembers the shock on Carla's face when she got the call from Ryan asking her who she is? Carla had checked him out and he could see she was quietly pleased. Steve needed somehow to get everyone he knew involved and obviously they will all have to get to know him again as he feels it is his duty to spend the next three or four weeks saving peoples life's again as the future has not happened and he will need friends to help. This is going to be tough, trying to get them to believe the life he has lived, but that's for tomorrow to think about. Today he wants to spend the time he should have had with Karen on this same day a lifetime ago. Karen asks him why his father seemed overjoyed about something he had passed to him? He smiles and tells her that he knows the lottery numbers for the big roll over next Saturday and he has given the numbers to his dad to win with,as Christopher would ensure it would be wisely spent. She tells him "You wish" and snuggles in, asking him if he has decided on a name? All the time he has been watching over his girl, he never once thought about a name and for once he is at a loss. Karen smiles and asks if she can call their baby Janis, after his mother? Steve kisses her tenderly, telling her he loves her and was looking forward to waking up with her on Monday. As Karen has got him between her fingers again, she uses her charm and asks him when her ankles have got back to their normal shapely look that they go shopping. What for, he asks, as if he didn't already know, and smiles.

"Shoes, my darling husband and because you love me and you would not want our little princess growing up with a mother with flat feet, I think it only fair that you buy me nice shoes. After all, it sounds like we are going to be rich," Karen joked.

Steve smiled to himself, knowing that they would be wealthy and the money would be put to good causes and that one of these will be to research the human soul. He has a feeling deep down that he may be the only person in the world walking around with two souls and believes research needs to be carried out in this field. He has an idea how the human race has managed to advance so quickly in such a short period of time compared to other life forms. This fourth dimensional apparition that attaches itself to the human conscience, Steve believes, has helped the human race evolve and he wants to know more.

Steve turns his attention back to Karen, playfully teasing her about having no income. He has given up his rights on fusion and has sent all his hard work to other organisations trying to create the fusion reactor. He has made sure to keep a few things back as he does not want others to repeat the same mistakes he himself has made. He will control the flow of information ensuring that proper procedures are followed and in time, the world will witness the first fusion reactor. He has already contacted Lucy and she is on his side already working on ideas. The future looks bright, he thinks to himself and leans into Karen, enjoying their little banter together.

"Karen, we are probably going to have to tighten our belts for a while. I'm afraid you are going to have to wait a long time before we can buy you a new pair of shoes," he teases.

Karen looks at him and pouts, pretending to cry, at the same time telling him it would be her last pair.

She promises, "Please, please, pretty please."

THE END